A LOVE TO LAST A LIFETIME

CLARE SWATMAN

Boldw**oo**d

First published in Great Britain in 2023 by Boldwood Books Ltd.

Copyright © Clare Swatman, 2023

Cover Design by Leah Jacobs-Gordon

Cover Photography: Shutterstock

A CIP catalogue record for this book is available from the British Library.

Paperback ISBN 978-1-80280-672-4

Large Print ISBN 978-1-80280-673-1

Hardback ISBN 978-1-80280-671-7

Ebook ISBN 978-1-80280-675-5

Kindle ISBN 978-1-80280-674-8

Audio CD ISBN 978-1-80280-666-3

MP3 CD ISBN 978-1-80280-667-0

Digital audio download ISBN 978-1-80280-670-0

Boldwood Books Ltd
23 Bowerdean Street
London SW6 3TN
www.boldwoodbooks.com

For Mark. Not just my little brother, but my friend for life.

Music expresses that which cannot be put into words and that which cannot remain silent.

— VICTOR HUGO

One good thing about music, when it hits you, you feel no pain.

— BOB MARLEY

PROLOGUE
THEN

The Beatles: 'Something'

A small group of teenagers crowded round a bench looking for all the world like a Topshop advert. From the centre drifted the strum of a guitar, the notes swirling and eddying in the breeze before floating away to meet fluffy white clouds that bobbed in a cyan sky. Below them, tiny buildings huddled along a cotton thread of river, thinning until nothing but fields and hills remained as far as the eye could see, all the way to the horizon. It was a beautiful view. But none of them were taking a single ounce of notice of it. Instead, they laughed and joked, swigged warm lager from cans in carrier bags, and occasionally sang along to whatever tune was being played.

Above all the laughter and singing rose one clear voice – and that was the one that eighteen-year-old Erin was mesmerised by as she hovered a few feet away from her group of friends. That deep, resonant voice was what she fell asleep dreaming about every night. Because it was the voice of Adam, the love of her life.

'E, want another beer?' Erin's reverie was rudely interrupted by a shout from Sam, one of her best friends, who was waving a can in the air nearby. She shook the can in her hand, discovered it was almost empty, and made her way over.

'Cheers,' she said, swiping it from him, snapping it open and taking a deep glug.

'What were you doing over there?' Sam eyed her suspiciously.

'Nothing. Just listening.'

Sam peered at her more closely, and grimaced. 'Ugh, you look all dreamy,' he said, his voice dripping with disgust. 'Are you so madly in love that even hearing Adam's voice turns you on?'

Erin shrugged. 'Just because you don't understand it,' she said haughtily, giving him a playful shove.

'What doesn't he understand?' Their friend Rose appeared at Erin's side.

'Being so sickeningly in love that just hearing someone sing can make you wet,' Sam said, laughing.

'Sam, don't be so gross,' Rose said.

'Well it's true. Look at the state of her.'

'Can you both keep your voices down,' Erin hissed, aware they were talking loudly and that Adam had briefly stopped playing.

'Oh come on E, it's not as though he doesn't know you adore him. You fawn all over him whenever he's anywhere near you.'

'I do not fawn all over him!' Erin could feel the indignation rising in her chest. So what if she was in love? What was wrong with that?

Sam put his hand on Erin's shoulder. 'I was only teasing. Don't be stroppy.'

'I'm not being stroppy.' She took a gulp of her beer. 'Anyway, so what if I love him? He loves me too.'

'We know Erin, honest,' Rose said, always the placater. 'Sam's just jealous because you go out with Adam every Saturday night instead of sitting at home with him watching Pop Idol like a saddo.'

'She's right. I'm well jealous.' He glanced over to the bench where Adam was sitting with his guitar on his knee, swigging from a whisky bottle. 'I mean, look at him. Who wouldn't fancy him, all dark good looks and sexy smouldering voice like some sort of Brandon Flowers wannabe.' He sighed. 'It's a shame I can't turn him.'

Erin giggled. 'Yes well, he's definitely not gay I'm afraid. But he is gorgeous.' She sighed. She did feel guilty that she kept abandoning her friends to spend all her time with Adam these days, but she couldn't help it. She felt consumed by him sometimes, as though she couldn't breathe properly if he wasn't there.

'Erin, what do you want me to play next?' Adam's voice drifted over. 'I don't mind.'

He raised his eyebrows and stuck a cigarette in his mouth, holding her gaze as he lit it, and she felt her legs go weak. He inhaled, blew out a puff of smoke, then balanced the fag on the bench beside him as he started strumming, the high-pitched chords instantly recognisable. She walked towards him as he began singing 'Something' by The Beatles, knowing the lyrics about the way she moved and her smile were meant just for her. She sat down beside him before her knees gave way.

As he played she tried not to stare at him, but instead studied her scruffy checked Vans and tuned out everything except Adam's voice: the babble of her friends' chatter, the occasional burst of laughter, the distant hum of cars on the road far below. They all melted into the background.

She jumped when she felt Adam move beside her, and before she knew what was happening he'd pressed his lips against hers and her whole body turned to jelly as she responded hungrily. He tasted of tobacco and whisky and something else, something musky and warm and deeply, deeply sexy. She felt as though she could float up into the air and drift away with the clouds, and never come back down again.

How could she ever live without this man?

1

NOW

The Verve: 'Bitter Sweet Symphony'

I've always known music can change your life. I just hadn't realised it was about to change mine so dramatically on an otherwise ordinary December afternoon.

It was already getting dark as I stepped out of the gift shop, the dusk creeping over the rooftops like reaching fingers, smothering the violets and greys of the day even though it was not yet 4 p.m. A streetlight flickered on as I turned a corner, casting orange smudges onto the frosty pavement, and I stomped my feet, trying to warm my numb toes.

I swerved to avoid a small gathering on the pavement outside the Fat Cat café, impatient to get home. But as I passed, the opening notes of 'Bitter Sweet Symphony' by The Verve rose above the heads of the crowd and I stopped for a moment, drawn in. I loved the song, and I listened, mesmerised, as the busker plucked out the familiar melody.

And then he started to sing, and the whole world ground to a halt.

Because I knew that voice.

I knew it.

On shaking legs, I pushed past a couple of women to the front of the crowd to see the singer more clearly. He had a beanie pulled tightly over his forehead and he was turned slightly away from me, his mouth pressed against the microphone. But I didn't need to see his face to know who it was. My heart hammered as I waited, concentrating on breathing in slowly, sucking air into my lungs and pushing it back out again. I'd forgotten all about the cold now; all I could focus on was the man singing in front of me.

Then he looked up, and my heart stopped.

It was him.

It was Adam Bowers.

I felt frozen, and I stood, locked in the moment, unable to move even though every single part of me was telling me to go, to get out of there. I hardly dared to breathe.

Then the song ended, there was a smattering of applause, and I came to my senses. And, before he could notice me, I turned and fled, ignoring the tuts as I shoved past people in my haste to get away. I ran all the way down the high street, past the shops and cafes and crowds and out to where the shops thinned and the terraced houses of the estate began. Only then did I stop, my lungs burning and my pulse thumping. I felt dizzy. I bent over and placed my hands on my knees while I waited for my breathing to return to normal, and then looked around me. I'd come further out of town than I'd intended so I started walking slowly back the way I came, trying to arrange my thoughts into some sort of order.

Adam Bowers.

What the hell was he doing back here after all this time?

Why was he busking?

Why did I care?

Rattled, I pulled my bobble hat down over my ears and tugged my scarf tighter, watching my breath rise in puffs in front of me as I marched along the pavement. I felt shaken, as though the world had tipped upside down, and I wasn't quite sure what to do with myself. I hadn't seen this man for almost two decades, but I'd thought about him many times. As I walked, my footsteps tapping out a rhythm on the pavement, memories flooded into my mind without warning.

Adam on stage, singing to me...

Adam playing his guitar in the park...

Adam's lips brushing mine...

Adam lying next to me, my skin burning beneath his touch...

Adam leaving, not even glancing behind as he walked away from me.

I stopped, pushed the memories away. Stop it. I couldn't do this.

When I looked up, I was almost at my best friend Sam's house, so I hurried the extra hundred metres to his front door and pressed the buzzer. Seconds later a tinny voice came over the intercom.

'Speak.'

'It's me.'

'Come up.' Sam buzzed me up and moments later I found him standing in his doorway in nothing but a towel, his bare chest glistening with drops of water.

'I was just out of the shower,' he said, rubbing his hair with a smaller towel and showering me with droplets at the same time. He looked sheepish. 'Sorry.'

I hugged him gingerly then stepped inside as he closed the door.

'Everything all right, E?' he said, looking me up and down

appraisingly in the way only a gay man can get away with. 'Well, apart from that ridiculous hat.' He grinned but I didn't return his smile.

'I saw Adam,' I said instead, breathless. I was still shaking.

'Adam who?' He stopped then, and gasped. '*Adam* Adam? As in the love of your life Adam?'

'The very one.'

'Fuck me, what's he doing back here?' He almost pushed me into the living room and pulled us both down to sit on the sofa. 'Tell me everything.'

'I—' I stopped, unsure where to start. Sam and I had been friends since we were eleven years old; he'd been through everything with me. He'd seen me at my worst – including when Adam left – and yet I still didn't know what to tell him. I couldn't work out how to form the words.

'Start with where and when,' he coaxed gently, taking hold of my fingers. His were icy and I realised he was still in nothing more than a towel in the chilly flat.

'Go and put some clothes on first and then I'll tell you everything,' I promised.

He stood reluctantly and headed towards his bedroom. 'Okay, but I'm ringing Rose.' And before I could object, he closed the door in my face.

Rose was my other best friend and the only other person in the whole world who knew me better than I knew myself. Rose and Sam and I had been friends since secondary school, so they'd both seen me through everything: boyfriends, parties, exams, heartbreak, the works. They both knew how much I'd loved Adam all those years ago, and how shattered I'd been when he'd left. If anyone could understand what I needed right now, it was them.

I was brought back to the present by the slam of Sam's door

and when I looked up he was dressed in a reindeer sweater and skinny jeans. His hair was still damp and he was holding his phone in one hand.

'Nice jumper.'

He looked down and did a twirl. 'Thanks. It's ironic, innit.' He sat down next to me and pulled a sock on. 'Rose is on her way. Now, tell me. Why is Adam bloody Bowers back?'

'Honestly Sam, I have no idea. I didn't exactly stop and speak to him.'

'But where was he, who was he with, what was he doing?' He rolled his hand impatiently, indicating that he expected more detail.

'He was busking on the high street.'

Sam stopped abruptly, one sock dangling in mid-air. '*Busking?* The international rock star breaking hearts all around the world, was *busking* in the high street of the town he always claimed to hate, in the middle of the day?'

I shrugged. 'What can I tell you? Although I think international rock star might be pushing it.' I gave a grimace.

He squinted at me. 'Are you absolutely *sure* it was him?'

'Of course I'm sure!'

'Okay, okay, I'm only asking.' He held his hands up in surrender. 'So what happened?'

'Nothing happened. I – I ran away.'

'Oh E.' Sam looked at me with pity. 'And did he see you?'

'I don't think so.'

The doorbell rang then, and Sam leapt up to let Rose in.

'Come in, sit down; Erin was just telling us about seeing Adam today.'

Rose perched on the sofa beside me, tucking her legs beneath her. 'I can't believe this Erin, what on earth did you *do?*'

'I didn't do anything,' I replied. 'I didn't even speak to him.'

'For God's sake, this is so frustrating!' Sam said, throwing himself down on the chair next to me.

'But it's a good thing, surely, given that she's happily married?' Rose tugged her hat off, leaving her curls wild around her head.

'Exactly. Thank you Rose.' I glared at Sam menacingly. 'My husband is something you seem to have conveniently forgotten about during this whole interrogation.'

'Moi?' Sam said, feigning indignation.

'Yes, you know what you're like Sam. Anything for a bit of juicy gossip.' Rose turned to me. 'But E, what on earth *is* Adam doing here?'

'I honestly don't know. I legged it,' I admitted sheepishly.

Rose studied me questioningly. 'But?'

'But what?'

'Come on, we know you, remember? There's no way you saw Adam Bowers and felt nothing at all.' She nodded at me. 'Look how flustered you are. You don't get that flustered when you see Mr Higgins walking his dog along the road do you?'

I grinned at the thought of our old geography teacher Mr Higgins setting anyone's pulse racing. 'I couldn't let him see me,' I said. 'I couldn't breathe.'

Rose crossed her legs and leant her chin on her fist. 'I wonder where he's been all this time.'

'We know where he's been Rosie,' Sam cut in. 'Travelling round the world playing his guitar and spreading his seed far and wide. The question is, why is he back?'

We fell silent for a few minutes, then Sam spoke.

'When did you last Google him?'

I looked up indignantly. 'I don't Google him!'

'Yeah you do. So come on, how long's it been?'

I sighed. 'Not for at least a year.'

Sam looked impressed. 'Wow, that's very restrained.' He stood, walked across the room and returned with his iPad. 'Let's look him up.'

'No!' I cried.

Sam's fingers hovered in mid-air. 'What do you mean, no?'

'Honestly Sam, please don't do it.'

Sam put the iPad down slowly and twisted round to face me. 'This has really rattled you, hasn't it?'

I nodded.

'And I take it you haven't mentioned this to Greg?'

I looked up. 'Of course not. I came straight here.'

Beside me, Rose nodded. 'Wise decision.'

'Poor Greg though,' Sam said.

'Why poor Greg?'

'Well, you know.' He shrugged. 'He always hated Adam for being the man you loved more than him, didn't he?'

'Sam!' Rose said.

'What? It's true.' He held his hands up in protest. 'I'm not saying you don't love Greg, E, I'm just saying, this is *Adam*. The love of your life Adam, who you had a mad, passionate affair with. Greg was your rebound guy who stuck around, and he knows it.'

'Sam that was years ago—' Rose started, but I interrupted her.

'It's okay Rose.' I ran my fingers through my hair. 'He's right, isn't he? I mean, if Adam is back for good, it's going to be weird for both of us. It's not as though I can pretend to Greg that Adam never meant anything to me. He was there.' I had a sudden urge to be by myself. I pulled myself to standing. 'I'm going to the loo.'

As I locked the toilet door behind me I let out a huge sigh. Seeing Adam for the first time in eighteen years had sent my mind into turmoil, flashbacks spiralling in uninvited until I couldn't work out what was up and what was down. I sat on the closed loo seat and dropped my head into my hands, letting the memories come.

I'd been relatively innocent before Adam had walked into my life. Of course I'd kissed a few boys, had a few boyfriends; a fumbling snog with Danny Hardman at a year nine party had been my first. He'd tasted of cigarettes and Pot Noodle and he'd put his hand in my bra as we'd kissed out the back of the social club by the bins. I'd even gone out with a couple of boys in my year after that first kiss. Trips to the cinema to see *Bend It Like Beckham* or *About a Boy*, an awkward dinner with Matty Sampson at a local Italian where we'd had nothing to talk about so had ended up getting outrageously drunk on Lambrusco to try and make up for it.

But I'd known Adam had been different the moment I set eyes on him. He didn't have the same identikit undercut haircut with a floppy fringe that all the boys at my school had – his had been longer, less styled, freer. He'd gone to a different school – no nylon blazers for him; no Friday night fish and chip suppers from the local chippy. His life was mysterious. Exciting. Dangerous.

And while the other boys had made me feel warm as we snogged, with Adam I felt as though my insides were poker hot, as though the desire could burn me from the inside out from our very first kiss.

When we'd split up, I'd struggled. How could my life possibly go on without him in it? I'd thought about him constantly for weeks, tortured myself imagining what he was up to, wondering whether he was thinking about me. I'd even pictured him walking back through the doors of the pub and declaring his undying love for me in front of everyone. And as I'd just admitted to Sam, I had looked him up online a few times too, but it was always from a step removed, the photos of him and his band on stage in various venues around the world lacking any relevance to my life back home.

Over the years the memories of him had gradually faded,

parcelled away on a high shelf away from harm so I could no longer picture his face clearly. And I knew it was for the best. After all, I had Greg, and Greg and I were happy. Greg loved me, I loved him.

Nothing could come between us, not after all this time.

Until now.

The trouble was, Greg and I were now in trouble. For the first time in our thirteen-year marriage, he was no longer the safe sanctuary I'd always assumed he would be, and it had pushed our marriage to the limit. Five months ago I'd discovered that Greg had gambled away almost everything we owned – including our house. The constant rows following the revelation meant that the bitterness had chipped away at the foundations of our marriage with every snide comment, every misplaced word. We'd been working hard to repair it, but things were still fragile, the stability we'd always had seriously compromised – and I knew that telling Greg about Adam being back in town would only set us back again.

I stood, washed my hands and headed back to the living room to find Rose and Sam. As I walked in, the pair of them abruptly stopped talking.

'So what are you going to do?' Sam said as I sat back down.

'She's not going to do anything, Samuel,' Rose cut in sharply before I could answer. She fixed me with a look. 'You're going to steer well clear of Adam, aren't you Erin?'

I nodded slowly. 'Absolutely,' I agreed.

'See?' Rose turned to Sam triumphantly. But Sam was watching me, and I could see from the look in his eyes that he didn't believe a word I was saying.

Kasabian: 'Club Foot'

Until recently, if anyone had ever asked me to describe Greg, I'd have said he was solid. Dependable. Kind. Thoughtful. Then they would say how wonderful he sounded, and how lucky I was. And of course, I was. Who didn't want to feel loved and safe?

For years – eighteen years to be exact – it had been more than enough for me. Greg's love had kept me grounded, focused. Happy. Things might be on more shaky ground at the moment, but Greg's mild manners and kind demeanour were what was on my mind and what was making me feel so wretched as I walked through the door after leaving Sam's flat, having spent the entire evening talking and thinking about another man.

As I closed the front door behind me I called his name and heard a muffled reply from the back of the house. I slipped off my shoes, hung up my coat, and made my way into the kitchen as my cat, named Dog (don't ask), purred round my feet. I bent to give him a stroke and found Greg in the kitchen chopping vegetables with his back to me. He turned when he heard me and smiled, waving a knife in the air.

'There's a bottle of white open in the fridge,' he said, indicating the half-drunk glass he already had next to him.

'Thanks.' I smiled gratefully, grabbed the bottle and poured myself a large glass and topped Greg's up. As I leant over him, he planted a kiss on my forehead and I forced another smile.

'Good day?' he mumbled into my ear as I pulled away.

'Not bad.'

'Get all your Christmas shopping done?'

'Most of it, yeah.'

He peered round the kitchen to see where the bags were, like a child searching for Father Christmas, and I felt a flame of anger.

'There's nothing for you; I can't afford it,' I snapped, and then instantly regretted it as I watched his face fall. 'Sorry.' I took a gulp of my wine and didn't meet his eyes.

'I wasn't—' He stopped, floundering. The knife in his hand hovered in mid-air, glinting off the kitchen spotlights. 'I know I fucked up, Erin, but you can't keep punishing me. I've said I'll make it up to you.'

I gave a curt nod, the words caught in my throat. I knew I was being unfair. Greg was doing his best to make up for his gambling mistakes. But right now I was feeling confused, thrown, and I didn't know how to handle it.

The trouble was, despite Greg's promises, I was terrified he was never going to be able to make things right again and that we'd never get over this.

When he first started gambling a few months ago I should have seen the warning signs. He'd begun being secretive for the first time since I'd known him, hiding away in his office after dinner, not letting me have the password to his bank account.

But the first thing I'd really noticed had been the empty space where his beloved collection of trainers had previously been carefully stashed away in their original boxes. On this day, though, when I'd opened the wardrobe door, there had been nothing there.

'I got into a bit of debt gambling online and had to sell them,' he later admitted. But when he insisted he could handle it, that he'd sort it out, I'd believed him. Why wouldn't I? Greg had never lied to me; I had no reason not to trust him. I'd even felt sorry for him, having to sell the trainers he'd spent so many years collecting.

But then I'd discovered the emails that had shattered our world, and that had revealed the true scale of his problem. While I'd been putting in increasingly long hours at the clinic where I worked as a counsellor and where, since the pandemic, I'd seen more and more patients struggling, Greg had been idling away the hours he usually spent in the office online, gambling – and losing – more and more money.

Our savings had all but gone, he'd maxed out four credit cards, and taken out a loan that he was struggling to pay back. But worst of all, he'd also been talking to someone about borrowing against the house. The house that we'd bought together, that we'd both poured all our time, money and energy into over the years to make it somewhere we loved. Our sanctuary.

And he had been prepared to risk it all.

Things had been tough since then. Something between us had broken that day, some thread of trust that had previously always existed. My husband became someone I didn't recognise and I felt untethered. And while Greg had been getting help for his addiction with another counsellor that I'd recommended but didn't know personally, and between us we'd been trying to pay back some of the debt, bit by bit, it meant that, for the first time since we'd met, I'd been the one to look after him, and it had made me feel less secure than I had for years.

Although I'd forgiven him, in theory, I still felt open, and vulnerable.

And now Adam had appeared out of the blue. No wonder I was feeling rattled.

I took a deep breath and pasted a smile on my face, then stepped forward and took the knife from his hand, laid it carefully on the side, and wrapped my arms around him, relief flooding through me as I felt his body relax. We stood there for a few minutes, letting the sounds of the house settle around us, until I pulled away and stared up at him. His eyes held a sadness I'd never seen before, and I knew he was still terrified I was going to leave him, despite my reassurances that we'd be fine.

Which was why there was no way I could tell him about seeing Adam today. He'd understood the depths of my love for Adam, and had always assumed that, if Adam had come back during those first few months, even years, of us being together, I would have left him at the drop of a hat. But for the last decade, he'd been more sure of us, more secure, happy to relax and let us be Greg and Erin, a solid, strong couple.

'Sorry,' I said at last, my voice soft. I felt a heaviness in my belly. 'Of course I've got you something. I didn't mean it.'

He smiled sadly. 'You did, but I don't blame you.' He cupped his hands round my face a little too firmly. 'I just – I don't know what else to say to make you forgive me.'

'I have forgiven you.'

He shook his head miserably 'No, you haven't, and I totally understand why. But I'll make sure you do one day. I promise.' He planted a soft kiss on the end of my nose then turned back to the worktop to resume chopping. 'Starting with this,' he said. I peered round him at the food he was preparing.

'What is it?'

He tapped the side of his nose and closed the recipe book so I couldn't peek. 'You'll see.'

I knew he was trying his best, and I loved the fact that he was cooking something special for me, but I couldn't help feeling a stab of sadness at the distance that had opened up between us. I hoped we could bridge it before it was too late.

* * *

Later, as we were finishing off the enormous selection of curries that Greg had spent the afternoon preparing, and a Christmas soundtrack played softly in the background, I finally began to relax. The events of the afternoon seemed a million miles away, and we cleared the plates away in companionable silence, Greg humming along to 'Fairytale of New York' absentmindedly as we stacked the dishwasher.

'Another glass?' he said, holding up the bottle of red we'd started over dinner.

'Why not?' I held my glass out and he filled it almost to the brim, and grinned. 'Trying to get me drunk?'

'Definitely.'

We made our way into the living room and settled on the sofa in our usual positions, me curled into the end, Greg spread along the length of it, his feet tucked beneath my thighs, Dog nestled in his lap.

'Alexa, play "Club Foot" by Kasabian,' he said, loudly and clearly, to the device in the corner.

'One of our songs,' I said softly.

'You remember.'

'The playlist you made for me? Of course I do.'

I tipped my head back, closed my eyes and let my mind

wander as the repetitive 'ooosh' of the song washed over me, bringing with it a sense of contentment I hadn't expected to feel. I forced Adam out of my mind and turned my thoughts to Greg, and how we'd got here.

I'd been in a bad place when Greg and I had finally got together. We'd known each other for a year, having met during Freshers' week, and lived in the same block of flats, but at first we were just friends. That was my choice – I was still officially with Adam, who was travelling round the country with his band, playing in pubs and bars and trying to make a name for himself. He came to stay whenever he was nearby, and I was still desperately in love with him.

'You can do better than him,' Greg told me one day after Adam had been to visit during those first few weeks.

'You don't know him,' I'd snapped, then felt bad. I knew by then – everyone did – that Greg had been in love with me from the moment we'd met. I'd never led him on, never promised him we could ever be anything more than friends, but I understood from experience how that didn't always stop the feelings from existing. He was just looking out for me.

Greg was important to me. As a friend, sure, but from the very beginning there was something about him that made me realise he was going to be in my life to stay. During our first week, a group of us had gone drinking together at what turned out to be a bit of a rough pub when a group of locals had got rowdy, goading the new students, seemingly desperate to start a fight. I'd hated it, hated any kind of threat of violence, and some of the others were getting riled. But Greg had handled it calmly, stepping in and asking them if they fancied a game of pool and getting in a round of drinks, instantly defusing the situation. He'd been a hero in my eyes after that, and we spent most days together. He'd come to my room and we'd listen to music, go to the library and study, or just hang out at the student union, drinking, smoking and laughing. He was unlike any of the other friends I had – and the complete opposite to Adam – but he was funny and kind and self-depre-cating and I liked being with him. Perhaps it was because he made me feel so safe during the times Adam was away. And even though everyone knew he wanted us to be more than friends, that he hated the way Adam treated me, he never pushed it, and he never, ever made me feel uncomfortable. With Sam and Rose off in different corners of the country, I loved having him as a friend.

Then two things happened: Mum was diagnosed with early onset dementia, and, shortly after, Adam and I split up. Just when I'd felt as though my entire world had fallen apart, Greg had been there for me. He'd become my world, and over the weeks that followed we'd fallen into a relationship.

Whether it should have developed into what it eventually became I couldn't say, but the truth was I *did* love Greg, and I'd never want to hurt him. The roots of our marriage ran deep, and I loved him with all of my heart. It perhaps wasn't the kind of all-consuming passion he'd always hoped for, but it had always been uncomplicated, absolute. Comfortable.

I pushed the memories away now, fearing my thoughts might slide back to Adam again, and how different it had always felt between us. Things were delicate enough between Greg and I, the last thing I needed to do was bring another problem into the equation – not to mention the fact that dreaming about some wild, unobtainable passion felt childish, naïve. Life doesn't work that way, Erin.

Slowly, I became aware of Greg running his fingers along my arm, and up to my shoulders. I opened my eyes to find him watching me, a question on his face. Was this okay? I smiled to let him know it was and tried not to feel guilty at the look of grati-tude in his eyes as he pulled himself up until his face was level with mine. As he lay alongside me on the too-narrow sofa, I felt the familiar press of his body against mine, the places where we'd learned to fit together, despite our bodies changing over the years. The truth was, physically, Greg had hardly changed from the trim boy he'd been when we met, and I was only slightly heavier. The familiarity was a comfort to us both.

'I love you,' he whispered, and his breath tickled my lips. In that moment I made a decision. I needed to show Greg how much I cared, and push Adam from my thoughts for good. And so, without reciprocating his words, I kissed him deeply.

3

THEN

Nirvana: 'Heart-Shaped Box'

The music was loud but the party was lame. Erin stood in the corner of the room tipping lukewarm beer down her neck faster than she should, feeling her head spin and her body relax. She'd had a shitty day after falling out with Sam – some misunderstanding that she was sure they'd clear up soon – she'd had a detention for forgetting her maths home-work, and when she'd got home, Mum and Dad had been in the middle of a huge row. It was so rare for them to argue it had freaked her out. She'd snuck in the back door so they didn't see her and hid in her room until she'd heard her mum storming out and slamming the front door.

In fact, Erin had been in such a bad mood she almost hadn't come to this party at all. But in the end Rose had convinced her, standing on the doorstep and practically dragging her out of the house.

'Come on, it'll be fun,' she'd insisted.

Rose had been wrong of course, as Erin had known she would be. And now here she was, standing on her own in a room full of writhing bodies deciding whether to just cut her losses and leave, while Sam sulked and Rose snogged the face off a boy she fancied in a dark corner.

She took a final swig from her bottle and left it on the floor, then made her way into the kitchen to find another one. Even though all the best parties were meant to end up in the kitchen, this one hadn't got going properly yet and the kitchen was still empty. Cans of Red Stripe and bottles of cheap wine were lined up along the worktop, and a bin bag was already starting to bulge with empties. Who was cleaning up at a teenage party?

Erin grabbed another bottle of beer and was about to step into the back garden when a voice behind her stopped her in her tracks.

'I don't think we've met.'

She turned to find a boy leaning against the doorframe. His long dark hair curled out from beneath a battered fedora, and he was dressed in a leather jacket and ripped jeans. But it was his piercing blue eyes that made her stomach flip over.

'Um, no. We haven't.'

'I'm Adam,' he said. When he smiled, his whole face lit up.

'Erin.'

'Nice to meet you Erin.'

'You too,' she mumbled.

'Are you going outside?'

'Yeah.'

'Mind if I join you? Could do with a smoke.'

'No, um, sure.'

Erin pushed the door open and was relieved when the cool air hit her damp skin. She breathed in deeply and waited while Adam followed her. There were some folding chairs round a small wooden table so they pulled one out each and sat down. Adam put his feet up on the table, ankles crossed, and rummaged around in his pocket. She'd felt grown up when she'd left the house in her satin camisole and white capri jeans, but now she just felt very young and very shy as she tried *not to stare at this mystery man who'd decided to come and sit with her.*

A lighter flared, and Adam inhaled deeply, blowing smoke out into the air and tipping his head back. It definitely didn't smell like tobacco.

'That's better.' He held his hand out. 'Want some?'

Erin hesitated. She'd only ever smoked weed once before and it had made her sick. But there was something different, something intoxicating about this boy that made her desperate to impress him, so she took it from him and inhaled gently. She couldn't help thinking about how her lips were touching the same place his had just been and she was glad it was dark so he couldn't see her face flame. She took a couple more tokes then handed the joint back, watching the smoke curl from her mouth into the darkness, her throat scratchy with tobacco.

'So, how come you're at this party all on your own too?'

'I'm not on my own.'

'Oh? With your boyfriend?'

'No, nothing like that.' She felt her words tumbling over each other, getting tied up, and she hated herself for it. 'I'm with my friends but they're off somewhere.'

'Gotcha.' He inhaled deeply again then ground the spliff out on the floor beneath him. Then he leaned back and studied her.

'I don't know anyone; will you be my friend?'

'Course.' Erin's stomach flipped again.

'Good. So, tell me about you.'

'Oh. Well, I'm Erin. I live not far from here, my friends are Rose and Sam, and I'm studying maths, chemistry and French. I want to do psychology at university and – well, that's it.'

'Nice CV, thanks.' He studied her for a moment and she tried to meet his gaze.

'What about you?' she said. 'I mean, how come you're here if you don't know anyone?'

'Well, long story short, I just got chucked out of Long Acre and now

my dad is refusing to pay for me to go anywhere else so I'm having to do my last year of A Levels at Grangemouth.' He shrugged. 'I'd be happy to just quit and play with my band, but my dad says he'll disown me if I do that, so here I am. Integrating.' He made speech marks in the air as he said the final word.

'Chucked out? How come?' Long Acre was the expensive private school nearby, and Erin couldn't help wondering what you'd have to do to get thrown out of a school with such high fees.

'I got caught selling weed.' He shrugged. 'Everyone does it, I just made the mistake of getting caught.'

'Oh.' She knocked open the bottle of beer on the edge of the table and took a swig. 'Well, sorry you have to mix with us lot now.'

He fixed her with a stare. 'Come on, don't get all offended. I mean, you've got to admit it's not the best party you've ever been to.'

Erin smiled despite herself. 'No, you're right. It is pretty shit.'

'See.' He dragged his chair towards her and she could make out the contours of his face in the watery light from the kitchen. She held her breath, unsure what was meant to happen next. He seemed wild to her, unpredictable, and she couldn't take her eyes off him. And when he touched her hand and threaded his fingers through hers, she thought she might burst into flames.

'So Erin, will you look after me? I'm not sure I can get through a whole year without you.'

'Yes,' she said, her voice a squeak. She coughed. 'Of course I will.'

'Thank you.'

In that moment everything else in the world fell away – the house, the party, the garden, the music. Everything. It was just Erin and Adam in the centre of the universe, like a TV that had faded to nothing but a tiny circle of light. The world was theirs, the possibilities endless, and she let herself drink it in.

'Let's go and dance; I love this song,' Adam said, and the world snapped back into sharp focus: the party, the stub of the spliff, the

warmth of his hand in hers, the rhythm of Nirvana's 'Heart-Shaped Box' on the stereo inside the house.

And so Erin let herself be led back into the hot, sweaty party to dance and drink beer with this boy, this intriguing man, who was so unlike anyone else she'd ever met. It could have been just the two of them for all the notice Erin paid to anyone else around them. The brush of his arm against hers, the feel of his breath on her cheek as he leant down to whisper in her ear, the pounding thump of the bass; it was all utterly intoxicating, and she felt swept away, powerless.

Did she realise it was the night that would change her life? Maybe not, while she was lost in that moment. But later, as they said their goodbyes and went their separate ways and Adam pressed his body against hers and kissed her goodnight for the very first time, his lips warm and tasting of tobacco – that was when she finally realised that this one thrilling, heady night had changed something in her. She had lost her heart.

4

NOW

The Rolling Stones: 'Wild Horses'

Have you ever had one of those moments where you're reminded of someone you haven't thought about for years, and then you keep hearing about them over and over again, almost as though you've conjured them up out of nowhere?

That's what happened to me after seeing Adam for the first time in eighteen years. Despite the promises I'd made to Rose and Sam to steer well clear of him and to concentrate instead on sorting out the problems between me and Greg, I just couldn't seem to shake Adam Bowers from my mind. It was almost as though seeing him had dislodged a memory and sent all the other ones tumbling down behind it, like a line of dominoes. And my unfaithful heart didn't know how to stop them.

I'd been down to see whether he was busking again three times in the last two days. He'd been there once so far, and I'd stayed well back so there was no chance of him spotting me, just studying him, but I hadn't yet plucked up the courage to speak to him.

Then a few days before Christmas I decided it was now or never. I headed into town with the excuse that I still needed some bits and pieces for Christmas Day – mince pies, a few cheeses, crackers (both kinds), more wine and a bottle of Baileys, my dad's favourite.

Shopping completed, I dumped everything in the car, then, before I could change my mind, I made my way back into town. Despite it only being mid-afternoon, the darkness was already folding itself over the high street, the sun having dipped behind the shops and offices long ago. It was chilly and I pulled my hat on and wrapped my scarf round my neck. It would serve a double purpose of keeping me warm while also making me less recognisable, on the off-chance that Adam *was* there.

I headed up the high street towards the café where he'd been each time. Lights twinkled in shop windows, the decorations strung between lampposts looked pretty in the fading daylight, and my heart thumped loudly as I rounded the final corner before the deli. As I got closer I heard music, and my stomach rolled over. *Was it him?*

A small crowd was gathered and I could hear the strains of 'Wild Horses' by The Rolling Stones floating above the heads of the gathered crowd. I inched closer, trying to see over the shoulder of a tall man in front of me. My body was like a ball of tightly wound string, ready to unravel.

Then I saw him.

Adam.

I felt as though I was suffocating, and I pulled my scarf away from my throat to let in some air, then looked back. Adam had his beanie pulled down low to his eyebrows like last time, so I couldn't tell whether his hair was still the same mess of dark curls that had once made my heart skip a beat, and I couldn't make out his mouth properly behind the microphone, but there was no doubt it was him. I'd recognise those piercing blue eyes anywhere. I felt a wave of pleasure deep in my belly as I remembered the first time those eyes had fixed themselves on me at a party in some long-forgotten friend's kitchen.

How long would it take him to notice me standing here, and how would he react when he did? I waited, poised, ready.

And then Adam looked up, and our eyes locked for a moment. I was frozen, unsure how to react... Was he happy to see me? Shocked? I held my breath in anticipation.

But then his gaze slid right over me, unseeing, on to the next person, and I snapped to attention, bewildered. Had he been looking at someone else behind me? I glanced over my shoulder, but there was no-one there.

What was going on?

I stood stiffly, waiting for the song to finish, torn between wanting to confront him and wanting to turn and run away again. But my legs weren't strong enough to take me anywhere this time. My pulse thumped through my body and my limbs felt weak so I just hovered, staring blankly over Adam's shoulder at the coffee shop sign behind him, and waited.

Suddenly, the song changed, and as he began playing 'Heart-Shaped Box' by Nirvana, relief flooded through me. This was our song. He *had* seen me, and this was his way of letting me know.

As I listened, I let my mind wander, the song conjuring memories – some that I'd spent years trying to keep hidden, but which were now flitting in and out of my mind like images on a broken movie reel: Adam playing on stage, his eyes never leaving mine;

Adam introducing himself at a party, sharing a spliff; Sam telling me Adam was no good for me, a flare of anger; Adam appearing at my door after weeks apart, smiling at me like I was the best thing he'd ever seen; Adam's naked body hovering above me in my single bed…

The song ended and the film reel stopped abruptly, bringing me back to the present with a jolt. I could hear the crowd clapping as my heart slowed down, and then Adam was on his feet, getting ready to pack up his guitar and microphone.

He still hadn't looked back at me.

'Adam!' I blurted the name out before I'd had time to think about it. He whipped his head up and, for the first time, his eyes met mine properly. 'Hi,' I said, suddenly shy.

'Hello.' He glanced at his guitar case and then back at me. My legs were trembling so much I was worried I might collapse. I waited for him to say something else.

But nothing.

I stepped forward and closed the gap between us. 'What are you doing back?'

A small crease appeared briefly between his eyebrows and he tilted his head to one side.

'Back?'

'Yes Adam. Back. Here, in this town.' My voice was calm, measured, despite my anger.

'I—' He stopped and let out a huge sigh. 'I'm really sorry, but do we know each other?'

What?

I stared at him hard. What was he playing at?

'Are you kidding?' He must be, surely?

But he shook his head. 'No. I—' He looked down at his feet, then seemed as though he was about to say something else, but changed his mind. 'Never mind.'

I couldn't speak. I didn't know what to say. How could he possibly have forgotten who I was when what we had between us had been so passionate, so all-consuming? I'd spent the last eighteen years trying to squeeze him out of my mind, to let myself live and be happy with someone else. God, I'd almost ruined my marriage for him more than once. And he was pretending he didn't know me?

Fury rose in me like a fire and I felt my body start to shake uncontrollably.

'How *dare* you,' I hissed, my hands clenched by my sides. 'How *dare* you pretend you don't know me?'

He took a step back and I realised how close I was standing to him. So close I could almost feel the warmth of his breath on my face.

'I'm sorry.' He shoved his guitar in its case and slammed the lid shut, folded up his stool and tucked it under his arm, then turned and almost ran away from me, away from the high street. I watched his retreating back in horror for a few moments, paralysed. Then my mind came back to itself and I set off after him, half-walking, half-running, yelling his name. In that moment I didn't care who saw me, or how mad I looked. All I could think about was reaching him and demanding to know what the hell he thought he was playing at.

He glanced behind as I closed the gap between us, and then before he could do anything about it, I was standing in front of him, blocking his path. He tried to go round me, but I blocked him again and he finally gave up, his shoulders slumping, and stopped. He was staring at a spot just above my shoulder, and I rose up on my toes, trying to get him to look me in the eye.

'Adam.'

Finally, he did look at me. It was dark now and I couldn't make out the vivid blue of his eyes, but there was no mistaking the sadness in them. The Adam I knew, the sparky, feisty, rebellious Adam, seemed to have evaporated, leaving behind a strange kind of melancholy in his place. I couldn't read him, and so I waited.

At last, he spoke.

5

NOW

Bush: 'The Chemicals Between Us'

'I was dreading this happening.' Adam's voice was low so I had to lean towards him to hear. After all these years his sudden proximity was making me feeling faint, and I reached out for the wall to steady myself.

'Dreading seeing me?' My heart felt like stone, but he shook his head.

'No, I don't mean that.' He let out a long breath and shuffled his feet. 'I was dreading meeting someone who clearly meant something to me.'

I frowned, confused.

'What do you mean, *clearly meant something to me?* You're speaking as though you don't remember who I am.' *But how could he possibly have forgotten?*

'I don't.' I stared at him, waiting for him to elaborate, or to break into a smile, or laugh and tell me he was only joking. But from the look in his eyes, I knew that wasn't going to happen.

'What – what do you mean?'

His eyes searched mine, and I studied the depths of his, looking for some clue as to what was going on. But then, instead of speaking, he picked up his guitar again and started striding off.

'Come on, come with me,' he called over his shoulder, and before I could consider what I was doing, I was scurrying to catch him up.

We set off along the high street, the shimmer from the Christmas window displays lighting our way. I stared down at the pavement as we walked. What was I doing, following him like this? What if Greg saw us? Or Sam, or Rose? But I couldn't think about that right now. The urge to find out what Adam had to say engulfed everything else.

We marched out of town towards the quieter residential streets on the outskirts, away from my house. The traffic was thinner here, and the sky had turned from grey to a deep navy, a stripe of orange drawn across the rooftops. I stopped, and Adam came to a halt a couple of footsteps ahead. 'Where are we going?' I demanded.

'To my house.'

'Your house? Where—' I stopped dead, mortified. 'You don't mean your parents' house do you?'

'Yes. Why?'

What could I tell him? I might not have known what was going on here, but I did know that the last people I wanted to see right now were Adam's parents. They'd hated me eighteen years ago, believing that I wasn't good enough for their precious son, that it was all my fault he'd gone off the rails rather than the fact they couldn't have cared less about him that had made him rebel. I'd spent the last two decades trying to avoid seeing them at all –

easy when they didn't deign to come into town with the common folk – so I couldn't imagine they'd exactly be thrilled to see me now.

'I can't,' I said. 'Can we go somewhere else?'

He hesitated, clearly torn. But in the end he nodded, then turned and walked in the other direction in silence. I hurried alongside him, throwing him the odd glance, and when I caught a glimpse of the angle of his jaw, my heart squeezed. I looked away before he noticed me staring.

He stopped abruptly outside the Slug and Lamb.

'How about here?'

'I—' I stopped. This was Greg's favourite pub and I couldn't risk him or his friends seeing me with Adam. 'How about that place?' I pointed across the road to The Crown, an old-fashioned pub with one gin to choose from and one type of cheap white house wine. Greg and his mates would never go in there.

'Okay?' He said it like a question but I didn't bother to explain. He had his secrets, I could have mine.

We entered the deserted pub. A quick glance round confirmed that not only was there no-one in here I knew, but there was barely anyone at all. We peeled off our coats and hats and hung them on the backs of chairs in the corner.

'What would you like?

'A glass of red please.'

'Coming up.'

As he was buying the drinks I gave my mind a moment to catch up with itself. I shouldn't be here. I should be at home, with my husband, shoring up our marriage so it was strong enough to survive the tsunami of his betrayal. But, just like he always did, Adam was drawing me to him like a shopaholic at a closing down sale, and I couldn't help myself. I couldn't leave now even if I wanted to.

I studied him for a moment. He'd taken off his hat, and I saw for the first time that his once-long, shaggy curls had gone, his hair shorn almost to the scalp. But otherwise he looked the same. A few more lines, his cheekbones a bit less pronounced, but he was basically still the same boy who'd set my heart alight all those years before.

Adam returned, placed the wine carefully on the table in front of me, one in front of him, and sat down. His knee bumped mine and I moved my leg away as though I'd had an electric shock.

'Thank you,' I said, and took a sip of the cheap red wine to cover for my lack of small talk. I felt as though my tongue had shrivelled up inside my mouth.

Luckily, he spoke first.

'So, I obviously know you, which means I owe you an explanation.' He drank some wine and licked his lips. 'But can you tell me how we know each other?'

I shook my head. 'How about you tell me what's happened first. Why can't you remember me? Then I'll tell you.'

He nodded. 'Fair enough.' He glanced up at the ceiling, then slowly lowered his gaze to meet mine.

'I had an accident.' He took another sip of his wine, building up to something. 'You have to bear in mind, I don't remember any of this, it's just what I've been told since. But apparently I was riding my bike, the road was wet, I skidded, and I lost control. I hit my head on impact with the central reservation and – well, that was that.' He shrugged. 'I woke up in hospital, and I didn't remember anything about who I was or what I was doing there.'

'Nothing?'

'Absolutely nothing. I didn't know who my parents were, my friends. I didn't recognise the house when I finally left hospital and was allowed back to my parents' place. I didn't know where I'd been living, whether I was married, had kids, a job. I was just an empty shell of a person, as though I'd never existed before. Still am.'

I didn't know what to say. If what he was telling me was true – and there was no reason to doubt him – then it wasn't just me he'd forgotten. He'd forgotten everything. He wouldn't remember the way his parents had treated him, or being thrown out of his private school, or falling in love, or playing in his band. He wouldn't remember the passion we'd had, or breaking my heart. It was hard to believe that it wasn't still in there somewhere.

'That must be...' I trailed off, aware no words could ever be enough.

'Terrifying? Yup. Frustrating? Absolutely.'

A silence fell between us. I heard the whir of the fruit machine in the corner, the clatter of glasses behind the bar, the tired squeak of the ale pump. 'Is there anything you remember at all?' I said finally. 'I mean, you remember how to play your guitar.'

'Yeah, I do. It's weird, that just felt natural from the moment I got home and saw them sitting there.' He picked at a beer mat in front of him. 'I sometimes get flashes of something, like a tiny fragment of a memory that's trying to reach me, but it always disappears again before I can quite get a grasp on it.'

'It's just like my mum,' I said.

'Your mum?'

'She has dementia.' I realised he wouldn't remember the day the terrible phone call had come to tell me about her diagnosis, even though he'd known about it once.

'She was really young when she found out.' I swallowed. I still found it hard to talk about, even now. 'At first she just forgot minor things like how to make a cup of tea, or she'd leave the house and forget where she was going. But over the years she's lost more and more of her memories. I guess it's different because all of yours went at once, and hers have slowly been extinguished, one by one, like the lights of a house going out. It's been tough.'

'It must be. Has she lost all of her memory now?'

I shook my head. 'No, some days she's lucid, and seems to remember a lot. Other days she doesn't have a clue who I am or what I'm doing there. We used to be so close, she was my best friend, and now she often stares right through me, or is terrified of me when I come into the room, which is even worse.'

'God. I'm sorry.' He stopped, and looked round the room, assessing it. 'Anyway, it's your turn now.'

'My turn?'

'I told you why I don't know who you are. Now you need to tell me how we know each other.' He smiled, and my skin tingled.

'Well. Wow. Okay. Where do I start?'

'How about you tell me this. Did we sleep together?'

I felt my face redden and I suddenly felt hot, and Adam banged the table.

'We did, didn't we? Oh God, was I any good?'

'Adam don't. It wasn't like that.'

'Sorry. Totally inappropriate.' He shook his head. 'One thing I've learned is that I can be a dick sometimes. Please carry on.'

I swallowed, trying to decide where to start. A cheer went up in the corner followed by the clatter of coins into a metal tray. 'Well, we haven't seen each other for a long time.'

'How long?'

'Eighteen years.'

He gave a low whistle. 'That is a long time. Was I hot then?'

I didn't answer. Instead I simply said: 'We were at school together. You'd joined our school for the last year because you'd been chucked out of your posh school.'

'Oh yeah. Mum and Dad have been sure to fill me in on that little detail. I think they're hoping they've got a brand new son this time round. A new and improved version.' He rolled his eyes and I was reminded of the way his parents used to treat him. Well, *not* treat him would be more accurate. Most of the time it was though he didn't exist, and his dad threatened to disown him more than once just in the year we were together. It was no wonder he kicked out against them so much.

'Anyway, you were different from the boys I knew from school. Exotic, really. We got talking at a party and – well, we kissed that night, and were together for more than a year.' It all sounded so pedestrian, so ordinary when I explained it like that. But how could I possibly put into words the thrill, the intoxication of the two of us together? How he'd made me feel like the sexiest girl in the world when he wanted to, how he'd consumed me? 'We were —' I hesitated. 'We were good together.'

'Right.' He rubbed his hand over his short hair several times and sighed. 'I can't believe I don't remember any of that. I mean, it sounds like it was pretty special.'

I nodded. 'It was. It was the most intense thing that's ever happened to me.' I paused, suddenly shy again. 'You sung to me once, from stage.'

'Did I?'

'Yeah. Do you know the song "The Chemicals Between Us" by Bush?'

He nodded. 'I think so.'

'You sang it to me. You were up on the stage and you held my gaze throughout the whole song and I couldn't take my eyes off you either. It was...' What? Sexy? Profound? Exhilarating? All of those things, but more. 'It was everything,' I said.

Adam didn't reply. Instead we sat for a beat, me remembering the way we had been when we were together, Adam no doubt trying to process this new knowledge, that there had been such fire between him and a woman he no longer recognised. It must have been a lot to take in. I couldn't help wondering whether he still found me as attractive as he once had, whether he was drawn to me in the same way as he had been back then, and I felt suddenly self-conscious. I'd come looking for him today so I had applied a bit of make-up and made an effort with my outfit, but it occurred to me now, under the spotlight of his gaze, that I must look dowdy and ordinary. He was probably wondering what on earth he'd ever seen in me.

'So, what about now?' he said.

'What about it?'

He shrugged. 'Tell me about you. Are you married, single? Have you got kids, what job do you do?'

'I don't have children, no.' I don't tell him that I suspect Greg wants kids but that I'm trying to ignore it because I'm not actually sure that I do. 'I am married, yes.'

'That's a shame.'

My face flamed. 'Is it?'

His gaze met mine and once again, just like the first time I'd met him, the rest of the world faded away to nothing, so there was no more tinkling of glasses, no more background chatter, no more pub, leaving just me and him in the centre of our own little universe. A beat, a wisp of breath, then: 'Well, I would like to get to know you better, Erin.' His voice was low. I could feel his leg pressing against mine under the table and I buzzed with anticipation. It was all I could do not to throw myself at him, and I was thankful when he looked away and took a sip of his wine.

I didn't trust myself to speak, so I stood, knocking my thigh against the table as I did. Wine splashed onto the tabletop and puddled round the bottom of the glass.

'I'm just going to the bathroom.' I left before he could say anything else.

Inside the loo I entered a cubicle, bolted the door and

dropped onto the toilet lid, pressing my fists into my eyes until I saw stars. What was I *doing?* What was I thinking, sitting here in a pub with the man who had once been the love of my life, when my husband was at home, oblivious to the turmoil I was going through? What sort of person did it make me that I'd sought Adam out, and then chosen to spend the evening with him rather than trying to fix my marriage?

I felt utterly overwhelmed. Firstly, by seeing Adam again after he'd filled my thoughts for so many years. But also by the fact that he'd forgotten me, that all his memories of what we'd once meant to each other had been erased forever.

In part, it felt as though an old wound had opened up and was refusing to stop bleeding, seeping into every nook, every corner of my life. But it also felt as though his return had revealed a whole realm of possibilities, one where anything might happen. Where, in other circumstances, we might just start up where we'd left off.

I was reminded suddenly of the first time Greg had met Adam. Greg and I had still just been friends, and Adam was visiting for a few days on a break from touring pubs and clubs with his band. It had been clear from the start that there was no love lost between the pair of them. Greg thought Adam wasn't good enough for me, that he didn't treat me the way I deserved – in his defence, he was right – while Adam thought Greg was a creep, hanging round to get my attention. It had been a nightmare.

If Greg knew where I was and who I was with right now, it would destroy him. I needed to get out of here and go home.

I stood, left the cubicle and took a deep breath before heading back out into the pub. It was filling up a bit now, and as I wound my way past tables, I kept my eyes peeled for anyone I knew. When I got back I didn't sit down, and Adam looked up at me questioningly.

'Are you going to finish your drink?' he said.

'No. I shouldn't be here. I need to go.' I grabbed my coat and bag and turned to leave. Adam stood and grabbed hold of my wrist. I didn't pull it away.

'Let me walk you home.'

'You can't. Greg can't see me with you.'

He stopped then, realisation dawning. 'Greg knows me.' It was a statement, not a question.

'Yes.'

'And he doesn't like me?'

How did I answer that? 'He – he was always jealous. Of me and you. And then, when you left, he—' I stopped, not wanting to tell him too much.

'He pounced?' Adam finished.

'No! It wasn't like that. He's a lovely man. He's good to me.' I pulled my arm away from his grasp, desperate suddenly to get away.

'But you don't love him?'

'I do. I do love him.'

He studied me for a moment, and I had to look away. I turned and pushed the door open, the freezing evening hitting me like a slap round the face. I didn't know whether Adam had followed me and I didn't dare look round, so I hurried away from the pub and back in the direction of home.

'Erin, wait!' Adam's voice cut through the air and I slowed, unsure whether to turn. But he shouted again and I stopped then turned haltingly to face him. He was bundled back up in his coat and hat, his guitar case in his left hand, an unlit cigarette in the other. When he reached me he touched my arm with his other hand and I felt it like a jolt, despite the layers of clothes between us.

'What is it Adam?' I kept my voice icy, unobtainable. He placed his guitar down on the ground, reached into his pocket and pulled out a lighter. The flame lit up his face as he inhaled, the cigarette sparking to life. It had been a while since I'd smelt cigarette smoke and it brought back unwanted memories.

'Sorry, seems to be one habit I can't break,' he said, blowing smoke out into the air. 'Can I see you again? As friends I mean? I just – I've got so much to find out about myself, and you're the first proper connection I've made outside my family.' He looked at his feet as he inhaled deeply on the cigarette again. 'I was so angry when I got back to my parents' house. Angry with life, with them, with everything. I've mended physically, but I still don't know who I am, Erin, and I feel as though you might be able to help me. Please?'

I blew a puff of warm breath into the space between us, considering. Would it really be so bad to see him one more time, to help him try and remember who he was? 'Okay,' I agreed before I could talk myself out of it.

'Really?'

I nodded. 'But we have to be careful. I can't hurt Greg. This is just one person helping another, nothing more. Okay?'

'Understood.' He rummaged in his pocket for a minute and pulled out a mobile phone. 'Can I give you my number? So you can ring me when you're ready.'

I took my own phone from my bag and typed in the number he read out from the screen, and saved it as 'AB'. Already keeping secrets from Greg.

'I'll ring you, okay?'

He nodded, and then I turned and walked away, without looking back. It wasn't until I was almost home that I realised I'd told him all about me, but he hadn't told me anything at all about where he'd been for the last eighteen years.

6

THEN

The Strokes: 'Last Nite'

'*D'ya want another beer?*'

'*Yeah, thanks.*'

Erin watched as the girl she'd only met a few minutes ago – Erica, maybe? – threaded her way to the bar where teenagers stood three-deep waiting to buy pints of watered-down lager at £1 a pop. It was Fresher's Week at Nottingham University and a group from the student accommodation they'd been housed in had come to the union for a few drinks with the aim of either making new friends (Erin's case) or getting off with someone (almost everyone else's). Erin knew she'd already been marked out as different because she had a boyfriend – at least one she wasn't planning to cheat on. Leaving Adam to come here had been such a wrench she'd almost changed her mind about coming to university altogether, but despite the fact she felt as though she had a limb missing, she was glad she was here now. This felt like the start of a new era. Adam had promised to come and visit the following week when he'd finished touring, and she was sure he'd be true to his word, so at least she had that to look forward to. Besides, being unavailable definitely made life easier. The girls liked you more because you were no competition, and it was easy to talk to boys without the worry of impressing anyone.

Erin sat for a moment, nursing the dregs of her pint and studying the room. It was huge, the union bar, built for practicality rather than style. Foam burst from rips in the fake leather seating, unidentifiable stains marked plastic tables, the bar was sticky, the carpet rough around the edges and the music thumpingly loud – and she loved it.

She was startled by a movement at her side.

'Hello,' said a voice and she turned to find a handsome man sliding into the seat next to her, placing a full pint on the table. His sandy hair was slightly long, and he had a classically handsome face, like a Disney prince, all strong jaw and big blue eyes. His style was the opposite of Adam's carefully curated scruffiness and dark good looks.

'Hi,' she replied.

He held out his hand and when she shook it his palm felt warm and soft. 'I'm Greg.'

'Erin.'

'I know.' She must have looked at him quizzically because he smiled sheepishly and said 'I'm two doors down from you and I saw you moving in.'

'Ah gotcha. Well, it's lovely to meet you.'

'You too. Can I get you another beer?' he asked, indicating her empty glass.

'Someone's getting me one now – I think,' she said, peering at the bar where she could see Erica was finally at the front of the queue. She appeared to be simultaneously ordering drinks and snogging the face off the boy next to her. Erin admired her skills.

An awkward silence descended, then Erin said, 'So what do you do?'

'Ah, classic student talk, eh?' Greg replied, smiling to let her know he *was only teasing. 'Sports Science, although God only knows what I'm going to do with that. Probably end up working behind a desk some-where. How about you?'*

'Psychology.'

'Oh that sounds cool. So does that mean you know what I'm thinking right now?'

Erin laughed. 'I'm a psychologist not a psychic.'

'Well that's a relief.' He grinned and she couldn't help noticing how straight and white his teeth were. What was she doing?

Luckily Erica's return saved her. Her new friend was balancing three pint glasses in her hands and beer spilt all over the table as she plonked them down unceremoniously. 'Bloody carnage up there,' she said, beer slopping over the side of her glass and splashing onto Greg's jacket.

'Oh God I'm so sorry.' She swiped ineffectually at his arm.

'Don't worry,' Greg said smoothly, and held his hand out to her. 'I'm Greg.' Erica shook it and then turned to the boy behind her. 'This is Mark.'

'Mike.'

'Ha sorry, this is Mike.' She slid onto the stool next to Greg and Mike sat beside her and put his hand straight onto her thigh. Erin's mind flashed to Adam, and she felt a sharp stab of regret that he wasn't here with her. She thought about the last time she'd seen him, more than a week ago when they'd said goodbye on the bench on the Common. She'd been sobbing uncontrollably, and he'd held her in his arms and she'd never wanted to let go. Stop it; she mustn't think about that now.

She turned back to Greg and plastered a smile on her face, deter-mined not to let the fact she was missing Adam ruin her chances of making some new friends.

'Let's have a toast,' Greg said, holding up his pint, which dripped all over the table in sticky pools.

'What are we toasting?' Erica said.

'New friends!' Greg said, and they clattered their glasses together, spilling even more cheap lager. For the next few minutes as the group chatted amiably, Erin studied Greg surreptitiously. He had a lovely, calming aura about him. He'd only known these people for a matter of minutes but he was already making them laugh, treating them like old friends. He reminded her of Sam, in the way he seemed to find it easy to talk to anyone. She wished she could be more like that. She tried not to notice the sparkle of his eyes, the way his hands moved as he spoke, as though he had more to say than the actual words could convey and this was the only way to express it. And she definitely *didn't* notice how handsome his face was, and the fact that he kept glancing over at her every now and then.

'Hey, this can be our song,' Greg said suddenly, wiping froth from his top lip. 'A reminder of the day we met.' 'Last Nite' by The Strokes thumped from the speakers.

'We?' Erin said, snapping out of her daydream and tuning back in.

'We,' Greg confirmed, sweeping his arm round the table as the song went on about girlfriends and grandsons not understanding. 'All of us.' He gave Erin a look she couldn't read.

'Yes!' Erica said, and Erin was saved the embarrassment of her misunderstanding, raising her glass once more to chink the others'.

'To us,' they chorused.

When Erica and Mike started snogging on the other side of the table, Greg turned to Erin, his arm resting on the back of the chair.

'So, Erin-who-can't-read-minds. Tell me about yourself.'

'What do you want to know?'

He shrugged. 'Where are you from? What music do you like? Do you have a boyfriend...' He trailed off, his face hopeful.

'Ah, right. Yes, I do,' she said, and tried to ignore his look of disappointment.

'Right.' He gave a small nod and took a sip of his beer. 'Well that's a *shame.'*

She smiled back and shifted awkwardly in her seat, trying to think of a way to move the conversation onto another topic before either of them said anything they might regret.

'He's a musician,' a voice piped up, and Erin turned in surprise to find that Erica and Mike had stopped chewing each other's faces off and that, in fact, Erica must have been listening earlier when Erin had been telling her about Adam.

'Is he now?' Greg said, eyebrows raised. 'What kind of musician?'

'He's in a band,' she said. 'A rock band.'

'Oh right. Too cool for me then.'

'Probably off shagging groupies most of the time,' Mike said.

'He isn't,' Erin said, indignant.

'Yeah right. Course he isn't.'

'He wouldn't do that,' Erin insisted more firmly, feeling the colour rise in her cheeks and slamming her pint down onto the table harder than she intended. 'He loves me.'

'Well I bloody would if I was him, girls throwing themselves at me all the time. He'll be shagging for Britain.'

'He won't!' Erin yelled, the thought of Adam with someone else making her feel sick, the beer in her bloodstream making her more emotional than usual.

Greg put his hand on Mike's arm firmly. 'She's said he wouldn't do that so let's leave it at that shall we?' His voice was low. Calm but commanding.

Mike stared at him for a few seconds, then gave a lazy grin. 'Yeah sure. Sorry.' He looked at Erin. 'He won't be doing any of those things, I'm sure,' he said, insincerely.

The trouble was, Mike had hit a nerve; it was all Erin thought about every night as she lay in bed, picturing Adam playing gigs in pubs and clubs. She knew girls would be throwing themselves at him, and as much as she told herself he would never cheat on her, that they loved each other too much for that, the truth was she wasn't as secure in their relationship as she made out.

But as the night wore on she found her thoughts turning to Adam less and less, and began properly enjoying the company of her new friends. Especially Greg, she realised. Not only was he nice to look at, but he was funny, thoughtful and intelligent. He asked questions of everyone and seemed genuinely interested in the answers, and told self-deprecating stories about his middle-class upbringing. He admitted his secret love for Saturday nights in watching Casualty and how he really preferred drinking alcopops but had trained himself to like beer, and he made everyone laugh when he did a spookily accurate impression of Mr Bean. She found herself drawn to him in a way she hadn't expected. He was, she realised, someone she could imagine getting close to, which, in the absence of Sam and Rose, was just what she needed to help get her through the weeks and months to come.

It wasn't until much later, after they'd spent the whole evening chatting and getting to know each other and drinking too much weak lager, Greg buying endless rounds of tequila, and dancing sweatily on the sticky student union dancefloor, that it occurred to her that most girls would have been throwing themselves at this man if he'd have paid them even a fraction of the attention he'd paid her that night.

When they got back to their halls of residence, Greg lingered at her door for a moment longer than strictly necessary. Erin was certain he wanted to kiss her, and it would have been easy to have let him. Part of her wanted to. But a bigger part of her knew she could never do anything to risk losing Adam. And so she leaned forward, gave him a chaste hug with her face turned away, and let herself into her room, leaving him to go back to his own room, two doors down, alone.

As she drifted off to sleep that night, she tried not to think too much about the handsome young man she'd spent the evening talking to, and tried to conjure up an image of her gorgeous, sexy boyfriend, pushing away all thoughts of him with some other girl, in some other town.

7

NOW

Linkin Park: 'Numb'

Greg was clattering about in the kitchen, and the smell of cooking wafted through the door. My mouth watered. He was trying so hard to make up for what he'd done that he'd been cooking for me every night, and doing everything he could to make me forgive him. Under normal circumstances, it would almost certainly have worked.

But right now, I was consumed with guilt; I felt as though my body was flooded with it. Because although Greg had betrayed my trust, there was no doubt that what I was doing was far, far worse. I couldn't even begin to imagine how hurt Greg would be if he found out I'd been spending time with Adam – the man he'd always resented; the man I'd been heartbroken over for months, years, even while Greg and I had been making a go of our own fledgling relationship. Adam had been like a shadow hanging over us back then, waiting to destroy everything at any moment.

That shadow had faded over the years from a deep, menacing black to a pale, wispy grey, but it had never quite gone away. And now he was back.

I needed to talk to someone who not only knew me well, but had known me when I was with Adam.

I popped my head round the kitchen door. 'Just going for a quick shower,' I told Greg.

He looked round, a smile on his face. 'Okay love. Dinner will be about half an hour.'

'Perfect thanks.'

I ran up the stairs and into the bathroom, locked the door behind me and pulled out my phone. I didn't want the judgement I knew I'd get from Sam when I told him I'd been to see Adam again, so I rang Rose instead. She sounded harassed when she answered.

'Can you talk?' I said.

'Yeah, give me a minute, I've just walked in.' I listened to her huffing and puffing for a few seconds, then she was back. 'Sorry E, I'm here. What's up?'

'I saw Adam.' No point in beating about the bush.

She didn't reply straight away. She sounded out of breath and I imagined her scrabbling to answer her phone as she ran up the stairs to her flat.

'Did you hear me?'

'Yes, I heard you. I was just trying to work out what to say.'

'You're angry with me.'

'Of course I'm angry with you. You're just lucky I'm not Sam.'

'Why do you think I rang you and not him?'

I heard her laugh and I relaxed. She might be cross with me – after all, she knew how unhappy Adam had made me, and she loved Greg – but a cross Rose was fine. I could cope with that. At least she'd listen to me and not just go off on a rant.

'So come on, tell me what happened.'

I told her about going to find Adam despite her and Sam's warnings not to, about his accident and about how he couldn't remember who I was, or who anyone was. And I admitted to her how he still made my heart skip a beat whenever I was near him, even though I didn't want him to.

'Oh Erin,' she said. I could hear her clattering around in the kitchen, the clink of a bottle and the glug of wine being poured into a glass.

'I know,' I said. 'I'm an idiot. But I can't help it, Rosie.'

'Don't think you can *Rosie* me and get my approval,' she said, but I heard the smile in her voice. 'So what now?'

'He wants to see me again. Just as a friend,' I added, before she could object.

'But he's not a friend. He was never a friend. You idolised him. Still do by the sounds of it.'

'I wouldn't say idolised is the right word.'

'Okay, you adored him. Worshipped him. Would have given up everything for him. Better?'

'No.'

'Don't sulk Erin, you know it's true. Why would you want to risk everything you've got with Greg just to see Adam one more time?'

I don't just want to see him one more time, I realised.

'I think I can help him.'

'What do you mean?'

'With my music therapy. You know, help him try and remember something.'

'But he's not a dementia patient Erin. He's got amnesia. You have no idea whether music therapy will help him.'

'I know, but it's got to be worth a try, hasn't it?'

'No, I don't think so.' She paused a moment, and then said:

'I'm not sure it's worth the risk. To you and Greg.' She cleared her throat. 'You know it will annihilate Greg if he finds out about this.'

I said nothing because she was right of course, and I'd already known that this was exactly what she was going to say. And yet something was drawing me to Adam, the way it always had, and I wasn't sure I could stop it happening even if I wanted to.

'I know you'll probably do it anyway,' she said, as if she could read my mind. 'But don't kid yourself you're doing this for Adam. You're doing this for you.'

'Now you sound like Sam.'

'I'm just telling you the truth. Sorry E.'

I had an overwhelming urge to stop talking about this, to move away from this conversation and think about something else.

'I need to go; Greg's made dinner,' I said abruptly.

'Okay. But don't be a fool. Promise?'

'I can't promise anything,' I replied. Then I hung up, wishing I'd kept the news to myself after all.

I got the shower running and stripped off, then stepped under the scalding jets. As the water ran down my face and over my body, pooling by my feet as it slowly drained away, I let my mind drift off to a long distant past; to the day when I saw such pain etched on Greg's face that I'd sworn to myself I'd never hurt him that way again. Adam had been gone for three months, and I was still struggling to come to terms with my mother's dementia diagnosis. Greg and I had become a couple, although it had taken me some time to be persuaded. I knew I was being distant with him, not giving all of myself to him the way he deserved, but I just couldn't help it. A part of me had felt as though it was lost to Adam forever. On this particular day Greg had confronted me, and asked me what the matter was. I'd broken down, and once I'd stopped sobbing uncontrollably, he'd said, 'Come on Erin, tell me the truth. Do you love me?'

I hadn't known what to say. I did love him. I just didn't know whether I was in love with him. The only thing I had to compare it to was the love I'd felt for Adam, and that had been all-consuming. It had felt dangerous and exciting. What I had with Greg felt safe, comfortable. Was that love? Who knew?

'I think so,' I'd said. His face had dropped and I'd instantly realised my mistake. He hadn't expected me to say that. I'd tried to backtrack. 'I do love you. I do.'

'But not as much as you loved Adam?' His voice was like shattered glass and my heart contracted. How could I agree with him? It would hurt him so much. And yet how could I deny it?

'I just...' I stopped, weighing up my words.

'Come on Erin, just tell me the truth.'

'I do love you. But a part of me will always love Adam too.'

'And would you—' His voice choked. 'If he came back here, right now, and told you he wanted you back, would you go? Would you choose him over me?'

I didn't answer immediately, and my hesitation told him everything he needed to know.

'Of course you would,' he'd said softly.

He'd left then, and it had been a few days before I'd gone to find him to try and sort it out, knowing he'd need time to cool down. We'd had a long discussion, and I'd managed to convince him that I loved him, that I wanted to be with him. But I'd never forgotten that look on his face when I'd more or less admitted that I'd always love Adam more than I could ever love him. That Greg would always be my second choice.

I turned the shower off and wrapped a towel round me. A glance at my phone revealed that Sam had left me a message – Rose had obviously rung him the second she'd put the phone down – and a knot of anxiety tugged at the pit of my belly. I knew he'd be cross and try and talk some sense into me, and right now I didn't want to hear it.

Because I'd already made my mind up that I was going to contact Adam again no matter what anyone else said, no matter how much it might hurt Greg. I couldn't even explain why, just that it was something I needed to do.

To exorcise the ghosts of our past maybe?

* * *

It was freezing as I set off, the mist hanging low, casting the town in a ghostly glow beneath the streetlights. Every now and then I passed a house whose Christmas lights flashed, piercing the darkness with their jollity, and it made me smile. I wrapped my scarf tighter round my neck, shoved my gloved hands into the pockets of my puffa coat, and stamped along.

I'd put on a brave face over dinner with Greg last night as we'd chatted about our days, terrified something in my face was going to give me away. I'd been with patients all day today too, so I'd barely had time to worry about the situation with Adam. But at lunchtime, instead of joining my colleague Kate for lunch as I usually did, I snuck out to send a text.

To Adam, of course.

I had to see him. Even if it was just to tell him I couldn't see him any more, I needed to lay that ghost to rest once and for all. But as I typed the words into my phone, I knew I was hoping it would be more than that. And I hated myself for it.

Hi Adam, it's Erin. Can we meet tonight? I have something to ask you.

It was only a simple message but it had taken several attempts to get it right. Should I end it with a kiss the way I usually did, or not? Should I tell him what I wanted to speak to him about? But what if I'd changed my mind by then? So in the end I'd kept it simple, straight-forward, and hoped he'd reply.

Which he had, of course. As I'd known he would.

I'd told Greg I was going out with Rose and Sam, and I knew he'd never check. He was going out for a few drinks with some cycling friends anyway, and as long as he wasn't gambling then I didn't care what he did. All I could think about was the evening ahead.

I hadn't wanted to meet in a pub – it was bad enough sneaking around behind Greg's back, I didn't want to risk being spotted by him or his friends too. So Adam had suggested meeting away from town at the entrance to the Common, the place where we'd spent so many hours together as teenagers. I felt nervous as I approached in case he didn't turn up, but when I rounded the corner and saw a figure beneath the streetlamp by the park entrance, I knew instantly it was Adam. My heart thumped and I stopped for a second to get my breathing under control. Come on Erin, stop behaving like a teenager. You're here as a friend, nothing more.

So why did it feel as though I was betraying Greg in the worst possible way?

Adam didn't spot me until I was almost by his side, and he smiled and stubbed a cigarette out under his boot and pulled an earbud out of his ear.

'You came!' The glee in his voice was obvious and it struck me that I'd never seen him this enthusiastic about anything; he always used to play it totally cool, as if it would be a show of weakness to do otherwise. I wondered what else had changed.

'I did.' I indicated his phone. 'What you listening to?'

He reached over and slotted the earbud gently into my ear, the back of his finger brushing against my skin. The soaring vocals of 'Numb' by Linkin Park flooded my ear, the lyrics about becoming so numb and losing control smacking me with a memory of Adam so hard that it almost took my breath away: the first night we spent together at his parents' house. It had been the first time we'd had the place to ourselves and had been able to spend the whole night curled up in each other's arms. This song had been playing while Adam had undressed me, and it brought back the breathless anticipation with full force. 'Oh,' I gasped.

'You okay?'

'Yes.' I pulled the headphone from my ear and handed it back with a shaking hand. 'It's just... nothing.' I stopped, aware he wouldn't have the same recollection of this song as me, the same frames of reference. Now didn't feel like the time to go into it.

He clapped his hands together, his gloves making a muffled flump, and I tried to focus on the here and now. 'Shall we go?'

'In here?' I peered through the gate into the darkness beyond. The innocuous trees and playground of the daytime had transformed into lurking, mysterious shapes under the cover of the foggy night, looming up at us out of the murk.

'You said you wanted to be discreet. You can't get much more discreet than this.'

'Okay,' I said uncertainly.

'Come on then.'

He grabbed my hand and pulled me through the gate and I shivered at his touch despite the layers between us.

Adam set off at a fast pace, marching across the grass.

'Do you even know where you're going?' I grumbled. 'I thought you couldn't remember anything.'

'I've been up here quite a bit since I've been back,' he admitted. 'My head injury means I can't work, and I'll go mad if I have to rattle around that house with my parents all day long.'

I couldn't reply – we were going so fast it was a struggle to catch my breath. The path had begun to slope upwards now, and we climbed the hill, up to a bench where, during the daytime, you could sit and look out across the town – the place where we'd spent so many hours together all those years ago, only back then we'd been trying to avoid our parents rather than my husband. I hoped we were going to stop there, but we reached the bench and walked right past it. I stopped for a minute. 'Wait!'

Adam turned round. 'You okay?'

'Just – let me catch my breath.'

'Sorry.' He walked back down to meet me.

'Can't you at least tell me where we're going?'

He shrugged. 'Let's sit.' He indicated the bench and I settled into it gratefully.

We were side by side and I was suddenly acutely aware of his proximity. His thigh pressed against mine and our shoulders touched through layers of clothing. I longed to study his face, remind myself of the lines and contours of his features, but instead I fixed my gaze on the lights of the town twinkling below us in the gloom, like a miniature railway set. I let my mind wander, thinking about all the times I'd come up here over the years – with Rose and Sam, with old school friends, swigging White Lightning from the bottle before puking it back up in the hedge – and, later, when Adam and I would come up here either with other people or just the two of us, the only place we could really be alone. It was incomprehensible to me as I looked out across the town I knew so well and that was filled with so many memories, that Adam couldn't remember any of it.

I squinted into the distance and tried to make out where my father's house was but I couldn't quite see it in the gloom, so I let my eyes wander to the right to seek out mine and Greg's house, the house we'd started saving for when we graduated and got our first jobs, that we'd spent the last fifteen years sprucing up and making our own – and that he'd very nearly lost – and then across a bit further to the edge of town where Sam's flat was, before finding Rose's a bit further on again. I wondered what they'd all say if they knew where I was right now.

'Penny for your thoughts.' Adam's voice broke into my reverie and I jumped.

'Sorry, I was miles away.'

'I could tell. What were you thinking about?'

'Just—' I stopped. 'All the things that have happened to me in this town over the years I suppose. It always makes me think, when I come up here and see it spread out before me like this. I mean, you realise how small you are, how insignificant. How you don't really matter.'

'Is that honestly what you think? That you don't really matter?'

I glanced at him. 'I guess so. To some extent. I mean I know I matter to some people, and I'm good at my job and that helps people. But at the end of the day, this is a tiny corner of a tiny part of a tiny country on a tiny planet in a vast, vast universe, and we're just – us. Two tiny specks sitting here on this bench.'

'Wow. I mean, I thought you might have some profound thoughts when we got to where I was taking you, but I didn't expect it to happen on the way there.' He grinned. 'Still want to go?'

'Definitely,' I said.

Adam stood and held out his hand and pulled me up. 'Follow me then.'

We walked for a few more minutes, following the trail as it snaked further up the hill, through the gorse bushes and bracken that had bedded down for winter until, finally, we were right at the very top. I rarely came up this far because it was so overgrown and remote, and it was so dark now I couldn't even see my own feet on the unfamiliar path in front of me. In fact, all I could make out was the occasional headlight passing on the road just below us. I turned on my phone torch just as we stopped beside a huge tree, its black arms reaching up into the inky sky.

'Here we are,' Adam said, and sat down and leaned against the trunk. He patted the ground beside him. 'Joining me?'

I lowered myself down to sit next to him and leaned my back against the tree too. The ground was damp and cold but I didn't care. 'You need to lie almost flat, and wait,' he said, and shuffled himself down until he was lying horizontal. Even though the earth felt frozen through my jeans, I did the same. I shivered.

'Look,' Adam said. 'Can you see?'

'What are we looking at?'

He swept his arm round in an arc. 'This. Just wait.'

We lay still for a few minutes. My body was stiffening, getting colder, but Adam's presence beside me was distracting me enough to make me want to stay here a little longer. I heard him light up another cigarette and watched the smoke evaporate into the air. Beneath me, I could almost feel the ground shifting, hear the animals deep below the earth burrowing and scurrying. Slowly the sky darkened another shade, and the stars shone through like lights on a Christmas tree, and suddenly it was just me, and Adam, and the huge, sweeping sky speckled with stars. And I could see instantly what he meant.

'This is amazing,' I whispered.

'I told you.'

We lay in silence for a moment, letting the wonder seep in.

'I come up here quite often,' Adam said into the darkness.

'Aren't you afraid, on your own?'

'Why would I be? There's nothing up here but trees.'

I didn't try and explain that it was different for me, as a

woman, to come somewhere like this at night by myself. I didn't want to spoil the moment. Adam carried on.

'Ever since the accident I've started coming up here and lying down to look at the stars,' he said.

'It must be so hard, not being able to remember anything at all about who you were before.'

'It is.'

'You don't seem very angry about it.' A root was digging into the back of my head and I shifted to get comfortable. 'I think I would be consumed with rage about losing more than thirty-five years of my life.'

A silence followed, filled with the distant hoots of owls, and I wondered whether I'd said the wrong thing. But then Adam spoke again.

'I was furious. Scratch that. I *am* furious. It's been awful, these last few months since it happened. I can't remember anything about the person I was before. I don't really know where I've been living, who with, or the places I've been to, apart from the few details my parents have filled in for me. I assume my band must have been fairly successful, but I don't even remember any of that.

'At first I was desperate to fill in all the blanks, and blamed everyone else for my memory failing me. But now I'm starting to realise that I can't change what's happened, and I can't force my memory to return, so what's the point in being angry for the rest of my life?' He stopped. 'Besides, perhaps it's a good thing.'

'What do you mean?' I turned to face him and tried to seek out his features in the dark, but it was almost impossible.

'Well, I don't seem to have anyone who cares about me. I mean, barely anyone has been to visit me since the accident, and even those who came at beginning have stopped bothering now. I guess it's pretty boring spending time with someone who doesn't have a clue who you are.' He stopped, sighed. 'And my parents don't like me very much either. At least, my dad doesn't. He hasn't said so of course, but it's pretty obvious I'm a complete disappointment to him.'

I didn't reply. I couldn't. If no-one else had bothered to fill Adam in on exactly how toxic his relationship was with his parents, I certainly wasn't going to be the one to break the news. *'Well, your dad was always threatening to disown you because he thought you were a disgrace to the family, he never spent any time with you and thought that throwing money at you made up for it, and your mum went along with all of it for an easy ride – she preferred lunching with her friends over spending any actual time being a mother.'*

No, there was absolutely no way I could say any of that.

'Don't worry, I'm not going to ask you,' he said, to my relief. 'But tell me one thing.' I felt him move beside me, and the back of his hand brushed against mine. I snatched it away and regretted it instantly.

'What?'

'Was I an arsehole?'

'No!' I sat up and shuffled until my back was against the solid trunk of the tree. Physically I might have been rooted to the earth, but for the first time in a long time, I felt unconstrained, free. I didn't know whether it was this place, far away from everything, or Adam's presence. I didn't want to analyse it too much. 'You weren't an arsehole. You were...' I stopped. How on earth could I explain to Adam what he'd been like when I knew him? How could I capture the essence of him, the ferocity of his emotions, the hunger, the longing between us? 'You were amazing.' My voice was quiet. 'But then I haven't spent time with you for a very long time.' I shrugged. 'So who knows what you're like these days?'

He didn't reply straight away, but a few seconds later I felt his hand brush against mine again, and this time neither of us pulled away. Instead we just lay there, peering at the stars, lost in our own thoughts, our fingers barely touching, letting the vastness fill our souls.

As I took it all in, I felt as though nothing else mattered, as though there were no problems to deal with: no amnesia, no dementia, no gambling, and no thoughts of infidelity. As though, actually, nothing was insurmountable.

I wasn't sure how much time had passed, but I suddenly realised my whole body was shivering. 'Can we walk?'

'Are you cold?'

'Frozen.'

'Come on then.' Adam leapt to his feet and pulled me up. As I stood I lost my balance slightly and tipped towards him. Our noses were almost touching, and even though I knew I should move away, create some space between us, I couldn't seem to make my body do as it was told. I could feel his warm breath against my lips and I was frozen to the spot.

'Was it always like this?' he whispered.

My legs shook and my whole body was tense with expectation. I didn't need to ask him what he meant. 'Yes.'

We stood there for a moment, the air fizzing between us, me thinking about the past, Adam no doubt trying to imagine it. Then suddenly the moment was broken when Adam moved away and smacked the tree trunk with the palm of his hand. 'Fuck!' He hit it again. 'Fuck, fuck, fuck. This stupid brain.' As I watched him I was reminded briefly of the young, volatile man he used to be, so quick to anger that it could sometimes be frightening. He turned to face me, his eyes filled with pain. 'I thought things were bad before, but this has made it ten times worse.'

'Meeting me?'

'Meeting you and realising that, even though I don't know you, there's something between us. Something magnetic.' He buried his face in his hands. 'I'm deeply drawn to you Erin.' His voice was low.

'Me too. To you I mean.' I was, despite the flash of the volatile side of Adam that had eventually led to us breaking up.

He looked up at me again. 'But you're married.'

'I am.'

He hesitated for a moment, then started striding away down the hill. I ran to catch him up. 'Where are you going?'

'Home.'

'Well wait for me.' The path was muddy and I found my feet sliding around beneath me in the dark. 'Adam, wait!'

He stopped and turned to face me in the darkness. I watched his breath rise in puffs as he waited for me to speak.

'Are you angry with me?'

He stepped towards me and took my hands in his again, gently this time. 'No Erin, I'm not angry with you. Just myself and my stupid brain.' He let out a breath. 'Do you have any idea how bloody difficult it is to not remember anything about yourself? About the things you like, the things you don't like; people you know and love, what programmes you enjoy, the music that means something to you, the places you've been...' He trailed off and tipped his head back to look at the sky. 'Fuck Erin, not a single day has gone by since my accident that I haven't wished, at least once, that I hadn't made it out of that wreckage alive. But now, standing here, I'm glad that I did.'

'I'm glad you did too.'

'It's just a shame I seem to be about eighteen years too late.'

We carried on down the hill and didn't speak again until we reached the gate that led back onto the road. I stopped and turned to face Adam. His face was flushed beneath the glow of the lamppost.

'Will you let me help you?' I said, remembering what I'd said to Rose yesterday.

'What do you mean?'

I paused, unsure how to explain it to him.

'As well as my counselling, I also work part-time with dementia patients.' I watched his face for a reaction but there was none, so I ploughed on. 'I play music to them, and I'm carrying out research into how music can unlock their memories.'

'Right?'

'Don't you see? Maybe that's the key for you, too? Music?'

He frowned. 'But I haven't got dementia. I've got a brain injury.'

'Yes I know that. And I know it's different. But there's some really amazing research into how music can trigger memories and I've seen it working first hand and I just thought...' I stopped. I was getting over-excited about the idea, but I didn't see the same enthusiasm reflected back in Adam's face. In fact, he looked decidedly unimpressed.

'I'm a musician Erin. I listen to music all the time, and I play it all the time too. And nothing has helped bring my memory back so far.' He sighed. 'Sorry, I know you're only trying to help but I just don't know what you think you might be able to do that the doctors haven't already done.'

I longed to explain it to him – about the amazing transformations I'd seen happen when a piece of music started, changing someone from an empty shell with no recollection at all, into a happy, complete person full of joy and a mind full of memories with just few notes of a familiar song, even if it was just for a few minutes. But now was neither the time nor the place.

'Okay. It was only an idea,' I said. Adam stepped forward and took my hands in his.

'Don't be upset,' he said. 'I know you want to help, but I also know it won't work. I listen to music all the time, and there's no point.'

I couldn't hide my disappointment. Even if it hadn't worked, at least it would have given me an excuse to legitimately spend some more time with him, carrying out the research. But now I didn't have a reason to see him again.

'I'd better go,' I said, taking a step away. The cold air rushed between us, as solid as a barrier. 'Let me know if you change your mind.' I took one last look at his face, then turned and walked away.

'Erin!' he called, and I turned back.

'Happy Christmas.'

'Happy Christmas Adam.'

8

NOW

Neil Young: 'Old Man'

Throughout history, where there have been humans, there has been music. Some of the oldest excavation sites in the world have uncovered flutes and drums made from animal skin stretched over tree stumps. Music has been created for every occasion and every gathering, whether it's a celebration, the start of something, the end of something, an African tribe celebrating or just a mother rocking her baby to sleep. Music soothes, music rouses; it's sewn into the fabric of everyday existence.

Scientists have long thought that the idea of using music to help memory is an exciting prospect, and after my mum was diagnosed with dementia so young, I decided to study music more seriously. I studied its importance in human evolution and development, and later, once I had my psychology degree under my belt, I started working with music and memory. The fact is, memory is the glue that holds us in our conscious present, and for those who have started to lose their memory – like my mother – the possibilities of using music and musical sounds to unlock those forgotten memories are endless.

For the last few years I'd been helping to develop a programme for people with dementia and had spent time visiting patients as a music therapist, learning, watching and recording how the music I played helped them. So far we had seen some amazing results: it seemed to unlock something in the patients' minds and either helped them remember who they were, or transported them back to a time when they felt happy and not scared by everything and everyone.

I loved my job and was frequently surprised by how lucky I was to be doing something that was so worthwhile. But today, on one of the last working days before Christmas, I was finding it hard to focus.

I only had two counselling clients booked in this morning, and then a couple of hospital visits with my music therapist hat on in the afternoon. I loved the variety, but still wished I could be somewhere else today.

When I'd got home from seeing Adam last night, Greg had been absorbed in an online chatroom with fellow recovering gamblers, so I'd left him to it and had soaked in the bath, grateful not to have had to explain where I'd been.

As I lay there in the scalding hot water, I wondered how long it would take for Greg to find out that Adam was back. It was a good sign that he'd already been back for a few months and Greg hadn't seen him. But then it was hardly a surprise, as Adam's family lived slightly out of town in a grand house behind electric gates. They weren't the type to frequent the high street, preferring to keep themselves separate from the rest of us mere mortals. Greg rarely went into town either. But he was bound to find out sooner or later. I knew I needed to do the right thing and tell him myself. I just didn't know when – or how.

Greg and I had agreed to move back to my hometown after university so I could be near my mum to help with her care if she needed it. Greg had been happy enough – probably because he knew that Adam was well out of the way, travelling the world with his band, sleeping with groupies, his lifestyle a million miles away from ours. At that distance, he'd posed no threat.

But I knew finding out about Adam's return would throw Greg off balance – not to mention what would happen if he found out I'd been spending time with his nemesis behind his back. We didn't need that drama right now. Greg had finally got his gambling under control, but he was still vulnerable to setbacks.

It was for the best that Adam didn't want me to help him.

So why did it feel as though there was a cavern opening up in my soul, hollowing me from the inside out?

I got through the morning, and made sure I really focused on what my clients were telling me. But later, as I was playing some gentle notes on my portable keyboard to a newly diagnosed dementia patient to see if I could stir any memories for him, I found myself drifting off, playing on autopilot.

Finally the day ended, Adam still on my mind. Not only did I feel overwhelmed at the emotions that seeing him again had stirred in me, but I couldn't help feeling frustrated at his refusal to let me help him. Response to music was such a deep-down, primal reaction, I was *certain* I could trigger something, if he'd let me try. But I couldn't force him to accept my offer.

I sat for a moment, suddenly exhausted by it all. I'd come a long way from the girl Adam had known all those years ago. Back then I'd been unsure of myself, so disbelieving that someone like Adam Bowers would pay me even the slightest bit of attention, and I'd lapped it up like a thirsty puppy. Now here I was with my own office, working as a counsellor, carrying out important research and making a difference to people who were losing themselves to dementia. And yet I seemed to be reverting, emotionally, to the teenager I'd been all those years ago.

I also missed my mum terribly. I missed our kitchen discos and our film afternoons, curled up on the sofa sharing a family-sized slab of Dairy Milk, blankets over our knees while my father was out playing squash. I missed her advice, her cooking. I missed her love.

I think back to the day that the phone call had come to tell me she'd been diagnosed with early onset dementia. I'd been in my room trying to get some work done, listening to Neil Young's haunting voice singing 'Old Man'— it was one of my dad's favourite songs and the melancholy lyrics reminded me of home. When the phone had rung, it was as though I'd had a sixth sense: I'd just known.

'Reeny?'

'Dad, what's wrong?'

There was a pause and my father cleared his throat.

'Now it's nothing to worry about Erin but – it's about your mum.' He stopped and I heard him sniff, and I had to stop myself from shouting at him to carry on. 'She's been having some... trouble.'

'Trouble? What do you mean?'

'She's been... forgetting a few things. Losing things.' He hesitated. 'And then the other day she got lost.'

'Lost? Where had she gone?'

'Just into town. The same as she always does.'

I waited for him to continue.

'She was brought home by two police officers in ever such a state. Seems she'd gone out but had forgotten how to get home and then... well, she went into a shop and asked for help. And the police were called.' His voice hitched a little. 'Anyway, we sat down and spoke about it later that evening once she'd calmed down, and it seems this wasn't the first time this sort of thing has happened.'

I went cold.

'And... is – is she okay now?'

I hardly dared to breathe as I waited for my father's response, my body perfectly still, my pulse roaring in my ears.

'I'm really sorry love, but the doctor said she has dementia.'

His words floored me. Mum was only forty; how could she have dementia?

On the phone, the hum of the long-distance connection filled one ear. I could hear my father's breathing and nothing else.

It wasn't what I'd been expecting Dad to say. I hadn't seen my parents much recently, too absorbed in university life – my work, new friends, missing Adam. But even I'd noticed Mum had seemed different when we'd spoken on the phone, or the few times I'd been home to see her. She'd been distracted, unable to fully concentrate on the thread of a conversation, flitting from one subject to another at will. But I hadn't really given it much more thought beyond simply noticing it. I had wondered vaguely whether it might be her hormones, and I'd even once considered she might have a brain tumour, but that had quickly been dismissed as being too dramatic.

'But she seems fine,' I said, aware I sounded like a little girl desperate for her father's reassurance.

'Yes, I know, she does most of the time. And most of the time she *is* fine. But she is getting worse. I made her go to the GP of course, after the police incident. She would never have gone on her own steam.'

I was reeling, struggling to make sense of it, but my father sounded so calm.

'You don't seem very upset.'

'Of course I'm upset. This is the worst possible news we could have had. But this isn't about me. It's about your mum, and what we're going to do.'

'You're right, sorry.' I paused. 'So what are we going to do?'

'Well that's just it love. *We're* not going to do anything. I am – I can look after her for the time being, while things are on an even keel. We're fine, me and your mum, as long as I stay with her most of the time. So I'm going to go part-time at work. It's not a big deal, I'll be retiring in a few years anyway. But—' He stopped and I heard him swallow. I knew this was just as hard for him as it was for me. 'As your mum deteriorates she's likely to be too bad to stay here with just me, and when that time comes we'll need to think about some help.'

'What sort of help?'

'I don't know yet. I suppose we'll cross that bridge when we come to it.' He swallowed again and my heart hurt at the thought of him having to deal with this all on his own. 'I'm so sorry to be the bearer of such bad news love. But promise me something?'

'What? Do you need me to come home?'

'Absolutely not. In fact, I want you to promise me the exact opposite of that – that you *won't* come rushing back here.'

'But—'

'Please love. Neither me nor your mum want this to be any harder than it needs to be, and that means you carrying on as normal, at least for now. These are the most important years of your life, and getting the actual diagnosis hasn't changed anything, not yet.'

I didn't speak for a few moments, letting my father's words sink in.

'How long have we got?'

He didn't ask what I meant; he knew. 'Nobody is really sure.

The doctors are saying it's progressing slowly but your guess is as good as mine. Which is why I don't want you rushing home. We might need you soon, but we're okay at the moment.' His voice cracked and he coughed to cover it up.

'Okay.' I hesitated. 'Dad?'

'Yes?'

'I love you.'

Dad let out an involuntary sound of surprise – we rarely expressed our feelings, just assumed the other one knew how we felt. 'I love you too Reeny.'

After he'd hung up, I'd sat there for a while, my mind numb. How could my mum – my vital, playful, fun-loving mum – be losing herself to such a cruel disease? Surely the doctors had to have made some mistake. And yet I knew deep down they hadn't.

It felt like my life had short-circuited and I longed to tell someone. Adam was away God only knew where with his band and wasn't due to visit for a few days, and it wasn't something I wanted to burden Rose or Sam with over the phone. That left Greg and, although we'd only known each other for a few months, he seemed like the natural choice so I'd sought him out. When I'd arrived at his room he'd been studying and I was about to leave, but he spotted me hovering in the half-open doorway and his face had lit up. He turned out to have been exactly what I'd needed that evening; he'd comforted me, listened to me, let me cry. He didn't tell me stories of other people he knew who had dementia, he didn't try and tell me that everything would be all right. He just let me get it off my chest, and sob. It was cathartic. Later that evening, when I'd been lying alongside him, squashed on top of the covers on his single bed, staring out of his tiny window at the dark night sky, a little thought started to settle and I realised I had no idea whether Adam would have been such a comfort. Sure, he would have listened, and would have done his best. But there was something about Greg that had been just what I'd needed in that moment. Perhaps that had been the night, months before we'd actually got together, that the foundations for us as a couple had been dug. Perhaps.

When I finally had gone home to see Mum a few weeks later, I'd been surprised – and relieved – at how normal she had been, for want of a better word. If I hadn't have known about the diagnosis, I would never have suspected that there was anything wrong at all. By the end of the two days I did start to notice the odd thing – she'd forget where the teabags were, or get stuck trying to remember the word for 'jacket' or 'newspaper' 'or 'radio'. But they were small things, minor memory lapses, the kind you have when you're tired or overwhelmed. Not dementia. Surely not. Not my mother, with her whole life ahead of her.

Not her.

And yet, as the months had passed, it had started to become clear that there really was something wrong. Conversations on the phone became harder as she'd sometimes forget who she was talking to, or ask me the same question she'd asked me just a moment before.

But while my heart broke to see this happening to Mum, Dad was a rock. I'd never doubted their love for each other, even if I'd never really understood it. How had two people so utterly different ever even met, let alone fallen in love? But they'd been happy, and when Mum had needed him the most, Dad had more than risen to the challenge.

'Erin?' I jumped at a voice beside me and realised my eyes were closed. I snapped them open to find my colleague Kate staring at me with a concerned look on her face. 'Is everything okay?'

'What? Yes, sorry.' How long had I been sitting here, lost in the past? I glanced up at the clock. It was getting late.

'Did you want to come for a drink? We're just popping for a quick one as it's the last day before Christmas.'

I shook my head. 'No I'd better not. Got a few things to do before the big day, you know what it's like.'

'Okay, if you're sure.' She tilted her head to one side. 'Are you sure you're okay? You're very pale.'

'Honestly, I'm fine, it's just been a busy week. I need to collapse tonight.' I plastered a smile on my face and she seemed reassured.

'Well, if you're positive, then have a fab Christmas and I'll see you when we're back in the new year, will I?'

'You will. Merry Christmas Kate.'

Once she'd gone, I stood and gathered my instruments together, put my little speakers in my rucksack, and headed out of the door. It was only a fifteen-minute drive home but I was in no hurry and after sticking my stuff in the boot of the car I meandered along the path that ran beside the river and breathed in deeply. The air was bitterly cold but it felt cleansing, as though it was helping to clear my mind. I reached a bench and sat for a few moments, watching the silent river flow by. As I tipped my head up to the stars I thought about last night when I'd studied this very same sky, with Adam by my side. I wondered where he was right now, and what he was doing. Whether he was thinking about me.

Then I stood, walked back to my car, and drove home to my husband.

* * *

I opened the door and the house was quiet. I could tell Greg was home though, because the house felt different when it was completely empty. I jumped at something brushing against my feet and then smiled when I looked down to see Dog curling round and round my feet, purring madly. I bent down to pick him up.

'Hello little dude, how's your day been?' I cooed into his ear, and he wriggled to be set free. I let him go and he ran off to wait expectantly by his food bowl. I rolled my eyes. Why did Greg always leave me to feed the cat?

I followed Dog into the kitchen and filled his bowl. He tucked in greedily. There was a bottle of red open on the worktop so I shrugged off my coat, slipped my boots off and poured myself a glass. I stood for a minute, sipping my wine, and felt the tension from the last few days seep away. It was the day before Christmas Eve tomorrow, and I was looking forward to seeing Greg, Rose and Sam, as well as Mum on Christmas Eve and Dad on Christmas Day. It would be good for us to spend some time together, I reassured myself, trying to ignore the niggle at the back of my mind that was telling me I was going to miss seeing Adam.

Before I headed upstairs, it occurred to me that I hadn't checked up on Mum for a couple of days. The care home she'd moved into a few years earlier was about ten miles away and I visited at least once a week, but I tried to call regularly as well. I dialled the number and waited for someone to pick up at the other end. I was relieved when a familiar voice answered and I knew instantly that it was Suzy, Mum's main carer.

'Hello Erin,' she said warmly. 'Merry Christmas.'

'Ah you too Suzy,' I replied. I loved Suzy and was forever grateful that Mum had her looking after her. She gave her almost as much love and attention as she would get at home living with me and Greg, or with Dad, but she also kept her safe. 'How is she?'

'She's had a good day today, although the sound of the wind

upset her a bit earlier. All good now though. She's looking forward to seeing you tomorrow.'

Bless Suzy. We both knew full well that Mum was unlikely to have registered that I was coming to see her, and even if she had, that she was even less likely to still remember it by tomorrow, but I loved her for trying.

'Thanks Suzy. See you then.'

I pocketed my phone and headed towards the stairs, trying not to slosh wine onto the carpet. Halfway up it occurred to me I should have brought Greg a fresh glass up, but then he was no doubt chatting to his gambling recovery group so I didn't really want to disturb him. I reached the top of the stairs and could see a crack of light coming from under the door to the spare room, and padded across the carpet towards it. I pushed the door open and saw Greg at his computer. It all happened so quickly. I glanced at his screen, and almost at the same moment he turned and spotted me, a look of horror on his face. In that frozen moment I didn't speak, and then he turned back to his computer, shut down the website he was looking at and turned back to me. There were spots of red high on both of his cheeks.

'I – I didn't hear you come in,' he stuttered.

I still didn't speak and he watched me hopefully. I glanced at the now-blank screen and back at his face, then turned and slammed the door, stalking back down the stairs towards the kitchen. By the time he caught up with me I was pulling on my boots.

'Erin, please. Don't run off.'

'I saw you, Greg. I saw what you were doing.'

He hung his head. 'I know. And I'm sorry. It was a one-off.'

'That's what you said last time. But you promised me. You promised me you'd stop gambling.'

'I know. And I have. I had. I...' He stepped towards me. 'It really was just this once. I promise. You have to believe me.'

I shook my head. 'I don't believe you though, that's the problem.'

'I...' He held his hand out. 'Come upstairs. I'll show you. It was just one bet, just today, I swear. It's been months; I've been doing really well.'

I wavered for a moment. He truly did seem sorry, and I knew I should give him the benefit of the doubt. But after everything that had happened over the last few months and all the hard work he'd put into his recovery so far, I just couldn't believe he'd let himself slip up like this, and I was struggling to forgive him.

'I just need to go out for a while,' I said. 'Clear my head.'

'But where? It's getting late.'

'I'm just going for a walk.' I pulled my coat on. 'Can we talk about this when I get home?'

'I'll make dinner.'

I studied him for a moment, and I nearly took my coat off and let him convince me he was better, but instead I nodded curtly. 'Okay.' Then I brushed past him, out of the door, and walked away, hoping that my whole world wasn't about to crumble down around me.

9

THEN

Gin Blossoms: 'Hey Jealousy'

The air simmered with heat, despite it being early October. Erin and Greg were standing on the edge of Highfields Park boating lake, squinting out at the water.

'You sure you've got time for this?' Greg said, as a small rowing boat bobbed in front of them.

Erin checked her watch. 'Yeah, there's plenty of time. Adam won't be here for ages.'

Greg tried not to flinch at the mention of Erin's boyfriend – this enigmatic man he'd heard so much about and who he already detested with every fibre of his being – and held out his hand.

'Come on then, let's get going.'

They clambered aboard and Greg pushed them away from the bank. The air was cooler out on the lake, the heat of the sun scattering across the water, sparkling back at them like diamonds as they headed out, away from the crowds. Erin leaned back, hooked her elbows over the edge of the boat and pulled her sun hat down over her eyes. She peered into the blue-green depths of the lake where fish moved about just below the surface. What else was down there, hidden in the depths?

'This is better than studying any day,' she said, squinting at Greg as he pulled the oars back and forth. She tried not to notice the way his biceps flexed, or the way the sun had turned his skin a golden brown.

'Too right. Might as well make the most of this last blast of sunshine.'

They might have only met two weeks before, but Erin and Greg had become best friends since then. A frisson shimmered between them, some unspoken connection, but they were both content to settle for friendship. For now at least, Greg told himself.

He was dreading this afternoon though, because Adam was coming to visit, and he wasn't sure if he'd be able to contain his contempt for the man who'd stolen Erin's heart so completely. He sounded, in Greg's humble opinion, like an utter arse.

He stopped rowing for a minute and let the boat float lazily. A breeze rippled across the surface of the water and lifted Greg's hair away from his face. He closed his eyes and held his face up to the sun.

'Are we stopping?' Erin said, leaning forward to poke him in the belly. He jumped as though he'd had an electric shock, and felt his face burn. He turned his head away and reached behind him for his rucksack.

'I've brought a few things.'

'Oooh, what is it?' Erin said, trying to peer into the bag. Greg snatched it away and held it in the air.

'Hey, hey, patience.' He grinned.

'Come on, what have you got in there?' Erin half-stood and tried to swipe for the bag. But as she did she lost her balance and tipped forward and, as if in slow motion, she fell, landing on top of Greg, her palms against his chest and her face pressed right up against his. He thought his heart might stop beating as they lay there, momentarily stunned. It would be the easiest thing in the world to snake his arm round her, turn his head ever so slightly and kiss her, gently. But before he could do anything, the moment had passed, and Erin pushed her body off him, leaving him lying there, flooded with desire.

'Oh God, I'm so sorry,' she said, her face flushed, laughter bubbling out of her.

'It's all right,' Greg said, sitting up and brushing non-existent dust from his shorts. 'But that's what you get for being impatient.'

'Sorry.' Erin stuck her bottom lip out and Greg had to look away. 'But come on, show me what you've got in there.'

'Well, it's probably not that exciting now you've built it up so much, but here you go.' He pulled a bottle out of his bag and handed it to Erin. 'Ooh, Asti Spumante,' she said, reading the label.

'Yeah, sorry, it's all I could afford. I reckon it'll be okay though.' He pulled out a couple of plastic pint glasses – 'I swiped them from the Union' – and a Tupperware box containing cheese slices, Jacob's cream crackers, a bunch of grapes and a melted bar of Dairy Milk. 'I got these too,' he said, pulling out a tube of Pringles. 'I know it's not exactly high-end dining, but I thought it would be nice to have a little picnic. A bit of a celebration, you know...' He trailed off, suddenly unsure of himself.

'That's so lovely,' Erin said, yanking the top off the Pringles and peeling a couple of crisps from the top. 'What are we celebrating?'

Greg looked at her for a moment as she chewed, watching her face for any reaction. Her eyes were wide and bright, her skin shone in the sunlight, her sunglasses pushed back on her head as the sun surrounded her like a halo. His own perfect angel, he thought.

'Just – well...' He stopped, took a breath. 'Me and you. You know, our friendship.' He gave a small smile. 'I know it's silly.'

'It's not silly at all; I think it's lovely.' She reached out and pressed her hand into his. His skin was warm where they touched and he pulled it away and picked up the bottle.

'Want some?'

'Of course!' she said, crunching down on a cracker and holding out a plastic glass. 'Fill me up!'

Those ninety minutes on the lake drinking cheap fizz and eating dry crackers on that sunny Friday afternoon were among the happiest of Greg's life so far. They were alone, just the two of them, and he could get to know this wonderful, funny woman without anyone else interrupting. He could have stayed there forever, but of course all good things must come to an end, and in this case, they were brought to an abrupt end by a text message. He knew it was all over the minute Erin's phone buzzed, and yet he still hoped otherwise.

'It's Adam,' she said, squinting down at her phone. 'He's arrived.'

'Oh, great,' Greg said without a hint of enthusiasm.

'Sorry Greg. This has been really lovely but do you mind if we head back now? I haven't seen him for two weeks.' The light that shone in her eyes felt like a dagger to his heart because he knew she was no longer thinking about him, but about Adam. Bloody Adam.

'Sure,' he said, taking up the oars once more and turning the boat round. The sun was behind him now and he rowed in silence, letting the lapping of the water and the occasional shriek from the nearby park fill his mind.

As they stepped onto the lake edge, there was a shout from a distance away. Greg turned and could make out the silhouette of a man heading their way.

'Oh it's him!' Erin squealed, taking off, and Greg watched with a heavy heart as she launched herself at Adam. When they eventually peeled apart, Greg slung his rucksack over his shoulder and planted his feet firmly on the grass, his fists clenched, taking the time to study his rival. He had the rockstar look down to a tee – long scraggly hair, leather jacket (in this heat!), tight ripped jeans, fag hanging between his fingers. He looked like a total fucking cliché. But worse was the air of arrogance as he swaggered towards him, and it was all Greg could do to force a smile.

'Greg, this is Adam,' Erin gushed, her hand still clasping Adam's tightly. 'Adam, this is my friend, Greg.'

Greg tried not to bristle at the word 'friend' and stuck his hand out in greeting. 'Nice to meet you,' he said, and Adam shook his hand with a smirk.

'I'm so excited you two can finally meet,' Erin said, seemingly oblivious to Greg's sudden change of mood. She turned and looked longingly at Adam. 'It's such a nice day; do you want to stay here and chill for a bit?'

Adam glanced round him, taking in the groups of students sitting in huddles, then looked at Greg. He shrugged. 'I guess so. We've got plenty of time to be alone later eh?'

Greg had never wanted to punch someone so much in his life.

Even though the last thing Greg felt like doing was spending the rest of the day being a gooseberry, he also wasn't ready to give up his day with Erin. So the three of them made their way to the slope of the riverbank, away from the boat hire, where Erin immediately pulled off her shoes and walked straight into the shallow water.

'God, it's freezing!' She fizzed with laughter and Greg had to tear his gaze away from her. As he did he found Adam staring at him.

'So, how long have you two been friends?'

'We met in Fresher's Week, so only a couple of weeks.'

Adam nodded. 'Right.' He looked back at Erin. 'Great, isn't she?'

Unsure whether it was a test, Greg hesitated. 'Yes, she is,' he said eventually. 'How – how long have you two been together?' He knew, but couldn't think of anything else to say.

'A year or so.' He took his hat off and lay back on the grass, his arms behind his head. Greg hugged his knees into his chest.

'Don't you miss her when you're away?'

'Yeah, course. But I've got the band as well, and Erin gets that.' He glanced over at Greg again. 'I'm glad she's met some new friends though. Someone to look after her.' Was it Greg's imagination or was *there emphasis on the word 'friends'? He met Adam's gaze pointedly. 'I'll definitely look after her, don't worry about that.'*

The meaning sizzled in the air between them, so many unspoken words filling the gaps it was a wonder they could breathe. And then the moment was broken by the sound of someone nearby blasting out music from their speakers.

'I love this song,' Erin said, appearing in front of them both like a mirage, water running down her pale legs.

'Oh, it's "Hey Jealousy" by the Gin Blossoms,' Adam said, deliberately not looking at Greg as he said the song title loud and clear.

'It's a great song,' Greg said, ignoring the jibe.

Adam snorted.

'What?' Erin sat down between them, dripping cold water over them both. 'It is a great song.'

'It's shit,' Adam said. 'Anodyne and trite.' He sat up and pulled his hat back on. 'You wouldn't catch me playing something like this.'

'Just as well we all like different things then, isn't it?' Greg said, the words 'arrogant prick' fortunately staying safely on the tip of his tongue.

Adam turned slowly to face him. 'Yes grandma, I suppose it is.' He grinned. 'It's still a shite song though.'

'Oh stop it you two, it doesn't really matter. You like it, you don't. Let's talk about something else now.' Erin looked from one to the other and neither spoke. 'Aren't you going to get your feet wet? It's gorgeous.'

'Nope,' Adam said, pointing down at his scuffed Doc Martens.

'Greg?' Erin said hopefully.

'Go on then,' he said, pulling off his pristine Reeboks and heading down to the water's edge. But by the time he'd hitched up his jeans and turned round to see if she was following him, Erin and Adam were lying back on the grass, their faces pressed so close they were almost kissing. Greg thought he might scream. He turned away again and swallowed down a lump in his throat.

'Sorry Greg, I think we're going to go back to mine for a bit. Will you be all right on your own?' Erin's voice sailed through the air. He turned to see Adam sliding his hand up her thigh and Erin swatting it away, and he had to look away again.

'Yeah, no worries. See you later.'

He watched the water lap against his feet, trying not to think about Erin and Adam together, trying not to think about anything. Out on the water there was a splash, trails of white flicking up as a couple had a water fight on a rowing boat. It had been such a lovely day, just him and Erin. But now the whole memory had been tainted, distorted by a feckless, selfish man who Erin was too blind to see was no good for her.

Well, it didn't matter how long it took her. One day he would make her see that it was him she wanted. One day, she would look at Greg the way she looked at Adam.

One day.

10

NOW

Madonna: 'Like a Prayer'

Gliding up the driveway in my beaten old Merc, the gravel crunching beneath the tyres, I felt the tension rising in my neck and shoulders, and my hands gripped the steering wheel tightly. I adored my mum, but seeing her was so hard when I had no idea each time I visited whether she would have any clue who I was.

I pulled up outside the care home, the grey stone building glowering menacingly at me beneath the dark clouds, and closed my eyes for a moment. I needed a second to prepare for my visits these days, to remind myself that this wasn't who Mum was. She wasn't this broken shell of a human who didn't know where she was or what she was doing there. She was the vibrant, funny, loving mum who had always looked after me, laughed with me, hugged me when I needed her. That mum, the one who made me feel safe, protected, was still in there somewhere, hidden beneath the cruel cloak of dementia. And by God, I missed her.

As I climbed out of the car, an icy gust of wind sent my hair flying and made me stumble. It was so hot in the care home I usually left my coat in the car, but not today. I made my way to the steps, ran up them, eager to get out of the cold, and stepped through the door. As it closed behind me the atmosphere transformed; there was an air of calm in here quite unlike anywhere else I'd ever been.

'Erin, hello,' said a voice and I turned and smiled.

'Suzy,' I said warmly. We didn't hug the way we used to – two years of living through a pandemic seemed to have put an end to niceties like that – but she did clutch my arm in greeting. I'd known Suzy for more than eight years, ever since Mum moved in, and she meant the world to me. Not only did she look after my mum, but she looked after me too. I honestly didn't know how I'd make it through these visits without her.

'How are you?' she said now.

'I'm good,' I replied, the way I always did. There was something about Suzy that made you want to confide in her, to spill all your secrets, confident that she'd make you feel better. And right now, what with Adam, the memory loss, Greg's gambling, it felt as though I needed someone to confide in. But I held back. 'Work's busy,' I said instead. 'How are things here?'

She nodded. 'Really good. Your mum's having a good day.'

I nodded and forced a smile. Suzy's idea of a good day was not always the same as mine, and if I allowed myself to hope that Mum might just know who I was today, I'd almost certainly end up disappointed.

'Come on, let's take you to her. She's in her room.'

Of course she was. She always was. She used to spend time in the common room, listening to music, watching TV or chatting to her fellow inmates – sorry, residents. But these days she hardly left her room because everything either confused or terrified her. My heart felt heavy in my chest as we trudged along the corridor.

'Penny, Erin's come to see you,' Suzy said, as we reached Mum's door, and she pushed it open softly and we stepped inside. The air in the room was still and dry as a desert, the modern radiator in the corner pumping out heat all day and all night. Mum's three-quarter size bed was pushed up against the far wall by the large window that overlooked the garden – something Dad had insisted on when we moved Mum in here – and her bedspread was pulled neatly up and tucked under the pillow. This was the work of a nurse, I knew, because even before she was ill Mum was never this fastidious. She hated dirt and clutter, but she didn't believe in spending too much time doing housework. *No-one will ever remember you for having a tidy house,* she always said. Not much about this room reflected Mum, even aside from the tidiness. Mum's favourite photos were placed haphazardly in frames on top of a plain pine chest of drawers, some of her make-up scattered beside them, crumbs of broken face powder and smears of lipstick marking the surface. But the artwork, the décor – it was all drab, generic, institutional, with none of Mum's flair and eye for colour. It felt as though the mum I'd always loved had been left at home with Dad, with just her body here for show.

Right now, Mum was sitting in one of the burgundy high-backed armchairs that had been turned to face the window, and I held my breath as I waited for her response to hearing my name. Slowly, she turned, her eyes taking their time to focus.

'Hello,' I said, taking care not to approach too quickly. I'd learned a few things over the last few years, including to move towards her slowly in case she got frightened, and not to call her Mum straight away in case she didn't recognise me. That could make her really stressed.

'Hello, who are you?' she said with a blank smile.

'I'm Erin,' I said, making my way slowly to the seat across from her and lowering myself down gently.

'That's a lovely name. Have you come to give me more medicine?'

'No Mu—' I stopped. 'No, I've just come to see you.'

Mum looked frightened and her eyes flicked to Suzy, who stepped forward.

'Do you know who Erin is, Penny?'

Mum shook her head, her eyes wide with fear, and my heart broke for her. We went through this, or something similar, almost every time I came. Sometimes Mum simply accepted my presence and let me spend time with her. On really good days Mum recognised me and we talked almost like we used to. But much more often, Mum became anxious and frightened when I arrived and I had to leave her to calm down. It already looked as though today was going to be one of those days.

'Why is she here?' Her voice wavered and the pitch rose in panic.

'I'd better go.' I stood to leave.

Suzy placed her hand on my arm gently. 'Thanks Erin. Just give me a moment to calm her down.'

I stepped outside the room and sucked in the over-warm air, trying to fill my lungs, to calm myself. It didn't matter how many times I told myself Mum's reaction wasn't personal, I couldn't help feeling a little bit broken every time this happened.

I took myself outside. I needed fresh air and time to think, to decompress. As I strode around the grounds – the grass was wet underfoot and the wind had got up even more now – I thought about the look on Mum's face when she hadn't recognised me. You'd think after fifteen years of this I'd be used to it, but it seemed to get harder rather than easier. You would also think that, given my job, I would understand it more. But this was too personal; I couldn't take a step back and be objective.

A few years ago I'd broached the subject of trying to help Mum's memory with music with Suzy. She'd agreed it was worth a go and so, that very first time, I came in armed with Mum's favourite songs loaded onto my iPad, and played them to her. The effect had been both instantaneous and overwhelming. From the moment the songs had started, Mum had been transformed. Her face had lit up, the anxiety in her eyes had disappeared, and her whole body had seemed to uncurl. She'd leapt up and begun whirling round the room, singing along with every word as if she'd heard the songs only yesterday. It had been so wonderful to see her like that, it felt as though the curtain that had hidden my mum from view for so long had momentarily lifted and it filled me with warmth. The second the music stopped she'd stopped too, like a tired old wind-up toy, as though it had only been the music fuelling her. But for those few moments, at least, I'd felt as though I had my mum back.

Since then, I'd experimented with how we used the songs we chose. Sometimes it was just a case of playing a piece as loud as I dared and letting Mum get lost in the memories it evoked, allowing her to believe she was the young woman she used to be again, dancing round the living room with me on a Saturday afternoon, or swaying with Dad in the kitchen. Other times though, I'd tried playing songs quietly in the background, and asking Mum questions about when she was younger to see if the music would trigger something in her brain that might otherwise have been lost. I'd had mixed results; sometimes Mum was lucid and talked openly, even if it wasn't quite clear whether she knew *when* in time she actually was. Other times the therapy didn't do much at all and I'd left her feeling deflated.

I walked on, the dampness in the air making my hair stick to my face. I should go back and see if Suzy had managed to calm Mum down, so reluctantly I turned and headed back towards the care home, my feet heavy. I climbed the front steps again, and this time when I pushed open the door the warm air felt oppressive. There was no-one around so I made my way towards Mum's room. Suzy came out, pulling the door gently behind her.

'Ah, you're back, excellent timing,' she said, smiling. I wished I had her serenity. She appeared to find it so easy to cope when everything seemed utterly out of control.

'How is she?'

'She's calm again now. She's ready for you.' She nodded at my bag. 'Have you got some songs for her?'

'I have. Do you think she'll be okay with them today?'

'I think she'll be fine.' She placed her hand on my arm and smiled. 'She lights up when you come in you know. I know it's really hard to see her distressed.'

'Thank you Suzy.'

Inside Mum's room I was relieved to find her back in her chair, calm. She turned when I walked in and smiled. 'Hello,' she said. Even though Mum was only fifty-seven, her once blonde hair was now completely white. It was still long, and I remembered when I used to spend hours plaiting it for her, or brushing it and pulling it into bunches back in the days when I dreamed of being a hairdresser. The colour made her look elegant and distinguished, but I couldn't help feeling a pang of melancholy when I saw the blankness behind her eyes, the only clue from the outside that her mind had played such a cruel trick on her. I tried not to think about how things would be if dementia hadn't snatched her from me, of the fun we'd have had together, because it hurt too much.

I sat down on the smaller chair opposite, then leaned over and took her hands gently in mine. She peered down at our clasped fingers then back up at me with a puzzled look in her eyes. She said nothing so I took a minute to study her, this face I knew so well and yet which also seemed so unfamiliar to me.

She was lucky to have this place, I knew. Dad paid for it every month without fail and it was one of the best homes around – when he'd finally had to admit he couldn't cope with Mum by himself any more, he'd made sure he did his research and found the very best place he could. But seeing her here, festering away, deteriorating month by month, dragging out the years in the same old room, the same old building, gave me a hollowed-out feeling, like homesickness. Sometimes I wondered whether she might be happier if she just left this world for good.

We sat in silence for a moment, only the sounds of the other residents and the nurses disturbing our peace. The radiator clunked beneath the window and I stared blindly into the lamp before looking back at Mum's face. Dark spots jumped in my vision.

'Would you like to listen to some music?' I said, eventually.

She nodded. 'Yes please.'

I took my hands away and leaned down to find my phone in the bag. I pulled out the wires, then the portable speakers, then scrolled through my playlists. Mum waited expectantly, her eyes wide and innocent. Finally finding the song I was looking for, I pressed play and the opening strains of 'Like a Prayer' rose out across the room; the guitars, the choir and Madonna's soaring vocals...

Mum clasped her hands together.

'Oh I like this one!' she cried, getting to her feet as the beat kicked in. Slowly, her hips started to sway and she bounced from foot to foot, transforming almost instantly from a frail woman to my young, fun-loving mum. The change in her face always hit me, as though the years had dropped from her and she was twenty again, dancing at her local disco, attracting the eyes of all the boys, not a care in the world. These moments, when her dementia mask slipped, made all the other difficult times worthwhile. God how I adored her.

I watched her for a moment more, then she beckoned for me to join her, so I did. And for a couple of minutes, while the song played, we danced round her small patch of carpet, arms in the air, singing along. Mum was never quite sure of the words but she sang at the top of her voice anyway. I wondered what her neighbours must think, if they even noticed. People were sometimes surprised by the songs I played to Mum when I explained to them what I did: her favourite pop songs from when she was younger; some of my father's favourites, older songs from the sixties and seventies; and sometimes more basic tunes, simple harmonies and notes plucked out from violin strings. It was the same with all my patients. People expected the therapy to rely on classical music, and sometimes it did. But actually, classical music could often be too involved, have too many layers of tones and rhythms. Some music therapists played simple sounds, particularly to newborn babies in ICUs, and rhythms that mimicked the heartbeat. For dementia patients, we were often guided by the individual's personal choice, and that was definitely the case for Mum.

The song came to an end, and before the next one could start, I pressed stop. I'd learned from experience that if I tried too much all at once it left Mum feeling exhausted and more confused than ever. One song at a time was the best way.

Mum was still standing in the middle of the room, adrift. She seemed bewildered, but a wisp of a smile remained on her face, and I longed to take a photo of her, to capture this rare moment when she looked truly happy again. Instead, I took her hands and guided her back to her armchair, helping her settle before sitting back down myself.

'That was fun, wasn't it?' I said, trying to regain Mum's attention. When it became clear she was still elsewhere, I fiddled with my phone again and found a different song. This time I turned the volume down low and let the song play softly in the background, a suggestion, in the hope it would filter through to her mind.

'Hello, have you just got here?' she said, as if noticing me for the first time.

'Yes,' I replied.

'How lovely,' she said. 'Have you brought your lovely young man with you?'

'Which young man would that be?' I smiled. She knew who I was.

She frowned, trying to locate a name that was just out of reach. 'You know.' She flapped her hands around her head. 'Long hair. A bit scruffy. Plays the guitar.'

My stomach went into freefall. She meant Adam.

It wasn't a coincidence that she'd mentioned him today, she did from time to time, and if Greg was with me we both tried to ignore it and move on. But today it stopped me in my tracks and I felt my cheeks grow hot.

'No it's just me today,' I said. 'Shall we have a cuppa?'

'Yes please.'

I was glad of the change of subject, and while I popped out to ask someone for a pot of tea – the kettle had had to be removed from Mum's room after she kept burning herself on boiling water – I left her looking out of the window, lost in her own little world. I hoped she'd have forgotten all about Adam by the time I got back.

Sure enough, when I returned with a tray loaded with a teapot, cups and a plate of ginger biscuits, Mum didn't mention Adam again, as though the few minutes I'd been away had been enough time to wipe her memory and perform a complete reset, like a faulty computer hard drive.

'Is Greg here?' she said instead, peering round me expectantly as I walked through the door.

I sighed. Our conversations could be hard work even for me sometimes, flitting from one year to another, one person to another in such quick succession. It must be utterly exhausting for her.

'He's not coming today, but he'll be here to see you after Christmas,' I said, carefully balancing the tray on the sideboard and pouring the tea. I placed a cup and saucer in front of her and sat back down with my own.

'Oh, is it Christmas?' Mum said, her eyes wide.

'Yes, in a couple of days,' I said, for what must have been the tenth time.

'Oh lovely, I do love Christmas.' Her face collapsed into a frown then, creases appearing as her eyes darted round the room. 'Where's the tree? You can't have Christmas without a tree, whatever your father thinks.'

'The tree is in the living room,' I said gently.

'But why haven't I got one in here? I must have one in here.' Mum seemed agitated so I put my cup back down and took her hand again. Her body stilled and her face gradually relaxed. Her eyes searched me out and a gentle smile appeared on her lips. 'I used to love decorating our tree you know. I always chose the biggest one I could find.'

I smiled, remembering the towering Christmas trees Mum insisted on squeezing into our house, trees big enough to fit into shopping centres, and the battle she had to make them fit into the room.

'Your dad thought I was mad of course. But then he usually did.' She was right. Mum had always had a mischievous streak which Dad definitely didn't share. At sixteen years older than her, he'd been the sensible one, the one to rein in her madcap ideas. The combination seemed to work somehow, the two of them. They were one of the happiest couples I knew. Mum clapped her hands together suddenly. 'Oh, do you remember the angel we always put on the top, the one you made at school?'

'I do,' I said. It was always a mystery to me how Mum could swing so wildly from not having a clue who I was to remembering tiny details like the Christmas fairy I made more than thirty years before.

'Can you find it? I want to put it on my tree,' she said.

'I haven't seen it for years Mum.' Her face crumpled again and I squeezed her hands gently. 'But I promise to look for it, okay?'

She looked up at me, her eyes sad. 'Thank you. You can't have a Christmas tree without a Christmas angel.'

I let go of her hands and took a sip of my almost-cold tea, relieved that she seemed to have calmed down.

'I'm quite tired,' she said. 'Can I go to sleep now?'

'Course you can. Do you want me to help you?'

'Yes please.'

As I helped Mum get herself ready for bed, removing her clothes, finding her nightie, assisting her while she cleaned her teeth and brushed her hair, and with the day darkening outside the window, I couldn't help thinking about all the times she had done this for me, and feeling a pang of sadness at how time had slipped away, for both of us.

I hoped, as her mind and her memories slowly disappeared, one by one like bubbles in the air, that she didn't regret any of the choices she'd made in her life.

I hoped I wouldn't either.

11

THEN

The Human League: 'Don't You Want Me'

Erin reached up and pressed the doorbell, her heart thumping wildly in her chest. She wiped her palms on her jeans and stood, rigid, staring at the solid wood of the front door.

'You're shaking Erin, are you all right?' Greg said beside her.

'What? Oh yes, I'm fine.' She smiled weakly. 'Sorry, you know I'm really nervous about you meeting Mum and Dad.'

'You make them sound like ogres,' Greg said, looking at her quizzically. 'Do you think they're going to hate me or something?'

'God no, they're going to love you. It's just – well, I haven't brought anyone back before. At least not since—' Erin stopped, not wanting to mention Adam's name. It hadn't just been Greg who had taken an instant dislike to Adam. Her dad hadn't been keen either, and it had made things awkward, meaning they rarely spent any time at her home. Her mum had liked Adam of course, but then she saw the good in everyone.

Erin was saved from explaining any more by the front door
swinging open, and she turned to find her mum smiling widely, her dad
hovering behind like a shadow.

'Hello love,' Penny said, throwing her arms wide and pulling Erin
into a hug. As she released her daughter she looked at Greg, a smile
lighting up her face. 'And you must be Greg,' she said, pulling him into a
hug too. 'It's really lovely to meet you; Erin's told me so much about
you.'

'Good to meet you Mrs Pearson,' Greg said, looking flustered. He
held out a bunch of flowers he'd bought at the station as they'd got on
the train.

'Oh thank you,' Penny said, taking the flowers and pressing her nose
against the petals. 'And please don't call me Mrs Pearson, that makes me
feel ancient. I'm Penny.' She turned then to introduce her husband. 'And
this is Michael, Erin's father.'

Her dad stepped forward out of the shadows and held his hand out
to Greg, who shook it stiffly. 'Very nice to meet you, young man,' he said.

'Oh Dad, you don't need to stand to attention,' Erin said, reaching
up and ruffling his hair the way she always did. She was desperate for
her dad to approve of Greg and, although she couldn't see any reason
why he wouldn't like him – after all, Greg was polite and kind and,
most importantly, he wasn't travelling round the country playing in a
band instead of looking after his girlfriend – she knew what her dad
could be like sometimes. What most dads could be like when it came to
their kids.

'Come on in,' her mum said, moving into the house, her long dress
wafting around her legs like a sprite, her feet bare on the cool ceramic
tiles. Erin followed them, Greg just behind her, and as she made her
way along the familiar hallway, she tried to see her childhood home
through Greg's eyes. She wondered what he'd make of the old-fashioned
furnishings, the tall ceilings, the huge ornate framed paintings, and the
rundown kitchen that nobody had ever had the heart to renovate

because it was so in keeping with the old rectory that they'd bought as their home all those years ago.

'Right, who wants a glass of wine?' Penny said, spinning round to face them.

'Please Mum,' Erin said.

'That would be lovely Mrs – Penny,' Greg replied, smiling.

As her mum fussed around pouring drinks, Erin watched her parents closely. Her father was doing a great job of hiding his feelings, but she thought she could see the beginnings of a thaw from him already, now he'd met Greg. But it was her mum she watched most closely, trying to see whether she could see any signs of the dementia that doctors insisted she had. As she studied her, pouring drinks, chatting away happily, smiling the way she always had, Erin couldn't help wondering whether they might have made a mistake. After all, surely dementia meant she'd be getting worse, not better? Erin made a mental note to ask her father about it later.

The rest of the day passed without incident. In the end, Greg and her dad hit it off like a house on fire, finding common ground in a few things including their mutual love of all sports, and a similar taste in music. At one point Dad even jumped up to put a record on, insisting that Greg must like 'Don't You Want Me' by The Human League as it was a classic of its time. Greg agreed, of course, that the synthesizer and the techno beat were both way ahead of their time, that the opening line about the waitress in the cocktail bar was one of the best opening lines to a song there had ever been, and that the entire thing was completely underrated. Erin and Penny rolled their eyes at each other indulgently.

Her dad didn't even seem to be fazed by Greg's wilder side, the stories he told him of spontaneous naked swims in the river, or of the huge amounts of money he'd lost at the greyhound racing when he was seventeen. Erin watched them happily as they chatted easily, and she felt so proud of this funny, kind, handsome man who had made her life so much better since he'd become part of it. She couldn't help comparing *this meeting to the first time Adam had met her parents. It had been one sunny Saturday a few weeks after they'd met, and Erin had invited Adam back for a barbecue at her parents' house. She'd been nervous then, too – and rightly so as it turned out, at least as far as her father was concerned.*

Adam had tried his best. He'd scrubbed up well, tied his hair back neatly, worn his best pair of jeans, and spoken politely. And it had started so well. But she could remember clearly the moment it had begun to go wrong, that the respectable veneer Adam had so far managed to maintain had begun to slip, and that her father had begun to dislike him. They had been standing in the garden, waiting for the sausages to cook, when Michael had asked Adam what he was going to do when he left school.

'I'm off to tour with my band,' Adam had replied.

Erin had watched, mortified, as her father's face had pinched itself into a mask of disapproval, and she waited anxiously for his response.

'But what about after that? I mean, what about a career?'

'Music is my career. At least it will be,' Adam had insisted.

'I see.' Dad had been reluctant to engage with Adam much after that, making it perfectly clear that he didn't think he was good enough for Erin, until they had all felt so uncomfortable that they'd left early, slinking off as soon as they'd eaten.

The trouble was, Erin understood her father's reaction. It wasn't as though her dad was particularly highly strung, or that he was being unreasonable. She could see that now, even more clearly in hindsight. What father would want their daughter to be caught up in the sort of lifestyle associated with a rock band: the groupies, the alcohol, drugs and everything else? Of course he was never going to think Adam was the perfect man for her.

Surprisingly, though, her mother hadn't agreed with her husband.

'Don't listen to your father,' she'd hissed in Erin's ear as they'd slipped out of the front door. Adam had been standing a few steps away

by the front gate, just out of earshot, and Erin had turned back, surprised.

'He's made it perfectly clear he doesn't like Adam,' Erin had said, anger tinting her words.

'Yes, yes, I know that. But don't let him put you off, promise me?' Her voice had sounded urgent, and she'd tugged on her daughter's sleeve. 'Your dad's just – set in his ways. You know what he's like.' Penny's eyes had been wide and staring, and Erin had wondered whether she'd had too much to drink. But then her mum had looked right at her. 'If you really love Adam, don't let him go. You might never find love like it again.'

The moment had lingered between them, but before Erin had been able to analyse it, or wonder what her mother had meant, Penny had let go of Erin's sleeve and stepped away, back into the house.

'Bye Adam,' her mum had called as they went, waving at the pair of them as they made their way down the street.

'Bye,' Adam had replied, bemused.

Erin had never repeated to Adam what her mum had said that night, but it had stayed with her – and when she'd eventually left Adam, the words had niggled at the back of her mind, worrying, making her doubt her decision.

But it was all too late to worry about that now. And at least it seemed to be going better this time around, with Greg. Of course it would; Greg was a university student, wanted to be a physio or a sports coach. He was a nice boy, and clearly loved Erin. What parent wouldn't love him?

It was as they were leaving, just before they said their goodbyes, that Penny pulled Erin to one side again as Greg was saying goodnight to her father.

'Mum, what's wrong?' Erin said when she saw her mother's face.

Penny shook her head and leaned in close to her daughter. 'Are you happy?' Her voice was a hiss, like a pantomime baddie trying to whis-

per, and this time Erin could tell for sure that her mother had drunk too much wine.

'Of course I am,' she said, confused.

Her mother nodded then, looking at the floor. Then she shook her head and looked at Erin again, and Erin searched her mother's eyes, wondering what she was about to say.

'Are you absolutely sure about Greg?'

'Yes!' Erin said, surprised.

'Good, good.' Her mum clutched her arm. 'But does he make you as happy as Adam?'

Erin's face clouded then, as realisation dawned.

'Oh that's what this is about? You think I should have stayed with Adam?'

'No, no, not necessarily Erin. I just...' She stopped, her eyes casting about while she searched for the right words. 'I know how much you loved Adam. I just – I want to make certain that you're doing the right thing.'

Erin pulled her arm away. 'I'm absolutely positive Mum,' she said. 'Greg's lovely.' She glanced over to where her father and Greg were standing, laughing at something together in the dim light of the hall-way. 'Dad likes him. I thought you would too.'

'I do like him Erin, he is lovely. But it's not me or your father who needs to love him. It's you.'

'And I do.'

'Good. Because I never want you to regret anything. I always want to you to be certain you're with the love of your life.'

12

NOW

Yeah Yeah Yeahs: 'Maps'

'Happy Christmas!' It was clear from the pink glow of her cheeks when she opened the door that Rose was already tipsy, and she dragged me inside, Greg following closely behind.

'Come through here you beautiful pair,' she cried.

Greg and I traipsed dutifully into her tiny kitchen, where assorted bottles were lined up on the worktop alongside a collection of mismatched glasses. She lifted a bottle of Prosecco and waved it in the air. 'Fizz?'

I grabbed a glass and held it out, and Greg did the same.

'Sam not here yet?' I said, peering through the open door into the living room, where I could hear Christmas songs playing.

'He's on his way. He had a hot date.'

'Did he? Why haven't I heard about this before now?'

'Oh don't worry, he wasn't going to tell me either, but I forced it out of him.'

We made our way into the living room, where a silver Christmas tree twinkled in the corner, and fairy lights were strung across every wall and surface. It looked like there had been an explosion in a Christmas shop, but I didn't say anything. It was so very kitsch – and so very Rose. That was one of the joys of living on your own I guess – there was no need to compromise to suit someone else's taste.

Rose threw herself down on the sofa, and I chose the armchair – a deliberate move so that Greg had to sit away from me. We hadn't properly talked about his gambling lapse the other night, and I still hadn't decided how I felt about it.

'So, what have you two been up to?' Rose said, tucking her feet underneath her and sipping her drink delicately.

I kept my gaze turned away from Greg. 'Just working. I only finished for the holidays yesterday.'

'Yeah me too,' she said. 'Bloody kids drive me mad.' Rose was a primary school teacher and even though she pretended she hated it, I knew she loved every minute really. She was still like a child herself in so many ways – mainly good ones, such as seeing the best in people.

'You love it,' Greg teased her and she gave a grimace.

'Not just before Christmas I don't. They're so excited they're like wild animals. Come to think of it I think I'd prefer trying to tame wild animals.'

I smiled and sipped my Prosecco, feeling my muscles relax. I needed this after the few days I'd had. There was so much whirling around my head I needed time to process it all.

'Erin?'

I realised Greg was saying my name and I looked up. 'Sorry, what?'

'I was just saying that we're going to your dad's for Christmas Day, aren't we?'

'Yeah, we are. Rose knows that already.' I tried not to snap, and failed.

'Oh I know E, I was just bugging Greg, seeing if you'd have any time to come round and see us.'

'Us?'

'Sam's coming round here.'

'I thought he was going to his parents' house?'

'He was but they decided to bugger off to Barbados at the last minute and left him in the lurch.' She shrugged. 'You know what they're like; poor old Sam has never been their priority.'

'Oh, right.' I glanced at Greg. 'Well, I'm not sure. We'll come over if we have time.'

'We probably won't though,' Greg said.

I felt a tug of anger flare in my belly. He'd never tried to keep me away from my friends, but there had been odd occasions, such as this, when I'd felt envious of Sam and Rose's single lifestyles. They had dates and even the odd relationship, but the fact that neither of them had settled down meant they were free to do things together that I wasn't able to join in with, and it bothered me more than it should – especially as I knew they'd both prefer to be in my shoes, and happily settled. I also knew that, while it wasn't Greg's fault, I was in no mood at the moment to try to hold back my resentment.

'We'll see,' I said, my voice low, glaring at Greg. I caught a look in Rose's eyes that told me she'd sensed the tension between the two of us and I clapped my hands to clear the air. 'Anyway, shall we get this party started?' I leaned down and pulled another bottle from my bag.

'Ooh Champagne!' squealed Rose.

'Yep. Nothing but the good stuff for us. Although...' I glanced at the door. 'Should we wait for Sam before we open it?'

'Did someone say my name in vain?' A voice floated through

from the hallway, and seconds later Sam appeared in the door, his eyes shining.

'How did you get in?'

'My key.' He grinned, waving it in the air.

'That was for emergencies only!' Rose cried, swatting the air in a pointless attempt to grab it from his hands. He just held it higher. At over six feet tall, he was almost a whole foot taller than Rose, and she looked like a little girl trying to grab a toy from a big boy in the playground.

'This *was* an emergency,' Sam said.

'Really?' I raised my eyebrows at him.

'I'll have you know I've cut a very successful date short to be here tonight, with you lot.' He glanced at the bottle in my hand. 'And I *need* some of that Champagne.'

I grabbed his hand and tugged his arm. 'Come on then,' I said, and pulled him into the kitchen, leaving Rose and Greg behind. I closed the door.

'Erin, are you pissed?' He peered closely at my face.

'No! We've only been here a few minutes.'

'Well what was all that about then? Why have you dragged me in here like that?'

I stuck the Champagne in the fridge and poured him a glass from the Prosecco bottle that Rose had left on the side, topped my own glass up then took a huge gulp.

'I've just had one of those days,' I said, resting my hip against the worktop.

Sam held his arms out. 'Do you need a Sam hug?'

'Do you know what, I really do,' I said, and I stepped into his embrace gratefully, collapsing against him. His chest felt solid, and he smelt divine, as usual. He rubbed circles on my back until I drew away.

'Now come on, tell Aunty Sam what's wrong. Is it Greg?'

I shrugged and looked down at my toes. 'Yes. No.' I looked up at him. 'Partly.'

'Well that's cleared that up.' He smiled to show he was teasing. 'What's happened?' He gasped. 'Has he had an affair?'

'No. Don't be daft.'

'No you're right. He'd never cheat on you.' He sighed. 'At least that's one good thing about marrying someone who worships you.'

'He does not worship me.'

'You know he does. He always has.' He folded his arms. 'So come on, spill. If he's not had an affair, what's he done?'

'He's been gambling again.'

'When?'

'Two days ago. I came home early and caught him in the act.'

'Most women would be relieved it was only a gambling site they caught their husbands on.'

I smiled sadly. 'I know. But he promised me, Sam. He swore he'd never do it again, never put our house or our marriage on the line again. I told him I'd leave him if he did. And yet he did it anyway.'

'And you feel betrayed.'

'Too right I do.' I sighed and took another gulp of my wine.

'And what else?'

I looked up at him. He was giving me a knowing look, and I was reminded that it could be inconvenient to have a friend who knew you as well as you knew yourself – better, sometimes.

'Nothing else,' I said, but even I could tell my voice was just a pitch too high, and Sam continued to watch me in silence. I let out a puff of air, and crumbled. 'Okay, okay.' I swallowed, unsure how to say it. Luckily Sam came to my rescue.

'Is this about Adam?'

I gave a small nod.

'You've seen him again, since he told you he didn't remember you?'

I nodded again.

'Oh E. After everything we said, you went back there?'

'I had to. How could I just carry on without finding out more?'

'Because no good could ever come of it!' He was clearly exasperated with me, and I didn't blame him. But I was desperate for him to understand.

'Okay listen.' I waited, then carried on when he didn't respond. 'We just went for a walk on the Common. I – I needed to be certain there was nothing there any more. You know, that there were no feelings left for him.'

'And?'

I sighed. 'There were fireworks, Sam. Bloody fireworks.' I rubbed my face and shook my head.

Sam took my hands. 'Listen E, it doesn't mean anything. It's just the residual memory of you and him that's making you feel this way. You and Greg have got something worth fighting for. Adam was just a flash in the pan, and the only reason he seems more appealing to you right now is because you've had him on such a pedestal for all these years, and you don't know all the bad bits. You don't know him warts and all, the way you do Greg.' He shrugged. 'The grass isn't always greener on the other side, you know.'

'I know. You're right.' My voice sounded weak, unconvincing.

He peered at me closely. 'Is there anything else you're not telling me? You didn't—' He stopped, his eyes like saucers. 'You didn't *kiss* him did you?'

'Of course I didn't! I wouldn't! But—'

'But you wanted to?'

I nodded miserably.

'Come here.' He pulled me into a hug again and this time he

rested his chin on my head. 'I'm guessing you haven't told Greg about this?'

'Of course not. It would break his heart.'

Sam pulled away, looked down at me. 'Exactly. And that's my point.'

'There is no point.'

'There is a point, and you know what it is. Adam is your weak spot. It didn't matter how unhappy he made you, you could never see any bad in him.'

'He didn't make me unhappy.' Even as I was saying the words I knew they weren't entirely true. But I could also remember the happy times, which were so passionate and exciting that they overshadowed everything else.

'Come on Erin, it's him with amnesia, not me.' He sniffed. 'You've always been in love with Adam – you know it, Rose and I know it, and Greg definitely knows it.' He flicked a glance at the door. 'Poor guy; he's always known he was your second choice, and it's bad enough having to live with that knowledge. Imagine how he'd feel if he knew you'd seen Adam and hadn't even told him about it.'

I felt my body deflate. Sam was right, of course. I'd known this all along. And yet I'd still seen Adam more than once, and had thought about him almost constantly.

'Is this because of Greg's gambling? Are you trying to punish him?' Sam said.

'No!'

'Are you sure? Because I'd be surprised if there wasn't an element of that going on here.' Sam grabbed the Prosecco bottle and drained the rest of it into his glass, then got another one from the fridge, flicked it open and topped my glass up again. I took a sip and could feel my head starting to spin. I really needed some food.

'What's going on with Greg has nothing to do with me seeing Adam. I swear. I just – it's just bad timing.'

'You know you can't see him again, don't you?'

I did, of course I did. Even if I hadn't been sure, Sam's reaction was enough to confirm that what I was doing was completely wrong. And I hadn't even told him about my suggestion to Adam that I could help him, or about the few minutes before we parted where we came so close to kissing. But how could I promise Sam I'd never see Adam again, when I knew it would be a lie?

Luckily, I was saved from having to make a promise I had no intention of keeping by Rose, who popped her head round the door.

'Are you two coming back in here any time today?'

'Sorry, I was just filling Erin in on my hot date.' Sam flashed her a grin.

Rose studied us both for a moment as though trying to work out whether we were lying, before giving a small tilt of her head. 'Come on then, come and tell us all.'

When the door closed behind her, Sam blocked my way, hand on his hip. 'This conversation isn't over, missy.'

'I know.' When Sam got a bee in his bonnet about something, he didn't easily let it go. But for now, I was off the hook, and it was with relief that I followed him back into the living room to join Rose and Greg and listen to ridiculous Christmas songs.

It was late by the time Greg and I staggered home from Rose's flat. It was black as ink outside and tiny stars prickled through the darkness. I tipped my head back and watched the distant planets, marvelling at the vastness of the universe. I tried not to think about lying on the frozen Common with Adam looking at this very same sky just two nights ago.

'It's soooo Christmassy,' I slurred. My arm was hooked through Greg's, and when I stumbled he pulled me back to standing. 'Sorry,' I muttered. I was aware that I was much more drunk than him, and it made me feel at a disadvantage.

We walked on in silence. I was concentrating hard on not falling over, and staying in a straight line, as though trying to prove to a police officer that I wasn't as drunk as I seemed. I was leaning heavily against Greg and I could feel the warmth of his body pressed into me. The tension radiated from him.

We walked in silence for a few moments, the only sound our footsteps ringing out on the frosty pavement, and the odd car rumbling past a street or two away. The pubs were all shut now, Christmas drinkers all gone home, tucked up in their beds ready for Christmas Eve tomorrow. The world was holding its breath, waiting for something to happen.

'I wish you'd forgive me.' Greg's voice pierced through the icy air, and I lifted my head off his shoulder to glance up at him. My vision was blurred around the edges, but I could see him as clear as day.

'Whaddyoo mean?' I studied the contours of his still handsome face: his high forehead, sandy hair curled around his ears, the long, straight lines of his nose and the curve of his lips. His face was almost as familiar to me as my own. I loved his face, I knew I did. But it didn't set me on fire. It didn't get my heart racing, my palms sweating, my stomach somersaulting. It made me feel safe and protected – or at least it had done until now. Now I just saw betrayal in its familiar lines.

Greg turned towards me, his grey eyes hidden beneath the shadows from the streetlights. His skin had a blue sheen. 'You know what I mean.' He stopped, suddenly, outside the Fat Cat café where I'd seen Adam busking, and I tried to concentrate on Greg's words and not get caught up in memories of that day. What he was saying was important, and I needed to listen. I stared at his nose in the hope it would keep me focused. 'I know what I did was wrong but I'm doing everything I can to make it up to you Erin.' He licked his lips and I studied the movement of his tongue across them. 'But you're so distant. So angry. I just...' He shrugged. 'Oh God I don't know why I'm bringing this up now. We're both too pissed.' He turned and started walking away again.

'No!' I tugged his arm and he spun back to face me. 'Don't walk away.'

'I was wrong to bring it up now. I – we just need to get home and go to bed.' His voice softened and he cupped my face in his hands. 'We can talk about it in the morning.'

I felt my shoulders drop. He was right. This wasn't the time or the place. 'Okay.'

He took my gloved hand in his and we sauntered home, me more unsteadily than him. When we walked through the front door we both kicked our shoes off as Dog threaded his way round our ankles, and headed into the kitchen.

'Coffee?' Greg asked.

'I probably should.'

I perched on one of the stools and watched as he pottered about spooning coffee granules into the cafetiere and boiling the kettle. The cold air had sobered me up a bit and a ball of melancholy sat heavily in my chest as I watched this man I'd loved and lived with for more than seventeen years. Aside from the gambling, which I knew he was trying his hardest to overcome, Greg was a good man, and he loved me. That had been enough for me until now.

So why was I trying to find ways to punish him? And why was I thinking about someone else?

I pushed the stool back and stood up. 'I'm going to put some music on,' I announced, and Greg looked up at me in surprise, a mug of milky coffee in each hand.

He followed me through to the living room where I scrolled through the songs on his iPad which was hooked up to the speakers until I found the song I was looking for. Then, as the guitar intro floated through the room followed by the rhythm of the drums, Greg's face broke into a smile.

'"Maps",' he whispered.

I nodded. The Yeah Yeah Yeah's song was one we listened to all the time in the days after we first met, when Greg was still just one of my best friends and Adam was still my (mostly absent) boyfriend. We would sit in either one of our tiny bedrooms, squashed onto the bed or the rough carpet and smoke and drink and laugh. It was part of the soundtrack to the days when we had no worries, no cares, when all we had to think about was delving deep into the other one's mind and excavating all there was to know. Right now I realised I needed to hear it to remind myself of how much Greg meant to me. To keep the fire burning, we needed to reignite the spark that had once been there.

As he placed the coffee cups carefully on the side table and walked towards me, I felt my heart rate picking up, and when he stepped into my arms and wrapped his own around me, I let myself relax into him, felt his chest press against me, breathed in his familiar citrus scent, and told myself he was all I needed.

We swayed gently, Greg's lips pressed against my hair, mouthing the words into my hair. Then he whispered something I didn't quite catch and I looked up at him quizzically.

'What did you say?'

'I just said I love you,' he said, his voice a whisper. 'It was part of the song. But it's true.'

'I love you too.' It was so easy to say, but I did mean it. I did. 'Shall we go to bed?'

He searched my face for a moment, the space between his eyes creased. 'Are you sure? You're not just drunk?'

I smiled lazily. 'I'm drunk but I'm also sure.'

He didn't need asking twice, and we raced up the stairs and fell onto the bed and for the first time in months we came together and forgot all of our problems…

* * *

When we'd both brushed our teeth and I'd climbed into my favourite pyjamas and we were lying next to each other in bed, Dog curled up on the end by my feet, I felt Greg shuffle to face me and I turned to look at him. His cheek was squashed into the pillow and he looked content.

'I'm sorry,' he said, softly.

'What for?'

'Everything. Letting you down. Not keeping my promise.'

I could have told him it was okay, that he had nothing to be sorry for, but despite our closeness tonight, I was still hurt by his betrayal. That, combined with my churning feelings, meant I wasn't finding it easy to reassure him.

'We will be all right, won't we?' he said.

I didn't answer immediately and I could see myself reflected back in the warmth of his eyes. 'I hope so,' I said eventually.

He reached out and pulled me towards him and I let myself tip forward. 'What do you want me to do, Erin?'

We were so close I couldn't make out his features. I pulled back to look at him. 'I don't know.'

'I'll get help.'

'You're already having counselling, and that hasn't worked.'

'I'll do anything. Anything to make you forgive me.' His eyes shone with tears.

'Will you go to Gamblers Anonymous?' It was something he'd refused to do until now, adamant he wasn't addicted, that he could stop whenever he wanted. But recent events had proven that theory wrong.

He studied me for a moment then gave a small tilt of his head. 'All right. If you think it will help.'

'I hope it will.'

'Then I'll go.'

As I wrapped my arms around him, I swallowed down the guilt I felt knowing I was treating him this way when the truth was, what I was doing was far, far worse.

Because I wasn't sure I could give up my addiction that easily either.

13

NOW

Pixies: 'Monkey Gone to Heaven'

The black metal gates towered above me like a warning. There was a bell on the pillar next to them so I climbed out of the car and pressed it firmly, trying to ignore the fact I was shaking with nerves. Seconds later there was a crackling sound and a mechanical voice said, 'Hello?'

'It's me.' My voice came out in a croak and I coughed. 'Erin.'

A loud buzzing filled the air and the gates creaked inward. I scurried back to my car, then drove through them and down the driveway. The house was set so far back from the road that the driveway wound a little, and it gave me time to study this house I hadn't been to for so many years.

Hidden away from the road behind imposing metal gates, the Bower House, as we always called it, had always been shrouded in mystery and all of its accompanying stories. The dark grey brick was worn, the darkened windows overlooking the grounds like sentries, while the lawn behind stretched down to the river, and trees yawned towards the over-reaching sky. The last time I'd been here had been more than nineteen years ago as a young, naïve girl of seventeen who had felt overwhelmed and in awe at being allowed to step inside this house to meet Adam's parents.

'They'll be nice to you but don't let it fool you,' Adam had warned me back then. 'Especially my father. He's a master at showing his charming side.'

I hadn't believed him, convinced they were going to be open and friendly despite what Adam had said. But I quickly realised his description of how cold they could be had been pretty accurate.

It was obvious from the outset that his father was the one in charge of the household and that, most importantly, he didn't approve of the way Adam was living his life.

'I understand you're at school with Adam?' his father had said as we 'took tea' in the drawing room.

'Yes.' My voice was small. I hated myself for feeling inferior in front of these people, but there was something about Adam's father that just made you feel that way. I suspected I wasn't the only one who'd been cowed before him.

He'd given a curt nod at my response. 'Well, I don't imagine he'll come out of that place with any qualifications worth having but at least it's better than nothing.' He'd spat the words 'that place', as though they were poison and, despite an overwhelming compulsion to defend my school and myself, I bit my tongue. What would it achieve, to retort, apart from hurting Adam?

Later, his father had made sure he told me all about the trouble Adam had got into at the public school he was thrown out of, and how he didn't approve of the choices his only son had made in life. It was also made perfectly clear that included me.

I couldn't wait to get out of there and, as we'd driven back up the drive afterwards in my mum's car, I'd wanted to scream. Adam had been silent beside me, as though all his spark had been extinguished by this man who called himself his father.

'I'm sorry I put you through that,' he said, his voice subdued.

'I'm sorry you have a father like that.' My hands gripped the steering wheel tightly.

'It's not just him though, is it? My mother's just as bad. She might not say much but the contempt for me is there in her eyes. Anyway, if she cared, she'd stick up for me, but she'd never do that.'

I turned to look at him but he stared out of the side window away from me. We approached the black gates and while we waited for them to open I reached out for his hands.

'Don't ever let them make you think you're not good enough,' I said, struggling to keep the anger out of my voice. 'You're the best person I know. They're the ones who should be sorry, not you.'

'But they're right though, aren't they? I have wasted my life.'

'No!' Fury raged in my chest. 'You're funny and kind and forgiving. You don't belong in an awful stuck-up school like that anyway. Your parents are just...' I'd struggled to find a word to express how angry I was. 'They're horrible, Adam. I'm sorry, but they are.'

The gates had swung open in front of us and I inched forward onto the road and drove back into town. I'd never been so grateful to be heading back to my own house. My father might not be the warmest, most demonstrative person, but I knew he loved me and he would never treat me the way Adam's parents treated him. No wonder Adam rebelled against them. Nothing he did would ever please them anyway.

A tapping at my window made me jump and I looked round to see Adam's face peering in at me. My stomach flipped and I wound the window down.

'Are you coming in then?'

I'd reached the house and must have been sitting here for a while, lost in thought. 'Yes, sorry,' I said, grabbing my bag and climbing out of the car. I stood in front of Adam for a moment, trying to still the thumping in my chest. I wasn't sure whether it was his presence or the fact that I was about to see his parents again, but I swallowed down my nerves and tried to remind myself that I was a grown woman now, not a shy seventeen-year-old girl. I could more than stand my own ground with these people.

'Thanks for coming,' Adam said. 'I didn't expect you to come on Christmas Eve.'

'It's fine,' I replied. 'We weren't doing anything special today.'

Adam couldn't remember what his parents had been like before – how they'd treated him or me – so I said nothing. But as I followed him towards the house a feeling of dread settled in me, mixed with the guilt I already felt at being here in the first place.

I've been thinking about what you said. I wondered if we could talk about it after Christmas? Adam x

Adam had sent me this text at ten o'clock that morning. I'd been nursing a hangover from the night before and Greg had been making us bacon sandwiches to ease the nausea we were both feeling. For the first time in weeks I'd felt as though Greg and I had got back some of our closeness again: we weren't treading on eggshells around each other as though one false move could crush everything. I'd felt a sense of peace that had been missing from our marriage for a while.

Then Adam's text had arrived, and I'd known instantly I was going to see him today.

Are you free today?

I'd replied while Greg had his back turned.

If you're sure, that would be perfect. Can you come to my house about lunchtime?

Although my heart had sunk a little at the thought of going back to his parents' house all these years later, and I knew I should be spending the day with my husband, I also knew I wasn't going to say no.

'I've got to pop out later,' I'd said as Greg slid my bacon sandwich in front of me. I took a huge bite and wiped ketchup from my chin.

'I thought we were spending the day together?' A small frown creased his forehead.

'I know, sorry, but I've realised I've still got a few last-minute bits and pieces to get for tomorrow.'

'Oh okay.' He hadn't said anything else but I could see the disappointment in his face and it pierced my heart like a needle.

But now I was here, I wasn't sure why I'd come. I'd had the chance to spend the day with my husband which, after the few months we'd been through, should have been my priority. Instead I'd chosen to see my ex-boyfriend who couldn't remember who I was, at the house where his awful parents lived. For what?

As we made our way through the expansive hallway towards the back of the house, all was quiet and my hopes soared. Maybe his parents were out after all.

But then they plummeted again when we reached the kitchen to find his mother sitting at the table, a glass of wine in hand. She stood when we entered and held her arms out in greeting as though we were old friends. I remained stock still as she walked unsteadily towards me.

'How lovely to see you,' she said, placing her hands on my upper arms and air kissing either side of my face. I flinched at her touch. 'Erin, isn't it?'

'You know it is Mum, I told you she was coming.' Adam's voice was sharp.

'All right dear, no need to be like that.' She stepped away from me and I relaxed. 'Adam tells me you've been spending some time together over the last few days.' She clapped her hands together like an excited child. 'How lovely for Adam to be back in touch with someone from his old life.' She glanced at her son. 'He says he can't remember a thing you know. Imagine that, not being able to remember your own mother!'

Lucky for him, I thought, but didn't say. 'Yes, it must be awful,' I replied. 'Well it's very nice to see you Mrs Bowers.' I turned to leave the room but she was having none of it. 'Oh won't you join me in a glass of wine? It is Christmas after all.'

'Thank you Mum but Erin doesn't have very long and we have things to discuss.' Adam steered me towards the sweeping staircase when a figure appeared at the bottom, and a chill ran through my bones.

'Hello Adam.' His father was as imposing as ever. His once dark hair was now steely grey, but his eyes were still as piercing.

'Erin and I were just going upstairs.' Adam started to walk round him but his father didn't move.

'Hello Erin. It's been a long time since I've seen you here. I believe you think you may be able to help Adam with his memories?'

I glanced at Adam, unsure how much he'd told them about our conversation.

'That's right. I work with music therapists helping people with dementia.'

He studied me for a moment the way a scientist studies an insect – knowing they could crush them with one fingertip in the blink of an eye should they so wish – then gave a small nod.

'Well, anything is worth a try I suppose.' He threaded his fingers together. 'Although if even the best doctors in the world can't help him I'm not exactly sure what good your *music therapy* is going to do.' He put a stress on the words music therapy as though they tasted vile on his tongue. But this time instead of letting his words make me feel small, I stuck my chin out in defiance.

'I'm a highly qualified psychologist and music therapy is a well-researched area,' I said, keeping my voice strong. 'I'm sure we'll have some success.'

He scrutinised me for a moment longer, then stepped aside. Adam and I walked up the stairs under his gaze, and it wasn't until we reached his bedroom that I let out a breath.

'I'm so sorry,' he said. 'I don't know why he has to be like that.' He ran his hands over his short hair.

'It's fine. It's nothing less than I expected.'

Adam seemed to deflate at those words. 'You mean he's been like that with you before?'

'Worse.'

'Oh God.' He buried his face in his hands. 'Is it wrong to detest your own father?'

'Detest is a strong word Adam.'

'Maybe. But I've seen the way he is with everyone he thinks is below him – which is most people, including my mother. He's just so – *ignorant*. I can't imagine why anyone would ever want to be with him.'

'Well, maybe he has some redeeming features.'

'I haven't seen them if he has. No wonder I hadn't seen my parents for years.'

We stood in silence for a moment and I took in the room I hadn't been in since I was a teenager. It had barely changed. I was surprised it hadn't been converted into a gym or something, although with so many rooms to choose from it probably wasn't necessary. It was a huge room, roughly the same size as my entire upstairs floor, with high ceilings and an enormous king-sized bed dominating the centre of it. I looked away from the bed where we'd spent so many hours together when his parents were out of the house, and headed towards the far corner where there was a desk and a couple of armchairs. Much safer ground. I settled in one of the chairs and Adam sat in the other, facing me. I tried not to look him directly in the eye, but focused on a spot behind his head instead.

'Thanks for coming today,' he said. 'I didn't expect you to come over on Christmas Eve. But I'm glad you have.'

'It's fine. I didn't have any plans and it was easier to get away.'

He nodded. I tried not to think about his breath against my skin, the feel of his body pressed against mine. My face felt hot.

'So, what did you want to talk to me about?' Business-like and professional, that was the best way.

He sat back and crossed his ankle over his knee. I averted my gaze from the sliver of leg the action revealed. 'I've been thinking about what you said. About songs helping to trigger memories.'

'Right.'

He looked down at his hands. 'Well first of all I'm sorry I was so rude to you about it. I know you were only trying to help.'

'It's fine.' I waved it away, desperate for him to get to the point.

'I've been doing some reading. About music, and memory and how it can help.' He scratched his ankle and looked up. 'I wondered if we could give it a go?'

I didn't reply immediately.

'It's okay if you don't want to. I get that it might be weird, and that we probably shouldn't be spending too much time together given – well, you know. Greg.'

I shook my head, trying to stay calm, but my insides were a mess. 'It's fine, really.' I swallowed. 'I'll help you.' I shouldn't be doing this; it was a total betrayal. I felt choked with shame – and yet Adam needed me. The truth was, no matter what else was going on here, I really might be able to help him. How could I refuse?

'Really?' He clapped his hands together and I was reminded momentarily of his mother. I shook the image away.

'Yes. Absolutely. I'd...' I paused, uncertain of what to say. I decided to stay professional. 'I'd be happy to give it a go.'

He smiled and I felt light-headed. 'Thank you.' He glanced behind him. 'Are you in a rush? Could we...' He hooked his thumb towards the other corner of the room and I looked over to see his old stereo.

'You want to start *now*?'

'Only if you don't mind. I mean, unless you have to get home?'

I checked my watch. It was only one-thirty. I'd left Greg making mince pies. I didn't need to be home for a while. 'We could make a start.' I jumped up and headed over to the stereo, Adam following close behind. There was a huge pile of old CDs on the floor, as well as vinyl records, and an iPad wired up to two enormous speakers. I also noticed a few guitars propped up against the wall, and I tried not to think about the times I'd watched him play when we were teenagers. An ashtray sat on the chest of drawers, half-full, a packet of tobacco beside it.

'Do you mind?' he said, indicating the packet.

'No, go ahead.'

'So, what should we try first?' He pulled a paper out of the packet and began lining the tobacco up inside it. His hands were strong, secure. I tried not to think about the times those fingers had touched me, or the places.

'What I usually do with my patients is have a chat about music they like, songs that mean something to them,' I said, getting back on track. 'That way we can collate a few songs that might help to unlock their brains.' I paused, cleared my throat. 'Sometimes I play to them as well.'

'You play guitar?' He rolled up the cigarette and brought it to his lips, lit the lighter and inhaled. Smoke blossomed out around us.

'A little. Nowhere near as good as you but enough to play some simple songs.'

'Wow. You just get better and better.' His gaze burned into me and I looked away. 'Sorry. Totally inappropriate.' He picked up a CD from the top of the pile. 'So what happens after that?'

'It depends. Sometimes I get a reaction the very first time I play a tune. If it's a song that reminds someone of their childhood, or of an important moment in their lives, it can fire up part of the amygdala – a part of the brain associated with processing emotions – to evoke memories connected to that song or those lyrics. Sometimes the reaction is less immediate, but comes more gradually, with repetition, and slowly a memory starts to resurface.

'But the thing you need to realise about the memory is that people with dementia find it frightening, not having a fully functioning memory – it means they don't know what's coming next in a pattern of events so they can't predict things, as well as not being able to recognise people, places or formerly familiar things. So in their case their brains *want* to be stimulated, and want to respond. In a case like yours, though, the lack of memory could be the brain's way of protecting you from the things it needs to forget – in which case it might be trickier to tease the memories out.'

I looked up to find Adam staring at me. I held his gaze, and the space between us hummed with so many unspoken words. Then Adam looked away, took another drag on his roll-up, and the moment was broken.

'So you're saying my brain might not want to do this?'

'It's possible. But it's worth a try.' I bent down and studied the CD collection, running my fingers down the edges of their spines.

'These are probably the best ones to start with,' he said, crouching down beside me. His leg brushed my thigh and I moved away. 'I haven't bought CDs for years, so these will all be older.' He pulled one from the middle, making the pile wobble, and handed me the plastic box.

'Would this one work?'

It was Pixies' *Doolittle* album, its brown and white monkey on the front an instant flashback to the hours Adam and I used to spend together listening to music in our bedrooms.

'It might.'

Smiling, he took the disc from my hands and slotted it into the CD player.

'Hang on.'

He looked at me, a question on his face.

'I need to ask you a few questions first.'

'Riiight...'

I coughed, preparing myself. 'Okay. Firstly, do you have any negative memories associated with any of these songs?'

'I don't have any memories associated with any songs.'

'No, course. Sorry.' I felt edgy and nervous. I needed to pull myself together. I was good at this. I knew what I was doing. 'To be honest these questions are probably irrelevant given your situation,' I said, changing tack. 'We might as well just dive straight in.'

Adam pressed 'play' and seconds later, the sludgy, distorted guitar riff filled the room – and my head filled with memories like a balloon that was about to burst. *Adam and I side by side on my single student bed, kissing. This song loud, blocking out any other sound. Adam's hand sliding up my thigh, under my shirt, unhooking my bra...* I opened my eyes with a start and forced my mind away from what had happened next. Instead I concentrated on trying to steady my breath, and listening to the song. And I watched Adam, who was cross-legged on the floor beside me. He had his eyes closed and his hands clasped in his lap, a look of deep concentration on his face. I took the opportunity to study that face, at once so familiar and yet so different from the boy I remembered. My eyes traced the outline of his jaw, the stubble scattered across his cheeks, the dark hair cut shorter than I'd ever seen it before and a well of desire surged in my belly.

Adam's eyes flipped open and I quickly averted my gaze. When I looked back he was still studying me. I leant over and stopped the music and the silence that followed felt deafening.

'Well?' I said. 'Anything?'

He shook his head, a look of dejection on his face. 'Nothing. I assume that song meant something to me? To us?'

I nodded, praying he didn't ask for more details. But rather than being curious he seemed pent up, frustrated. 'I should have known it wouldn't work,' he said. He punched his fist into the rug.

'You can't give up that easily. That was the very first song; there are so many others we can try.' Without thinking, I reached over and placed my hand on his knee. Before I could pull it away again, his hand was on mine, and the skin where we were touching felt like I'd been branded. The moment stretched on forever, everything else forgotten except the feel of his skin against mine.

I pulled my hand away first.

'Shall we try another one?' I hoped he couldn't tell that I was shaking as I picked up a couple more CDs from the pile without checking what they were. I kept my gaze down, desperate not to see the look in his eyes. I couldn't go there.

'What's the point?' His voice was angry.

'Surely it's worth at least one more go before we give up?'

He stared at the jumble of CDs for a moment, then snatched one up seemingly at random and shoved it in the CD player. PJ Harvey's 'This Is Love' started up and I braced myself to be assaulted by yet more inappropriate memories about the two of us together. But this time, as the lyrics about life being so complex began, it wasn't happy images of Adam and me that flashed through my mind, but rather glimpses of a different type of recollection – a night I had forgotten until now. Adam and Greg were squaring up to each other at a party as this song thumped in the background; I'd watched them from across the room, frozen, as I wondered whether they were about to start fighting. Then as quickly as it had all started, they had broken away, Greg shoving Adam in the chest before storming off. Later, Adam had told me Greg had got mad about nothing, but Greg had admitted to me that Adam had been boasting about all the women who swarmed round him after gigs, and he'd been sticking up for me. I hadn't known who to believe, and so we never mentioned it again. But this song had brought the memory to the forefront in perfect HD clarity and I recalled the intense sense of sorrow I'd felt at the time.

I was pulled out of the moment by a sudden silence, and I looked up to find Adam had pressed stop, and was staring into space, his brow knitted into a frown.

'Sorry Erin. It's just so frustrating, not being able to remember anything at all.' His voice was low and he studied me intently, as though trying to work out who I was. I supposed he was, in a way. After all, he only had my word for it that I was who I said I was. It struck me for the first time how vulnerable it must make you feel to have no memories of your life, to not recognise people who claimed to have known you well. How could you ever know who to trust?

'It's fine.' I fumbled with another CD case and the disc fell out and rolled across the floor. We both reached for it at the same time and our fingers met. I froze.

'What did I do to you, Erin? Why didn't we stay together?'

The words rained down on me like rocks, and I struggled to catch my breath. This was wrong. I shouldn't be here, having this conversation with this man. I should be at home, with my husband, watching *Elf* and drinking Baileys in front of a roaring fire. I stood. Adam stayed where he was, looking up at me.

'I need to go home.'

'To Greg?'

'Of course to Greg.'

He pushed himself to standing so that I had to look up at him. He was only inches away from me and I was sure he must be able to hear the rush of blood in my ears as loudly as I could.

'Does he know you're here?'

I hesitated. Should I admit to him that Greg didn't even know Adam was back? What would that sound like? That I had something to hide?

'Yes, he knows. He's fine with it. It's my job.'

He didn't move for a moment and I wondered whether he believed me. 'Yes, I suppose it is, isn't it?' he said, eventually. 'In that case I should be paying you for your time.'

'That's not what I meant. I want to help. We're friends.'

'Are we?'

'What do you mean?'

'Were we ever actually friends Erin? Or were we always lovers?'

I felt my face flush at the memories that word brought back in just two short syllables.

'We were both.' I stood defiantly, challenging him to contradict me. I felt as though I was suffocating. Finally, he smiled.

'Good. I'm glad. Because that means we can be friends now, right?'

'Right.' I smiled back, glad to be on safer ground again.

He looked down at his feet, humble now, so unlike the old Adam it almost took my breath away. 'I don't think I had many friends.'

'What makes you say that?'

He shrugged. 'Nobody has bothered to come and see me, since the accident. Well, not for ages anyway. A few people came at first – a couple who claimed they were friends and brought flowers and grapes the way you do for old people you don't know very well, and a woman who said she was my girlfriend but didn't bother coming back again when she realised I didn't know her at all.' He rubbed his hand over his face. 'I just – I can't help thinking I must have been a pretty shoddy person if nobody cared enough to come and spend some proper time with me, to check I really was all right.' He shifted his weight from one leg to the other. 'You're the first person who's seemed even vaguely bothered that I've lost my memory, and has actually tried to help me.' His voice cracked and I didn't know how to respond. What could I say? I had absolutely no idea what he'd been like over the last eighteen years. All I knew was, if it had been me in his position, I knew at least four people who would be there for me instantly – Dad, Greg, Sam and Rose – and the fact that Adam didn't have anyone like that – no close friends, no wife, no loyal girlfriend – to worry about him suggested he could be right.

Instead of answering I glanced down at my hands.

'I'll do whatever I can Adam. But I can't promise it will work.'

'I know that. But just the fact that you care enough to try means the world.'

I inhaled slowly, trying to stop the thumping in my head, my arms, my legs. I felt heavy, as though I was being weighted down, and the more I tried to battle, the harder it became to stay afloat. I knew if I let myself it would be all too easy to reach for Adam, to use him as a life raft to rescue me. To save me.

But I also knew it could destroy everything, and that I'd regret it the instant I did.

'I do need to go soon,' I said, the words tumbling out as I stepped back. The distance between us hummed with electricity.

'Could...' He stopped. 'Couldn't we just try a few more songs before you go? Please?'

My mind was screaming at me to get away, to go home. My body on the other hand, was desperate to stay. I was also acutely aware that I hadn't done what I'd promised to do today, and if I didn't at least try and help him then the whole thing would have been a complete waste of time.

'Okay.'

He cocked his head. 'You sure?'

'Sure.' I bent and picked up a few CDs from the top of the pile and stepped towards the stereo.

For the next hour we tried song after song. Each time I started a new CD, a new song, I felt hopeful. And, although Adam seemed to remember the lyrics to some, it soon became clear that nothing was working. Nothing was triggering any memories.

At least, not in him. There were plenty cascading into my mind though – some of them more welcome than others.

'It must mean something if I can remember the lyrics, mustn't it?' he said eagerly between songs. 'That it's working a bit?'

I shook my head, tried to explain. 'I'm really sorry, but I don't think so. The thing is, the memories of lyrics and tunes are stored in a different part of the brain from the rest of our memories. It's almost an instinct, to sing along to a tune.'

He looked utterly dejected.

'Sorry.'

'It's not your fault.' His voice was tired, defeated.

It was almost three o'clock, and I'd left Greg alone for much longer than I'd intended.

'I'm sorry, but I really do have to go now.'

'Of course. Sorry I kept you here so long.' He smiled sadly. 'But thank you for trying.'

'We can give it another go, if you like, after Christmas?'

'I'd like that.'

I gathered my bag and coat and headed towards the bedroom door.

'Hang on.'

I spun round to find Adam right behind me, so close. He was holding a small, wrapped gift in his hands. 'I bought you something.'

'Oh. But —'

'I've been thinking about you more than I should, and although I obviously don't remember what you like, I saw this and it reminded me of you.' He shrugged. 'But don't open it now.'

'Wow. Thank you Adam. I haven't got you anything.'

'That's not why I gave it to you. Think of it as a thank you gift, rather than a Christmas present, if you prefer. Thank you for helping me, but also thank you for making my return home less depressing and lonely. I hope – I hope we can see each other a lot more next year. As friends, of course.'

In all the time I'd known Adam, I'd never seen him so hesitant, so unassured. Young Adam had been confident, cocky, so certain of his place in the world. At least on the outside. But this Adam was more cautious, more unsure of himself. It wasn't clear to me what it meant yet, but I hoped I'd get the chance to work it out.

'I'd like that. Thank you.'

Then I left, and went home to my husband.

* * *

Greg had made mince pies and the house smelt divine.

'Sorry I'm so late,' I called, and he appeared in the kitchen doorway, apron on, his face flushed.

'I thought you'd got lost,' he said, wiping his hands on a tea towel.

'Sorry, I lost track of time.'

His eyes flicked down to my empty hands and back up again. 'Didn't you find what you went for?'

'What?' I realised, too late, that I'd told Greg I was going last-minute Christmas shopping. 'Oh, yes. I got something for Sam and dropped it off before I came home. And I got this.' I pulled a bottle out of my bag and grinned.

'Great. Baileys and mince pies work perfectly.' He turned and headed back into the kitchen and I swallowed down a pang of guilt. I knew I couldn't keep Adam's return from him forever, but I didn't want to ruin Christmas. I followed Greg and watched him for a moment as he pottered around the kitchen. He'd always enjoyed cooking, but he'd been almost fervent with it recently, as though baking took his mind off the urge to gamble.

'Thank you,' I said, wrapping my arms round his waist and squeezing him. He spun round and rested his arms on my shoulders. He paused, a frown creasing his forehead, and inhaled deeply.

'You smell of fags,' he said snuffling into my neck. I stiffened. *Adam*. Greg peered at my face and nausea rose in my throat.

'I—'

'Have you started smoking again after all this time?'

'I—' I started again, then hung my head. 'You got me.' I looked up at him. 'I just fancied one, that's all. It's not going to be a regular thing, I promise.' He studied me for a moment and I held my breath.

'Ah you silly sausage, you don't need to answer to me.' He grinned. 'But you *do* stink.'

'Thanks a lot.'

He kissed my forehead. 'Anyway, Fag Ash Lil, what have I done to deserve this unexpected display of affection?'

I shrugged, hardly able to believe I'd got away with it. 'Nothing wrong with giving my husband a cuddle is there?'

'Nothing wrong at all. It's just unusual, that's all.'

'I'm proud of you,' I said.

'Proud of me? For what?'

'Tackling your gambling. I know it's hard, but I know you're doing your best.'

He watched me for a moment, then leant down and planted a gentle kiss on my lips.

'Thank you Erin. I promise not to slip up any more.' He held three fingers to his forehead. 'Scouts honour.'

'Good.' I pulled away. 'Now, where are these mince pies you promised?'

'Right here,' he said, sliding a tray of golden brown pies across the worktop.

'I might just go and get changed and have one when I come back down, okay?'

'Sure. I'll pour you a Baileys as well.'

I headed up the stairs and into our en suite bathroom. I locked the door and sat on the toilet lid, then pulled Adam's present out of my bag. It had been burning a hole in my side since I'd left his house. I tore the paper off and there was a small box inside. Carefully, I lifted the lid off. There, nestled in pink tissue paper, was a black musical note, a crotchet, on a delicate silver chain. I picked it up and put it round my neck and did up the clasp. It nestled neatly between my collar bones. I touched it with my fingertips and shivered. Then I gathered up the wrapping paper and was about to shove it into the bottom of my handbag when I noticed a small piece of paper tucked inside. I pulled it out and read the writing scrawled there.

Dear Erin. I might not remember you, but you're music to my ears. Merry Christmas. Love A. x

Trying not to think too much about what this meant, I tucked the necklace beneath my jumper, hid the note at the bottom of my handbag, and headed back downstairs, trying to ignore the guilt that sat like a rock in the bottom of my belly.

14

THEN

Pearl Jam: 'Black'

There was a loud, insistent banging at the door and Erin sat bolt upright, her heart pounding. Beside her, fully clothed, Greg snored away, oblivious.

Bang bang bang bang. 'Erin, let me in!'

Adam.

Erin shook Greg awake and he groaned sleepily and peeled his eyes open.

'Wha'?'

'Adam's here. Get up!' she hissed, yanking his arm.

As Greg sat up and slid off the bed and onto the chair by her desk, bleary-eyed and befuddled, Erin stumbled over to the door. They had fallen asleep last night after sharing a bottle of gin – Greg had sat an exam that hadn't gone very well and Erin had helped him drown his sorrows. But now Adam was here and even Greg was aware that it looked bad that she had another man in her room.

Especially him, who, Greg knew, Adam was suspicious enough of anyway.

With a quick glance over her shoulder to check that Greg was out of her bed, Erin took a deep breath and pulled the door open with a flourish.

'Adam!' she cried, and fell into him. As Greg watched, a ball of fury rose in his chest as Adam tried to wrap his arms around Erin but instead stumbled sideways into the door frame. He looked rough, his hair unwashed, his eyes bloodshot. There was an undeniable fug of whisky fumes around him. He was pissed. Great.

'Are you drunk?' Erin said, peering up at him.

'Maybe a little.' His words slurred into each other and Erin stepped back into the room.

'It's nine o'clock in the morning.'

He gave a lopsided grin. 'Yeah I know. Can I come in then?' Adam lurched forward and swiped for her, but she ducked out of the way so he fell against the wall. 'Hey, come here sexy.'

'Adam, stop it.' Erin grabbed for his hand and led him inside. 'Come in.' He bounced off the door frame and almost tripped. Then he looked up and saw Greg.

'Woss he doin' here?' He pointed accusingly and Greg felt his whole body tense. He held his hands up in surrender. 'Nothing, nothing. I was just helping Erin with something.' He gestured towards Erin's empty desk but Adam didn't even notice the lack of papers on it. He was pawing Erin instead, trying to kiss her neck. She shoved him away.

'Sorry Greg; I think he's a bit drunk,' she said over her shoulder.

'It's fine.' Greg stood and edged around Adam, towards the door. 'Are you all right?'

'Yeah, she's fine mate. I'm her boyfriend *in case you'd forgotten. Now bugger off.' Adam fell onto Erin's bed and stretched out.*

'Are you sure you're okay?' Greg whispered.

Erin glanced over her shoulder and back at him. 'I'll be fine. Sorry.'

She pushed him gently out of the door and blew him a kiss. 'See you later?'

Greg nodded, and trudged slowly along the corridor towards his own room. He would give anything to be the sort of person to storm back in there and insist Adam leave right now. But he knew it would do no good. It would only end badly for him. But he would check up on her later, no matter what she said.

The door closed firmly and Erin turned back to face Adam, swallowing down the shame she felt about her boyfriend being in such a state. The trouble was, it wasn't the first time Adam had turned up at her door like this, and it seemed to be getting worse each time. There was only so long she could keep making excuses for him.

'What are you doing here Adam?' she said, crossing her arms. 'I thought you were touring this week?'

He struggled to sit up. He looked terrible, worse than she'd first thought. It had been almost a month since she'd last seen him; he'd been off touring somewhere up north, and he'd lost weight. His clothes hung off him and his T-shirt was stained.

'I thought you'd be pleased to see me.' He held his arms up. 'Come here.'

Reluctantly, she sat down next to him. He pressed himself against her and pulled her shirt open so hard the buttons popped off. Despite his appearance, Erin felt a stirring of desire and for a moment she let herself get lost in him. They fell back onto the bed and moments later they were both naked, his lithe body pressing into her.

But then she noticed a mark on his neck and she stiffened.

'What's wrong?' His face was so close she couldn't make out his features, only smell his stale-smoke breath.

'What's that?' She ran her finger along his neck and across the livid red mark.

'What's what?'

'This bite mark?'

'It's nothing. Don't worry about it.' He pressed his lips against her again but she turned away and wriggled out from underneath him. She was cold now, and wrapped her flimsy duvet around herself. Adam pushed himself up to sitting, the moment gone. 'Fuck's sake Erin.'

'Adam, why have you got a bite mark on your neck?' Her voice was icy.

'I dunno.' He leaned towards her. 'Pleeease can we just get back into bed?'

She pulled away, suddenly disgusted by this man. She thought about all the times she'd defended him to Greg, to all of her friends, insisting that, no matter how many women Adam was surrounded by every night, he would never cheat on her. But of course she'd known, deep down, that it was inevitable. How could she have been so naïve?

'You need to leave.'

'What?'

'You're pissed.'

'So?'

She sighed. 'I've had enough.'

'Of me?'

'Of us. This.' Erin couldn't believe she was saying it. She worshipped Adam, still loved him ferociously. But there was no way she could deal with him turning up out of the blue like this any more, expecting her to welcome him with open arms, but knowing he was about to go back on tour and – probably – sleep with anyone who threw themselves at him.

'But I love you.'

She shook her head. 'I don't think you do. You just like me being here whenever you want me.'

He didn't answer for a moment, then he stood with a jerk, and started pulling his jeans on, then his filthy T-shirt. As she watched him she nearly shouted at him to stop, that she loved him, that she wanted him to stay. And the truth was she really did want him to. But she also *knew that she couldn't keep doing this, that things would only continue to spiral if she gave in again now. It took all her willpower to let him walk away.*

When he finally shut the door of her student room behind him, her legs collapsed beneath her, and she dragged herself onto her bed, dug out her favourite Pearl Jam CD, and listened to 'Black', the lyrics about being a star in someone else's sky torturing her as the thought of never seeing Adam again filled her with a terrible, agonising ache, like a bruise that was too tender to touch.

* * *

That's where Greg found her, hours later. 'Black' was playing for the hundredth, two-hundredth time, and she'd cried so much she had no more tears left to shed. She felt like an empty husk, hollowed out, and when Greg tapped on the door, she ignored it at first. But when there was no answer the tapping became more insistent until she couldn't stand it any longer, and she leapt up and yanked the door open.

'What?'

'Oh Erin.' Greg stepped into the room and wrapped his arms around her and she collapsed into his chest, let him walk her to her bed and curled up with her head on his lap. As she lay peacefully with this lovely, lovely man comforting her, stroking her hair back from her face, his hands so soft and gentle, she felt the pain seeping away. Greg had turned the music off and Erin could hear the thump of his pulse, and his skin felt so warm, and smelt so good. She sat up, finally, utterly spent. Her face was so close to his she could see the veins in his eyes, the tiny lines on his lips. He was so kind to her, so different to the man she'd loved for the last year, and she felt his desire for her so brightly it was as though it was seeping out of him and into her. Her skin pulsed with expectation.

Did she love him? Could it be that she'd been so blinded by Adam that she'd missed what had been right in front of her all this time? That, in fact, it was kind-hearted, handsome Greg who she loved, who she was supposed to be with? Greg, who adored her, who treated her like a princess? And so what if she didn't feel the same heat between them as she felt when Adam was near her – what good had that done her anyway? Greg's love was stronger; it made her feel warm, safe. Adored.

Without breaking eye contact, she moved closer, closer, closer, until she felt his warm lips on hers, and she pressed her hand against his cheek. He hesitated a moment, pulled back.

'Are you sure you want to do this?'

'Absolutely sure,' she whispered.

He didn't need telling twice. And as their kiss deepened, as Greg felt his way hesitantly around this body he'd only been allowed to admire from afar until now, he felt as though he had everything he'd ever wanted, everything he'd ever need.

And that was the moment Erin knew she'd do everything she could to make sure he was everything she would ever need too.

15

NOW

Fleetwood Mac: 'Everywhere'

My father was a hoarder, by which I don't just mean that he had a couple of rooms full of junk waiting to be sorted out. My father's house – my childhood home – was so packed full of *stuff* that I could barely squeeze my way inside. Newspapers and books teetered in precarious mountains along both sides of the entrance hall; boxes and pieces of furniture and suitcases and old TVs were shoved into every single room, sometimes piled as high as the ceiling. Some rooms were entirely inaccessible as items had fallen and blocked the doorway. The ones you could get into were so crammed there was barely room to turn around to come back out again. The only rooms he now used were the kitchen – where the cooker and the fridge were about the only things anyone could get close to, the ancient dining table having long been surrendered to the piles of junk on top of it – the lounge, where an ancient sofa, an armchair and a TV were still visible among the junk – and his bedroom where there was no floor space but he could just about climb onto one side of the bed.

Of course I knew that hoarding was meaningful, that it could be a sign of unprocessed grief – even if I weren't a psychologist it would be obvious to me. After all, my father had always been so neat and tidy when my mother was around, as though by being that way she'd feel as though he were looking after her. But he'd always liked to collect *things* – shells, a collection of pipes, novelty ties, vinyl records – and when my mother had moved into the care home eight years previously, there was no longer any reason for my father to stop filling his home with the junk that comforted him. And so he didn't.

I'd tried to talk to him about it, but he didn't want to listen, he couldn't admit that there was anything wrong with what he was doing, or that he was so obviously trying to fill the gaping hole my mum had left in his life with *things*. So instead, I did what I always did, which was to try and convince him to let me help him sort it out – usually without much success.

Even though I visited him at least once a week, it didn't stop my heart from sinking every time I got there and was confronted with the true state of the house I'd always loved. Today was no different.

Greg and I usually spent Christmas Day alone or with Rose and Sam, but this year I'd promised my father we'd spend it with him. I wasn't sure what to expect, given that we could barely access the kitchen, let alone the oven. But we'd come prepared.

'Here we go,' I said as we pulled up outside the house.

'Have we got everything?' Greg peered over his shoulder to where the bags were piled on the back seat.

'I bloody hope so.' I grimaced. Greg reached over and took my hand and squeezed it and I felt a ripple of guilt at the image of Adam that flitted through my mind at his touch.

'Just try not to let it bother you too much for today, okay?'

'Easier said than done,' I grumbled, but acquiesced. I reached over and grabbed a bag from the back seat, and handed it to Greg. 'Let's go.'

We climbed out of the car and I pushed open the metal gate, which was half hanging off its hinges, and squeaked as though we were in a horror film. This garden had always been overgrown, but now it was something else; ivy and honeysuckle tugged at the fence, roses extended their creeping hands round the window-frames and knocked gently on the glass. A tree I used to climb had grown so huge it covered most of the windows and soared well beyond the rooftop. The house would be completely buried in the undergrowth before too long if someone didn't do some-thing about it soon. I made a note to call a gardener in the new year, whether my father liked it or not.

I reached the door and knocked. The door probably wasn't locked but I didn't like to just let myself in. But as the seconds ticked past and nobody came, my heart began to race. Had some-thing happened to him? Had he been crushed beneath one of the towering piles of junk, the way I'd always feared he would be? I was about to try the door handle when a silhouette appeared through the stained glass. When the door swung open I smiled with relief.

'Merry Christmas Dad,' I said, holding out my arms. Every time I saw him I was shocked at his appearance. He used to be so imposing, his dark hair immaculately neat, his almost six-foot frame ramrod straight, towering over me and my mother; he'd been so strong, capable. But now he was only a shade taller than me, and hunched over a walking stick as though his spine had given in to gravity. He was still wearing a shirt and tie though, the way he always did for special occasions, his shirt tucked neatly into belted trousers, which were so loose they were threatening to win their fight with gravity too. His frame felt tiny as I hugged him.

'Hello you two,' he said, pulling away and beckoning us inside. We followed.

The piles of junk – books, magazines, newspapers – that had lined the hallway for years had become even more out of control now, and there was a double layer of them so that the once wide, spacious hallway was now a thin, narrow alley leading from the front door into the back of the house. It was dark, the windows having been blocked by books, and the old black and white tiles that had once been one of the best features of the rundown place were now varying shades of grey, buried under years' worth of grime.

His stick tapped on the tiles as he walked, and my heart cracked a little as I watched the back of his head, looking old and frail even from behind.

'We're in here,' Dad said, gesturing at the living room point-lessly, even though it was the only room in the house apart from the kitchen that we could actually get into. A ribbon of sunlight slipped through the net-covered windows, but the room was still dim, lit by a single bare bulb despite the sunny day outside. As always, I was hit not only by a sense of fury for what my father had done to the house I'd once loved, but by a sense of melancholy for what felt like the loss of a friend.

'What have you got there?' Dad said, pointing at the box in my hand as he lowered himself into his armchair.

I pulled a small, pre-lit Christmas tree out of the box. 'Ta-da!'

He smiled but said nothing.

'I knew you wouldn't have one, so I thought I'd help us get in the Christmas spirit,' I said.

'Thank you Reeny, that's very thoughtful.' I smiled at his pet name for me as he glanced round. 'Although I don't know quite where you're going to put it.'

I followed his gaze round the room.

'Hang on,' Greg said. He shuffled a few boxes around then took the tree from my hands and placed it on the makeshift table. It was battery controlled, so he flicked the switch and the lights came on instantly, twinkling incongruously.

'That's better.' Dad studied the tree, a small smile playing on his lips and I knew bringing the tree had been the right thing to do. He pushed himself to standing again and grabbed his stick.

'Sit down you two,' he said, waving his hand towards the sofa. 'I've got something for you.'

'Do you want me to get it?'

He shot me a look. 'No thank you, I'm perfectly capable of walking into another room. I manage it perfectly well 95 per cent of the time when you're not here.'

Chastened, Greg and I did as we were told and perched on the sofa while Dad shuffled away.

'Whoa, it's got *much* worse,' Greg whispered as soon as Dad was out of earshot. Greg hadn't been round for a few weeks and as I looked round now I realised he was right. Things in here had deteriorated despite my attempts to help Dad clear it. I'd seen Dad's hoarding increase over the years, and I'd been vaguely aware that it had been getting out of control recently. But sitting here now, with the Christmas tree I'd brought dwarfed by the piles of – well, crap – that were shoved into this space, I felt my heart pinch with sadness at just how bad it had become. My mind reeled back to a time when my mother was still living here with us. As I stared at the piles of boxes I could almost see the ghosts of our former selves, dancing round the room to our favourite songs, drinking Dr Pepper and laughing our heads off. My mother's golden hair flying wild around her head, her dress flaring, my heart full of joy. Then I focused on the room as it was now, and I felt a deep, lingering sadness for everything that had been lost.

My father returned before I could reply, a couple of small packages tucked under the arm that held his stick, a plate full of mince pies in the other hand. I took the plate from him and balanced it on the tiny table, then Dad handed Greg and me a parcel each. They were both neatly wrapped in midnight blue paper covered in tiny silver stars. This was the first surprise. I usually got something hurriedly wrapped in utilitarian brown paper, or even squashed into a paper bag, not a ribbon or a bow in sight.

'Thank you.' I reached for my bag. 'We've got your present here too.' Dad was so difficult to buy for – with a house full of more things than he could ever possibly use, most of them utterly useless, there really wasn't anything he could ever need – but I always tried to find him something thoughtful every year. I was quite pleased with this Christmas's offering.

'Aren't you going to open it then?' he said, indicating the package he'd handed me.

'Oh, yes,' I said. I couldn't work out why he was so eager for me to see what he'd bought me. He never had a clue what I liked and often just bought me a voucher or something for the kitchen. Intrigued, I unwrapped it carefully, picking the Sellotape off and peeling the corners back.

'Oh!' I gasped when the gift was revealed. It was a bottle of perfume.

'It was your mother's favourite, if you remember,' he said.

'Yes. Yes I do remember. Thank you Dad.'

'Yes, well. You always liked it. You're very welcome.'

I peeled the cellophane off the box, tipped the bottle into my hand and squirted it onto my wrist. In that instant I was transported back to my childhood, the scent of Mum's perfume lingering in every room, and I felt an unexpected rush of love for my dad for choosing something so thoughtful. I blinked back the tears that threatened to spill. Music might transport us back in time, but the power of scent shouldn't be under-estimated too.

'Are you going to open yours?'

He picked the parcel up from his lap and I watched his once-strong fingers fumble with the paper, but resisted the urge to help him. He didn't like to show any weakness.

'Please have a mince pie,' he said as he picked fruitlessly at the Sellotape. 'Dinner won't be ready for a while.'

Greg and I both reached for one at the same time. There were no plates so I took a bite and crumbs spilled all over my trousers.

Finally, Dad had eased the paper off his present and he held it up to take a closer look. It was a clock exactly like the one he'd always loved that had sat on the mantelpiece throughout my childhood, but that he had lost many years ago, no doubt buried somewhere deep in one of these boxes. Although this would almost certainly follow the same fate, I'd always loved it and hoped he'd understand why I'd chosen it.

'It's wonderful, thank you.' He looked around for somewhere to put it to no avail, so I took it from his hand and placed it next to the Christmas tree on the makeshift table. Its quiet tick was the only sound we could hear for a few seconds as we all munched on slightly dry pastry.

'Shall I open a bottle of wine?' I said.

'Not before dinner.'

'Oh, I brought you this,' I said, remembering the bottle of Baileys.

'Ah thank you Reeny.' Dad smiled. 'It's not Christmas without a bottle of Baileys eh?'

'Exactly.'

'Is there anything I can do to help with dinner?' Greg asked.

'No it's all under control. It will be ready in an hour or so.' Greg and I had offered to cook but Dad had insisted. I had no idea how he'd even managed to find the oven let alone pots and pans but I didn't question it.

I sat back for a moment and fiddled with the perfume bottle. The scent was strong, and it was making me feel nostalgic.

'Can I put some music on?' I said suddenly.

'If you like.' Dad shrugged. 'Although I don't know whether the stereo is working; I only ever listen to the radio.'

A quick glance at the stereo didn't look promising. There was a thick layer of dust across its cover and a wire trailing out from behind it. It was wedged tightly behind a heavy looking box.

Not to be put off, I stood and hauled the box away, coughing as dust floated up my nose.

'The CDs are in there I think,' Dad said. I wondered how he knew where anything was among the chaos. Carefully, I prised open the flaps of the tatty cardboard box to reveal dozens and dozens of plastic CD cases. The dust was just as thick in here, and I wiped the top layer away with my sleeve. I pulled a few from the top, then some more. Finally, right down at the bottom, I found what I was looking for.

'Got it!' I exclaimed.

'What is it?' Greg said.

'Just you wait.' I got down on my hands and knees, pulled the plug free and clipped it into the socket, then switched the stereo on. To my surprise it lit up instantly, and I placed the CD carefully in the drawer and closed it, then pressed play. Seconds later, jingling bells crackled from the ancient music station, and it was as though I was eight years old again, Mum and Dad opening presents by the fire, and me surrounded by discarded wrapping paper and endless, forgettable toys, and a soaring, overly large Christmas tree towering over me. A sense of happi-

ness filled me and I stood and brushed the dust from my hands
and shuffled my feet in the tiny section of floorspace that was
free.

'Dance Dance Christmas man,' Dad said, a smile spreading
across his face.

'Isn't this Jim Reeves?' Greg said.

'It is. But I used to call it Dance Dance Christmas man when I
was little,' I said, smiling.

'Your mother always loved this,' Dad said. 'It went on the
moment the Christmas tree arrived, do you remember?'

'I do.' It was so rare for Dad to talk about my mum these days I
didn't say any more. He'd always loved her so intensely, in a way
that he'd never loved anything or anyone else – including me –
that I understood how hard it had been for him when she'd
stopped recognising him. It had broken his heart and I knew he
found it easier not to talk about her at all, although I was in no
doubt that he thought about her all the time.

'Dance with me Dad,' I said, holding my hands out.

'Oh I can't,' he said.

But I refused to give up, and eventually he pushed himself up
and took my hands in his and we stood, swaying gently along to
the song until it came to an end. Dad looked happier than I'd seen
him in years.

I let the album continue to play in the background as we sat
back down.

'I visited your mother yesterday.'

I started in surprise at Dad's words. I knew he visited her occasionally, but he rarely mentioned it and I knew better than to ask.

'How was she?'

'The same as ever.' He closed his eyes briefly. 'I still miss her
you know.'

I studied my father's face. 'I do too, Dad.'

'I know you do. You were thick as thieves you two, weren't you? Hardly needed me around.' His voice was filled with melancholy.

'We were. She was...' I hesitated, trying to pick a word that didn't sound like a criticism of my father. 'She was fun. And I always knew she loved me.'

'Unlike me you mean.'

'No I don't mean that at all. I always knew you loved me too.'

'Well good.' He shook his head. 'Gosh I don't know why I've become so sentimental all of a sudden.'

'It's all right Dad. It is okay to talk about your feelings sometimes you know.'

He nodded, but barely. 'I will never understand what your glorious mother saw in an old fuddy-duddy like me,' he continued, seemingly out of the blue. 'But she bowled me off my feet you know.' Greg leaned forward to listen, nodding in agreement. 'Everyone wondered what on earth she was doing with me, but I was always grateful for her. I treasured every second we had together, even if I didn't always know how to show it.'

'She knew you loved her,' I said, my voice a whisper.

'Maybe. But she deserved better.'

'Don't say that.'

He shrugged. 'But it's true.' He stopped. 'When I saw her yesterday she knew who I was, at least for a few minutes. And in those few minutes I saw the Penny I'd always known and loved, and it made all the other difficult times worthwhile.' He sniffed and I realised he was trying not to cry. I had never seen my father cry. 'She loved you more than you can ever know too.'

'I know.' I reached out and took his hand, and he let me. Then he pulled it away and the moment had gone, evaporating into the air like smoke. He pushed himself to standing. 'Anyway, enough sentimentality. I'd better go and check the dinner before it gets burnt to a crisp.' Then he shuffled off to the kitchen, one small step at a time, and I was so shocked I watched him until he disappeared out of sight.

* * *

After dinner – a turkey meal from Marks and Spencer followed by Christmas pudding and brandy cream – I decided to do some clearing. I hadn't planned to, but I couldn't just sit here in this stuffy room any longer without feeling the claustrophobia closing in. I didn't know how Dad could stand it. Besides, I'd also remembered my promise to Mum to look for her Christmas angel, and now seemed as good a time as any.

'Are you leaving already?' Dad said as I stood up, looking up from the table where he was pouring three generous glasses of Baileys.

'Not yet. I thought I might crack on with clearing some more of that room I started on the other day.'

'Surely you can leave it for today?'

But I was desperate to get out of this room and clear my head, and think through everything that had happened over the last few days.

'Just an hour or so. I need to stretch my legs,' I said.

'Need a hand?' Greg said. He was reclining like a lion on the tatty old rug in front of the electric fire, sleepy from the wine we'd shared over dinner.

'No, you stay here and chat, or have a snooze, you poor old men.'

Before either of them could object, I left the room. I picked my way carefully up the stairs, along the small gap that still remained between the piles of junk and the handrail. I hated the thought of my father climbing these stairs to bed every evening. I had visions of him tripping and falling head over heels, snapping every bone as he fell. It was an accident waiting to happen and I vowed to clear some of this as well before I left today.

At the top, the landing was barely visible either. Two of the bedroom doors were completely blocked, and the other two had so much junk piled round them they were only just accessible. The bathroom door was missing and I could see even that room hadn't escaped my father's mania for collecting things. Bottles of shampoo and body wash, sponges, flannels, tubes of toothpaste and towels were all piled in the bath and the floor was half-covered with the same.

Turning away from it, I headed along the corridor towards my old room. I pushed the door open but it got stuck halfway, blocked by something. I could see enough to make out my old bed, piled high with stuff – of course – the windows grimy and dark, the room a shadow of the warm, welcoming place I'd made it when I'd slept here, and my ancient CD player, covered in so much dust it looked like a museum relic. If I hadn't known where I was I would hardly have recognised it, despite the picture of the Coca-Cola can that still hung crookedly on the one visible wall, its edges curling and ripped.

I went back to the spare room, which I'd started sorting out a few weeks ago, and was relieved to see that the tiny patch I'd already cleared hadn't been re-filled with something else yet. Small progress, but progress all the same. I sat on the floor, legs crossed, and pulled a few bags from the top of the next pile. I didn't hold out much hope of finding Mum's Christmas angel but it had to be worth a go. Sadly, after twenty minutes of sifting through three bags of mostly junk I'd had no luck, and didn't know where to try next. It literally was like trying to find a needle in a haystack. Or an angel in a rubbish pile.

I hauled the binbags straight down the stairs and out of the front door before my father could demand to check them, then headed back upstairs. There were a few more tatty-looking bags which I quickly checked inside, and then a couple of boxes, large and square. I dragged them towards me and pulled open the flaps of the first one. It was full of LPs, top-edge up so I couldn't see what any of them were. I pulled out a few at random and it quickly became clear that these were some of my father's old albums. Neil Young. Bob Dylan. Fleetwood Mac. The Rolling Stones. They were the songs of my childhood; rainy days, listening to the rain pummel the roof, watching the droplets slide down the glass, like some lovestruck kid in a teenage drama. Nostalgia overwhelmed me.

I opened the next box and was surprised to find Dad's old record player. Why had it been shoved up here with all this junk? Did he even know it was here? I lifted it carefully out of the box and placed it on the floor and blew the dust off the top, watched it shoot into the air and dissipate, resettle. There was a wire and plug sticking out the back and I searched round for a socket. I could just make out the edge of one poking out from behind a pile of boxes by the bedroom door, so I yanked the boxes away and plugged it in. Just like the old stereo downstairs, it came to life instantly. Then I pulled out the first record my hand landed on, removed it from its sleeve and placed it carefully on the turntable before flicking the switch. There was a second of silence, a loud crackle from the dusty needle, then 'Everywhere' by Fleetwood Mac began, the familiar line about hearing me calling out your name bringing the memories flooding back. I sat back, leaning against a box, and closed my eyes, letting the images fill my mind for a moment... the parties Mum and Dad used to hold, music and laughter and the tinkle of glasses being filled... Mum and Dad holding each other, Dad standing stiffly while Mum spun out from his arms, her skirt flaring, giggling as he watched her ador-ingly. Mum singing the lyrics to Dad and him rolling his eyes and laughing as I peered at them through a crack in the door, thrilled by how much they adored each other.

As the song came to an end and the next one began, my mind drifted to Greg. As a child I'd always seen how much my parents had loved each other despite being such an unlikely pairing, and I'd dreamed of having a love like theirs – it had always felt like a fairy tale. I'd believed I'd found it with Adam, once, but it had soon become clear it was different – more fiery, passionate. Thrilling.

Greg's love had been like a beam of adoration that had pointed my way and I'd soaked it up, hoping that one day it would seep in so far that I'd realise it was exactly what I'd been looking for all along. And I truly believed it had worked.

But Adam's return had made me doubt myself. It had made me reassess what I had with Greg, what we'd built up over the years, and made me question whether our marriage wasn't what I'd been searching for after all.

That maybe I'd only find that with someone else.

With someone like Adam.

I jerked upright and lifted the needle off the record with shaking hands. I felt panicky, the sudden silence making my ears hum as I watched tiny dust particles bounce around in the disturbed air. My breathing was shallow and I forced myself to take some deep breaths, filling my lungs with the dusty air until it slowed and deepened.

My hand fluttered to the chain around my neck, the crotchet which nestled against my heart that I'd hidden underneath my polo neck, and my stomach rolled over. What the hell was *wrong* with me?

I hurried to my feet and was about to head back downstairs when something in the bottom of the box caught my eye. I reached my hand in and clasped my fingers round the rectangles of hard plastic and pulled them out – five or six old cassette tapes, the CD90s that had already been almost obsolete when I was a child but that I'd still used to make mixtapes on Mum's old cassette recorder. I picked the top one off the pile. There was my handwriting, the neat, round letters telling me that this tape contained the top 20 from November 1995. I smiled and picked up the next one, and my heart stopped. On the front, on the white insert card, was a scrawled note, which just said:

To E. To remember me. Love A x

It was a tape Adam had made me. I'd forgotten all about it, but seeing it brought the memory of the day he gave it to me flooding back. It had been a few days before I'd been due to leave for university, and he was about to head off with his band on a tour of pubs in the north-east. I was beside myself, desperate not to be apart, and had cried non-stop for several days. We'd gone for a final drink with our friends before we'd all left, and as we'd arrived, Adam had handed the tape to me, shyly. I'd never seen him look so coy before, and he'd shoved his hands in the pockets of his jeans as soon as I'd taken it from him.

'I just thought you could take a piece of me with you,' he'd said, his voice low. His eyes darted back and forth as though to make sure no-one was listening.

I'd stared at the tape in amazement, my heart soaring. 'Wow, thank you,' I'd said, my voice cracking.

'It's not much but – well, I'll miss you.'

A tear had slipped down my cheek and I'd wiped it away. 'I'll miss you too,' I'd said, and almost thrown myself at him. We'd held each other tightly, locked in our own cocoon, before the moment had been shattered by Sam. 'Come on you two love birds, let's get this show on the road!'

I didn't get a chance to listen to the tape until much later that night when I'd got home and played it on Mum's old Walkman, lying in bed listening to all the songs Adam had deemed were important to me and him: Bush, 'The Chemicals Between Us'; Ash, 'Girl From Mars'; Nirvana, 'Heart-Shaped Box'... I'd played it endlessly for those first few weeks at university too, almost wearing the tape out between Adam's visits.

I hadn't seen it since those days, but now here it was, back in my hand. Was it fate, me finding this now?

Suddenly aware of the time, I stuck the tape in my pocket to take home with me, and was about to put the rest back in the box when I noticed something scribbled on the one below it. It looked much older than the one I'd just found, the insert card yellowed, and I pulled it out and studied it.

To Penny with all my love, J xx

I frowned. That wasn't my father's writing. His was curly and elaborate, while this was blocky and slightly childlike. I turned it over, opened the box and slid the tape out. But there was nothing else on there, no song titles, nothing. I slipped it into my pocket as well, and headed back downstairs.

16

NOW

Cyndi Lauper: 'Time After Time'

It was late on Boxing Day by the time I got round to listening to the tape I'd found in my father's house. Greg and I had spent the day drinking coffee in our dressing gowns, and I'd been for a walk to clear my head. At about three o'clock Greg suddenly announced he was going for a run.

'A run?' Greg hadn't been for a run for at least a year. As his gambling addiction had taken hold, early evening jogs and bike rides had slowly gone out of the window as he holed himself up in his room for hours on end. This was quite a turn-round.

'Yep. New year, new me,' he said, lacing up his slightly tatty trainers.

'It's not New Year yet.'

'I know.' He patted his belly. 'But it's never too soon to try and get rid of this paunch.'

I eyed him suspiciously, ignoring the fact that he obviously didn't have a hint of a belly. 'But you hate running. You said you were never doing it again.'

He sat down next to me and placed his hand on my leg. 'I do hate running. But I think it will help me, when I feel the urge to gamble.'

I met his gaze. 'Do you feel the urge now?'

He nodded. 'Always.'

'Well then I won't stop you.' I removed his hand from my thigh and stood, pulling my cardigan tighter round me.

When the door shut behind him, I waited a couple of minutes to make sure he wasn't about to change his mind and come straight back home again, then, when I was sure the coast was clear, I raced upstairs and retrieved the tape from my knicker drawer where I'd stashed it the previous evening after we'd got home from Dad's. Luckily, thanks to my job, I had an old tape recorder as well as a CD player just in case the songs my patients wanted to listen to were only on ancient cassettes, so I pulled it out of my holdall and plugged it in, then slipped the first cassette inside – the one Adam had made me all those years ago. I rewound it to the beginning. It felt important, somehow, to listen to it in the order in which it was intended. Then I pressed play...

The opening notes of 'Heart-Shaped Box' soared into the room and I smiled. I could picture exactly where we'd been when this had played for the first time: at the pub down the road. I was back there in an instant. I let the song play out, and then another song, and another, getting more and more lost in the memories, of me and Adam, young and in love.

I snapped my eyes open and pressed stop then sat for a moment, as an idea occurred to me. It wasn't doing me any good, listening to this: all it was doing was making me feel even more confused. But it could be useful, perhaps, in helping to unlock some memories for Adam. If the music was sending me back in time, surely it might be able to do the same for him too? I removed the tape from the recorder, placed it back into its case and tucked it into my bag for later. Then I picked up Mum's tape, the one from the mystery 'J', and placed that inside and pressed play.

Instantly, the opening bars to 'Time After Time' by Cyndi Lauper started, and I smiled. Mum had always loved this song so I wasn't surprised to find it on here. As the song played I took a closer look at the tape case, pulling the cardboard insert out to see if there was anything else written on it. I unravelled it and there, tucked inside, was a small piece of paper, folded several times. I picked it up and carefully opened it up, my heart thumping. What was I going to find? Would there be something Mum would never have wanted me or anyone else to see? Should I put it away and forget about it, pretend I'd never found it?

But I knew I wasn't going to do that.

Finally, I opened it fully. The paper was fragile and thin, so I gently smoothed it out on the carpet and read the words which were written in the same blocky handwriting as before.

Penny.
If you find this note, it means you have to say yes.
Marry me, and not him.
Say you will.
I adore you.
J xx

J? Who on earth was J? And why was he telling my mum to marry him instead of someone else? Was the someone else my dad? It must have been. I'd never heard her mention anyone else other than my dad, but then why would she? She must have been very young – after all, she'd married Dad when she was only twenty-one.

My mind raced with possibilities. Who could this 'J' be? And how different would my life have been if she'd have said yes to him and not my dad?

Maybe this tape could be the key to unlocking Mum's memories at last. It had to be worth a try.

* * *

'Are you sure you don't know who he is?' Rose said, after I'd filled her in on what I'd found. It was two days after Christmas and I'd popped round for a quick drink and to tell her all about my Christmas Day discoveries.

'Positive.'

'The cheeky little minx,' Sam said, handing me a full-to-the-brim glass of gin and tonic. I took a sip and almost spat it back out again. 'Christ, is there any tonic in here at all?' I spluttered, blood rushing to my head with the unadulterated hit of alcohol.

'A splash.' Sam grinned, holding his glass up. 'Cheers.'

'Cheers you two. And Happy Christmas.'

Despite the paint-stripper-like qualities of the drink, I took another sip and let the alcohol spread through my body, relaxing every limb. I'd felt like a wound-up toy recently and was so grateful to have these two to talk to whenever I needed – even if they did tell me the truth a little too easily.

'I guess you'll never know who this J was now then?' Rose said, a frown creasing her forehead.

I shuffled to sit up and placed my elbows on my knees. 'That's just it. I wondered whether there might actually be a way to find out.'

'Ooh I love a mystery; tell me more,' Sam said. His eyes shone with delight.

'You know I play Mum songs to try and get her to remember things?' I began.

'Yep.'

'Well, I always stick to the same songs – you know, the ones I know she loves, tunes that remind her of Dad, or of me, or of happy times, because I don't want anything to freak her out. I've spent hours carefully curating Mum's playlist so nothing takes her by surprise or upsets her too much. But what if, for a change, I played her some of the songs from this tape, the ones she might not have heard for years, to see if it helps her to remember who this J is?'

Rose scrutinised me for so long I wondered whether she'd even heard what I'd said. Eventually, she spoke, her words slow and deliberate. 'The thing is, Erin, don't you think she would have mentioned him before, if he'd been anyone important? I mean, your mum never really knows what day and time it is these days, and her mind definitely has no filter, so it's not as if she could deliberately stop herself talking about someone to protect yours or your dad's feelings, even if she wanted to.'

'She sounds like me,' Sam said, grinning.

'What, no filter?'

'Yup.' He took another sip and gave an innocent look. I rolled my eyes and turned back to Rose.

'I've thought about that. But what if – I dunno. What if she'd locked this J away in her mind until she almost *had* forgotten about him? I mean, our minds do this sort of thing all the time. Sometimes in response to trauma, sometimes just to protect us from feelings that might hurt us. But what if I played her some of these songs, and *because* her mind is more pliable than most, she does remember?'

'I suppose so,' Rose said, cautiously. 'But I still don't really understand why you need to know so desperately?'

I sighed. Rose had a point. Why *did* I feel such an urgent need to know who this mystery 'J' was? Was it because of the things Dad had said to me about never knowing why Mum had chosen him, or because of the turmoil my mind was in about my own self-inflicted mess?

'I'm just nosy I suppose,' I said.

'Me too,' Sam said, sloshing his drink around so the ice cubes clinked in the glass.

I sighed. The truth was, my instinct was to stay well clear of letting Mum listen to any of these songs. And yet there was something about the note I'd found hidden in the tape that made me need to find out who this man was, and that made me wonder whether this wasn't the key to getting my mum back: music made Mum open up, it lifted her out of her broken mind and let her believe she was somewhere else, some*time* else. It made her happy; it made her Penny again.

What if one of these songs could do that, and unlock the secret of this mystery man at the same time?

My thoughts were interrupted by a tug at my neck. Sam was leaning over me, pulling at something.

'What's this?'

It took me a second to realise what he was talking about and my heart stopped. Oh shit.

'It's a necklace,' I said, trying to hide the wobble in my voice.

'I can see that smarty pants. It's new though, isn't it? Who bought that for you? It can't have been Greg.'

Poor Greg. Lovely as he was, he wasn't the world's most creative present buyer, usually opting for something practical like a pair of walking boots or a hairdryer over something useless but thoughtful.

'Okay, it wasn't Greg.'

Rose was intrigued now too, and was peering at it questioningly.

'Oh my God, it's from Adam isn't it? You've seen him again!' Sam smacked the sofa, which emitted a cloud of dust.

'No!'

'It is; you've gone bright red.' Sam wriggled round to face me and leaned his elbows on his knees, legs crossed. 'Come on Donnelly. Spill. What's going on with you and sexy rock star Adam Bowers?'

Despite these two having been my best friends for so long, the time I'd been spending with Adam was something I'd wanted to keep to myself for a while longer. I hadn't wanted it to be analysed, to make it more or less than it actually was. I'd wanted to hold it to myself, to keep it secret just a little bit longer, because the more we talked about it the more obvious it would be to us all that what I was doing was wrong.

'I helped him, that's all.'

Sam waited, not saying a word. I crumbled first.

'He asked me if we could try and find some of his memories with music, and I agreed.' I kept my eyes trained on my hands in front of me. 'I mean, it is my job.'

'Okaaay. And you're sure there's absolutely no other reason why you'd want to help him?'

'Of course not.'

'Mm hmm,' Sam said. 'So, where did it happen, this little therapy session?'

'At his house.'

'His house as in the Bower House?! You went there for this professional assessment?'

I nodded.

'And were his parents there?'

'Yes, they were.' I looked at them both defiantly. 'There's nothing more to this you know. You're making a drama out of nothing.'

'Oh come on Erin, we all know it's not nothing. Sexy Adam comes back into town years after breaking your heart, and which, by the way, you never got over.' I was about to object but he held his hand up to stop me. 'And by some miracle he's forgotten everything that happened between you, and you're spending time with him and helping him... and you're telling me you don't feel anything for him at all, aside from a professional relationship?'

I let out a long breath and held my hands up. 'Okay, busted. Of course I feel something for him. But there's nothing going on, I swear. I wouldn't do that to Greg.'

'Not even for Adam?'

'No!'

'Okay, okay.' He leaned further forward. 'So, tell me more about this meeting. When was it?'

'Christmas Eve.'

'Interesting. Where?'

'I already said, at his house.'

'Which room?'

'His bedroom...'

'Ah ha!'

'Sam, leave her alone,' Rose interjected.

'What? I'm only getting to the bottom of it because she's so reluctant to tell us, her two very best friends in the whole wide world and the two people who know as much about her as she knows about herself, the truth.' He turned back to me, his voice softer this time. 'Seriously E, what's going on? Are you considering cheating on Greg?'

I should have denied it. I should have said no, of course not, I loved Greg.

But I knew, and they both knew, how things had been between us for the last few months and we all also knew how I had always felt about Adam. My lack of reply spoke volumes.

'Oh E, you need to be careful,' Sam said.

'I am being careful. I'm not doing anything wrong, I swear.'

His look stopped me in my tracks, and Rose reached for me, placing her hand on my forearm.

'We remember,' she said. I was about to object but the look in her eyes made me think twice. 'Me and Sam were both there when you were with Adam, and afterwards, when you split up. He didn't—' She stopped and glanced at Sam as if looking for reassurance about what she was about to say next. 'The thing is, E, we're worried about you. We both think that you...' She coughed. 'We think you only remember the good times. That you look back at the time when you were with Adam as being the best months of your life, and as him being the best thing that ever happened to you. But we were there, remember? We saw how it really was.'

'What do you mean, how it really was?' I spat the last words, feeling my hackles rise.

'What Rose means, E, is that Adam could be a shit sometimes, that he didn't always treat you very well, and we worry that you've forgotten that,' Sam interjected. 'We love you and we would never tell you what to do, but you know that me and Rose were both relieved when you and Adam split up and you met Greg. He was – is – much more deserving of you.'

I stilled for a moment, trying to absorb Sam's words. I wanted to feel angry, to shout at them both that they had it all wrong, that Adam had been the love of my life. I also wanted to tell them that of course I remembered Adam hadn't been perfect. But the truth was that, since his return, I *had* mainly only remembered how passionate our relationship had been, how intensely I'd loved him. But Rose and Sam were right. When I took off the rose-tinted glasses I remembered that Adam hadn't always treated me as well as he should have done. Sometimes he'd be distant, dismissing me when he was with the rest of his band, or when there were other girls around; other times he was downright rude to me in front of his friends, belittling me and making me feel like a silly little girl. How could I have forgotten those times so easily?

Shame flooded my body.

'You're right,' I said weakly. 'But he's changed, I swear.'

'Erin—' Sam started, but I cut him off.

'Really Sam. I promise. He's softer than he used to be. He's grown up I guess. And the accident, it's made him more – gentle. Kinder.'

'Okay. But remember you haven't seen him for eighteen years. You don't have any idea what he's really like these days. And you'd be a total fool to throw away your marriage for someone like Adam.' He swallowed and corrected himself. 'I mean like the old Adam.'

'I'm not planning to throw my marriage away. At least not for him,' I said.

But as the words left my mouth, I realised I didn't know for certain whether they were true.

17

THEN

Ash: 'Girl From Mars'

The music was loud, the bass thumping through the sticky floor as Erin, Rose and Sam pushed their way through the crowds towards the bar. The pub was packed and Erin felt a ripple of pride at the thought that all of these people were here to watch her boyfriend playing tonight.

'I'll get the beers, you find us a good spot to watch from,' Sam yelled, turning towards the bar to battle his way to the front. Erin and Rose elbowed their way to the back of the room and squeezed themselves next to a table where they could at least rest their drinks.

'What time are they on?' Rose yelled.

'Not sure.' Erin pulled a leaflet from the back pocket of her jeans and squinted at it. This was the first time Adam's band The Night Crawlers had headlined at this pub – they were usually second on the bill – and Adam had been really excited about it.

'This is a big deal Erin,' he'd said the previous night, pacing up and down in his parents' outbuilding where the band rehearsed.

'It's brilliant,' she'd said, reaching to hug him, but he'd pushed her away, agitated.

'Not now.' His body fizzed with anticipation and she took a step away, trying not to show she was hurt. He ran his fingers through his wild curls and crouched down, elbows on his knees. 'What if we fuck it up?'

'Why would you?' She squatted down beside him. 'You've played there loads of times. You'll smash it.'

He'd leapt up and picked up his guitar. 'You'd better go; we've got to get some more practice in.'

She'd left then, dismissed. Now she felt nervous about seeing him again.

'It doesn't say,' she said, folding the flyer up carefully and shoving it back in her pocket. 'They're usually on by nine though, aren't they?'

Rose glanced at her watch. 'Half an hour then?'

They turned to face the small makeshift stage the current band were playing on, and settled in to listen. But Erin wasn't really paying attention. Instead, she surveyed the room. It hadn't gone unnoticed that, dotted among the usual crowd were huddles of young, leggy girls, hovering around in their tiny cropped tops, tight jeans, high heels and back-combed hair. They were The Night Crawlers fans, and although she knew they existed, this was the first time she'd seen them in the flesh, these young women who followed Adam and his band round the country like lemmings.

She knew, too, that they were really only here for the charismatic front man, that Adam's dark good looks and deep, throaty voice were the main draw.

'Stop it E.' Rose nudged her in the side and she snapped her head round.

'Stop what?'

'Stressing.' She nodded towards the crowd. 'They're just groupies; you don't have anything to worry about.'

Erin nodded. 'I know.' She wasn't going to relax that easily though. It wasn't that she didn't trust Adam. She did, of course she did. He loved her, even if he didn't say it very often. But it was these girls who weren't to be trusted. She knew they'd throw themselves into bed with her boyfriend without a backwards glance if they got the chance.

She was here to make sure they didn't get that chance.

'Here you go.' Sam slammed three pints down, sloshing beer over the sides onto the already sticky table. He removed the crisps that were clamped between his teeth and threw them down too. Erin tipped half a pint down her neck and wiped the back of her hand across her mouth.

'Blimey, thirsty?' Sam smirked.

'Just needed a drink.'

'She's upset about the groupies,' Rose said.

Sam snaked his arm around her shoulders and gave her a squeeze. 'E, you know you've got nothing to worry about, don't you? Even if they throw themselves at Adam, we're here to drag them off him.' He grinned and she gave a weak smile back.

They sipped their beer and munched the crisps. The first band's set came to an end and they bought more beer. Erin could feel herself pulsing, both excited and nervous about seeing Adam on the stage. She wondered if he would spot her here, right at the back.

'I'm just nipping to the loo,' she said, disappearing before anyone could object.

In the harsh light of the toilet she studied herself in the speckled mirror. Her face looked pale and the eye liner she'd so carefully applied earlier that evening had smudged under her eyes. Her lipstick had faded and her lacy trim vest top and bootcut jeans looked immature and boring compared to the outfits her rivals – as she thought of them – were wearing. She dug in her bag and re-applied her lipstick, pinching her cheeks to give her some colour. She sighed. She'd have to do. She wished she wasn't so anxious.

Everything would be fine.

She went back to the pub, the noise hitting her the moment she pushed the door open. And as she arrived back at the table, a hush fell over the pub and the lights dimmed.

'Just in time,' Rose whispered.

There was a beat of almost-silence – then Adam strode onto the stage, followed by the guitarist, the bassist and the drummer. The place erupted, the screams from the girls who had pushed themselves to the front right by the stage the loudest. Erin's hand gripped her pint tightly.

She watched Adam as he began to sing. He had such undeniable presence and seemed to command the room. He took total control of the audience and she began to wonder whether he even knew she was there as he bent down to sing to the girls crowded round his feet.

'I'm going forward,' she yelled, but as she stepped away Sam pressed his hand against her arm and gave a little shake of his head. 'Stay here E.'

She looked at the stage and back at Sam, and knew he was right. She'd only make a fool of herself.

It was about halfway through the set when the band launched into 'Girl From Mars' by Ash. As the opening guitar began, Adam looked out across the pub. Was he seeking her out? She stood a little taller, and willed him to see her. And then, as his eyes landed on her and he gave a little wink and started singing about loving his girl from Mars, she felt herself puff out, try to fill the space.

'See?' Rose shouted in her ear. 'Nothing to worry about.'

Erin felt herself begin to relax, and by the time they had played their last song, she was glad she'd come. But as the band left the stage Erin found herself glancing round every couple of minutes, waiting for Adam to come over and find her.

'Erin, are you even listening to me?' Sam demanded, waving his hand in front of her face.

'Sorry. Miles away.' Her vision was a bit blurry, and she realised she was more than a little drunk.

'Miles away in lover boy's changing room you mean,' Sam slurred and Rose giggled.

'When is he going to introduce me to the sexy guitarist?' Rose said, her speech just as slurred as Sam's.

'Dan?' Erin said, incredulous. He was the quiet one, and usually the last one the girls fancied. Erin cast her gaze distractedly over to the side of the bar where she knew the band would emerge, and where there was an increasingly large group of girls hanging around.

'Yes, Dan.' Rose slapped her arm. 'Come on Erin, you two have been seeing each other for three months now and I'm still single.'

'I'll ask Adam,' she promised half-heartedly, her voice trailing off, the conversation fading into the background as she stared fixedly at the gaggle of girls waiting to throw themselves at her boyfriend. Her teeth were clenched and her whole body thrummed with tension. Where was he?

Suddenly there was a stirring over by the bar and Erin held her breath, waiting for Adam to spot her. She could see the top of his head now, his dark curls slicked back with sweat, as he pushed his way through the crowd. Then he stopped and she watched as one of the cropped-top girls slid her arms round his neck like a snake. Erin waited for Adam to shake her off, to move away and put some distance between them, but as the seconds ticked by she realised he wasn't going to do that. In fact, he didn't seem to mind at all that this girl was draping herself all over him.

Her world seemed to still as she watched the scene unfold before her. A leg hitched round her boyfriend's waist, his hand moving up it, along the smooth brown skin, under the skirt... lips nuzzling his neck, a look of pleasure on his face... and then the girl peeled off, and someone else grabbed his hand, pressing themselves against him.

Erin felt frozen to the spot, unable to tear her eyes away as her boyfriend enjoyed the advances of several girls, all desperate for his attention.

She jumped at a hand on her shoulder and turned to see Sam watching her with concern. 'Do you want to go home E?'

She gave a tight nod and tried to ignore the rising wave of nausea in her throat.

Sam took hold of her elbow and steered her towards the door. They were almost there when Erin heard her name being called above the buzz of the pub and she turned to see Adam weaving his way towards her.

'Are you leaving already?'

She nodded.

'Can't you stay? The guys are all hanging out for a bit.' Anger coursed through her. How dare he pretend nothing had happened? Did he really think she hadn't seen him lapping up the attention just now?

'You've got your groupies here,' I said, my voice in danger of breaking.

He glanced behind me and rolled his eyes. 'Them? Don't worry about them. You're my girl.' He held his arms out. She stood rooted to the spot. Every part of her body was screaming at her to believe him, to go to him. Yet it was battling with the rational part of her mind that told her she'd be a fool to trust him now.

'I think Erin wants to go home,' Sam said, no trace of drunkenness left in his voice. Adam looked at him with a frown, then back at Erin.

'Erin? Do you?'

'I—' She stopped, swallowed. 'Who was that girl?'

Adam glanced behind him. 'Which girl?'

'The one who was all over you like a rash just now,' Sam said, his voice icy.

Adam sighed heavily. 'No-one was all over me. I was just trying to walk past and get to you and she threw herself at me.' He took Erin's elbow. 'Erin, I promise. I don't even know who she is.'

'Okay.' She nodded, and forced a smile.

'So are you coming with me? Or are you going to go home and leave me here all on my own?' He stuck his bottom lip out and Erin couldn't help it: she melted. Of course Adam wasn't flirting with someone else in front of her; why would he do that? She must have misunderstood. She stepped towards him into his arms and he kissed her lightly on the nose.

'I'll stay.'

'Good choice.' His hands ran down her back and onto her bottom, making her entire body fizz.

She turned to find Rose standing next to Sam, her arms folded across her chest.

'Are you staying too?' she said.

'No, I think we'll head home.' Sam looked angry but Erin knew he'd forgive her. He always did.

'Rose?' she pleaded. 'You can come and meet the band.'

Rose hesitated a minute, torn between her loyalty for Sam and her desperation to meet Dan. But in the end, loyalty won. 'I'll go with Sam,' she said, pulling on her coat and hooking her arm through his. As the pair of them disappeared out of the door, Erin turned back to Adam, and as his eyes fixed on her, the guilt she felt at letting her friends down flew out of her mind. She was here, with Adam, and he wanted her. She kissed him, molten with desire, and felt a spark of triumph as he took her hand and led her backstage, away from the groups of girls still hanging around, who were watching them go with obvious envy. She'd won, for now. She could only hope things stayed that way.

18

NOW

The Psychedelic Furs: 'Pretty in Pink'

'Hello Mum,' I said, momentarily forgetting I wasn't meant to call her that.

'Hello,' Mum replied, smiling. It was three days after Christmas and to my relief she seemed in a good mood. She was sitting up in bed and looked as though she'd put on some make-up and brushed her hair. 'Have you come to see me?'

'I have. Is that okay?' I perched on the chair nearby and waited.

Mum looked at Suzy questioningly, and Suzy gave a small nod. 'You like talking to Erin,' she reassured her.

Mum turned back to me and smiled again. 'Oh good.'

'I'll leave you two for a while shall I?' Suzy said, heading towards the door.

'Thank you,' I replied.

A silence hung in the air for a few seconds after she left. I stared out of the window behind Mum at the gardens where, in the misty distance, a small figure trudged across the grass, and wondered whether they were supposed to be out there alone. My attention was brought back into the room by Mum's voice. Despite everything that had happened to her mind over the years, she still sounded the same, and when I wasn't looking at her I felt consumed with joy when I heard her and truly believed I had her back again. Until reality crashed back in.

'Sorry,' I said, turning my attention to her. 'What did you say?'

'What dear? What did who say?'

I sighed. 'Never mind.' I held out a small package wrapped in red and silver paper. 'Merry Christmas.'

'What's this for?' she said, eyeing it suspiciously.

'It's your Christmas present.'

'Ooh, is it Christmas? I love Christmas.' She snatched it from me and held it in both hands, gazing at it excitedly.

'Are you going to open it?' I encouraged her gently.

'What? Oh yes, in a minute.' I'd lost her again; her mind had wandered off somewhere else, to some far-away place. I hoped it was nice there. Minutes ticked by, and when Mum started to slowly peel the tape from her present I took a moment to study her. The last few years hadn't been kind to her. Even as her mind had begun to give up on her and she'd lost a little bit more of herself with each and every day, the vibrant, happy woman she'd always been hadn't disappeared completely. It had always been there, if you'd known where to look, in the subtle upturn of her mouth at some small piece of joy, or the glisten in her eye when she remembered some happier time. Now though, it seemed as though Mum's last sliver of sparkle had finally disappeared, and most of the time she was just an empty, sad shell. Her eyes were blank, her youthful glow had become a dull grey despite the make-up, and she dressed in baggy, shapeless clothes that made her look at least ten years older than her fifty-seven years. My heart ached for her.

Finally, Mum had her present unwrapped and she stared at it.

'It's a necklace Mum,' I explained, leaning over and lifting the delicate silver daisy from its silky base.

'But I have one of these already.' She looked up at me in confusion.

'Yes you did, but you lost it.'

'I don't think I did.'

I smiled patiently and pulled it from the box.

'Do you want me to put it on for you?'

'Yes please.' I stood and moved behind Mum's chair, carefully closing the clasp and letting the daisy hang against her chest. Her fingers flew up to touch it.

'Does it look pretty?'

'It does.'

'Michael bought this for me you know, for our tenth wedding anniversary.'

I smiled. 'I do know.'

She smiled back, the memory pleasing her.

'I have something else for you,' I said.

'You do?'

I stuck my hand into my bag again and this time I pulled out a Christmas angel. When I hadn't been able to find the one Mum had wanted at Dad's house, I'd taken mine from the top of the tree and wrapped it up for her, hoping it would suffice. I held it out to her now, and she took it gently and pulled the paper off. I studied her face for a reaction as she saw what it was. Then, completely out of the blue, she threw the angel on the floor in anger. 'That's not mine,' she said, and when she looked up, her eyes glistened with tears.

'I know it's not exactly the same, but you wanted an angel for your tree didn't you?' I said.

She shook her head vigorously and I waited for her to calm down before reaching for her hands which were fluttering in her lap.

'It's okay Mum. It's fine. We don't need to talk about it any more.' She sat staring into the distance just over my shoulder for a moment, her confusion clearing. I was furious with myself. I should have known any old angel wouldn't do. Mum might not know who I was, but she knew that wasn't the Christmas angel her daughter had made her thirty years ago. The mind was such a cruel place sometimes.

When I was sure she'd calmed down, I said, 'Would you like to listen to some music?'

'Ooh yes please,' she said, any upset seemingly forgotten already.

Relieved, I reached into my bag and pulled out the mixtape and a tape player. Mum watched with the interest of a small child but didn't register any recognition at the box or the handwriting on it, so I carried on.

I'd decided to play it safe and try one of our regular songs first. Seconds later the room was filled with the sound of David Bowie telling us to dance. I watched closely for Mum's reaction as she let the music wash over her, transporting her back to another time, another place. It never ceased to amaze me how instant the reaction could be. Mum's face relaxed, all the lines and creases softening, her worried frown smoothing out and her shoulders dropping. For a few minutes, as she listened to one of her favourite songs, she was no longer Penny the dementia patient, waiting in her residential home for her time to come, scared of everyone and everything. She was Penny, the funny, crazy, inspirational, independent woman who was loved by everyone who knew her. She was my mum again and my heart felt like it might snap in two. These moments, when I had my mum back again, were both amazing and heart-breaking all at the same time.

The song came to an end and her face changed almost instantly. I pressed stop on my phone and reached for her hands. She looked down with confusion at where our fingers were inter-laced and I squeezed them gently. She peered up at me, her grey eyes intense as though she desperately wanted me to know some-thing she couldn't remember how to express. Then her gaze slid to my phone again.

'More?'

I nodded and released her fingers. I loaded the mixtape into the player this time, then found the right track. 'I thought I'd play you something a bit different today Mum, is that okay?' She nodded, so I pressed play and waited for something to happen. My heart thumped. This was it.

And sure enough, seconds after the first jangly notes of 'Pretty in Pink' by The Psychedelic Furs floated through the room, Mum's face lit up again, a look of intense adoration in her eyes.

'Who's there?' I said, turning the volume down a notch so she could hear me. 'What's happening?'

'He's here,' she said, her voice soft, younger than usual.

'Who's here?' I said, gently, trying not to interrupt her thoughts, to keep her in the moment. She didn't reply for a while and I wondered whether I should change the song, try a different one. But then Mum stood up, clasped her hands together and held them below her chin. I waited.

'It's Johnny.' Her voice was almost a whisper as she swayed from side to side, and I leaned a little closer to hear her better.

'Who's Johnny?' I whispered. She snapped her eyes open, eyes wide with surprise.

'You're having me on,' she said, grinning. 'You know who Johnny is.'

I hesitated. 'Is he – your boyfriend?'

'You silly sausage,' she said, laughing. 'We're getting *married*.'

I held my breath. 'Married?'

'Yes. He asked me and I said yes and we're getting married next year.'

My head swam. I'd seen the note from 'J', of course, but I'd assumed that the talk of marriage had been more from him than from Mum. After all, she'd married my father, hadn't she?

Mum ran her thumb over her finger where her wedding ring still sat.

'He's going to get a good job and get me a proper ring one day. Daddy will let me marry him then, I know he will.'

'Granda—' I stopped. 'Your father doesn't want you to marry him?'

She shook her head. 'He wants me to marry Michael.'

I tried not to gasp at the mention of Dad's name. 'But you don't want to marry Michael.' It was a statement rather than a question and I held my breath as she replied.

'No. Michael is lovely but...' Mum looked me in the eye. 'Johnny is the love of my life.' Her words pierced me like darts as my mind reeled back through the years; to all the times I'd watched my parents, seemingly madly in love; to the video of their wedding day that I'd devoured, dreaming of having a fairy tale marriage just like theirs one day; and then to all the times Mum had told me not to let the love of my life slip through my fingers, and I'd assumed she'd been thinking about Dad. I watched as everything I believed in crumbled around me, like dust.

Poor Dad.

I couldn't speak, so I gave her a moment to get lost in the past, free from worries.

When the song stopped I clicked it off before a new one began, my hand shaking. Slowly, Mum's eyes started to refocus and she slumped in her chair, exhausted.

'Where's Johnny?' she said, her eyes flicking round the room, and I felt a dart of guilt. In all these years, Johnny must have been so deeply locked away that she'd never mentioned him before. Now, just one play of this song from the tape he'd made her, and he was back to torment her all over again.

'He's not here,' I said, my voice wavering.

'But where did he go?'

'He had to leave.' Sometimes it was best not to argue, and I could see Mum was becoming agitated.

'Oh. Will he be back?'

'He will.'

Her hands were clasped in her lap, her knuckles white, and she was fiddling with her wedding ring. When she looked up, her eyes shone with tears.

'He loves me so much you know,' she said. 'I don't know why he had to leave.'

'It's okay,' I said. 'He'll be back soon.'

We sat in silence for a moment, my mind reeling from what I'd just learned. I felt untethered, and scared.

'Are you okay?' I said, wondering what was going on in her mind now.

She looked at me and frowned. 'Who are you?'

'I'm Erin,' I said, clearly.

'And why are you here?' Her tone wasn't angry or accusatory, just curious, and I smiled at her.

'I've just come to see you, to see how you are,' I explained.

'Oh okay.' She hesitated, her eyes darting round the room uncertainly. 'And I know you, do I?'

'You do. I'm your daughter.' I tried to ignore the look of fear on her face and continued to smile sweetly until I saw her body start to relax again.

'Course you are, course you are,' she said as if to reassure herself. 'And where's your lovely Adam?'

My heart stopped beating for a minute. This was the second time she'd mentioned Adam in just a few days. She'd done it a few times over the years too – she'd even occasionally talked about him in front of Greg in her confusion, who, to his credit, had always managed not to take it personally even though it must have felt like a dagger to the heart. But this time I felt rattled.

'He's not here Mum,' I said. 'You mean Greg.'

She looked round. 'Who's Greg?'

'Never mind.'

'Is Adam not coming?'

I shook my head. 'No, not today.'

'Shame.' She rubbed her hands back and forth as though she was wringing out an old cloth. Suddenly, she reached over and grabbed my wrist.

'Erin. You must never let Adam go. Promise me.' Her voice was urgent, a whisper. I placed my hand on top of hers to try and soothe her, but she just leaned closer. 'Don't listen to your father. He doesn't like Adam, but you do and that's all that matters.' She shook her head and rocked from side to side. 'Never let anyone tell you who to love.'

As the words spilled from her mouth I was reminded of the time I'd taken Adam home to meet her and she'd said something similar. I waited, hardly daring to breathe, as Mum continued. 'Never settle for second best, Erin. Not like I did. You'll always regret it.' She looked me right in the eye then, her gaze hard. 'Always follow your heart.'

It was as though the air had left her like a deflated balloon as she slumped back into her chair. I didn't know what to say, so we sat quietly for a few minutes, listening to the low drone of voices outside in the hallway, and the occasional shout. I tried to swallow down the lump that was blocking my throat.

'Do you mind if I close my eyes? I'm ever so tired,' Mum said.

'Of course. Let me help you into bed.'

'I'm not going to sleep, just resting my eyes.'

'I know. But let's get you into bed anyway.'

She let me help her stand and waited patiently like a little girl while I pulled the covers down and plumped her pillows for her.

'There you go,' I said, standing back as she climbed beneath the covers, fully clothed. I was struck by how life had turned on a pin, how my mum, who had once tucked me in at night and sung to me, was now the one who needed the constant care and reassurance. I cupped her hand gently between mine and sat with her as she slowly drifted off to sleep. At least there she could dream, and pretend she was in some other place, some other time. A time when she knew who she was and what she wanted. A time before her mind betrayed her.

She was peaceful now, but my mind was all over the place. And I couldn't get Mum's words out of my head.

Never settle for second best, Erin. Not like I did.

Always follow your heart.

Although my heart bled for my father, who had always loved my mother with every fibre of his being, I couldn't stop thinking about Greg, and Adam, and wondering whether I had made the wrong choice all those years ago after all.

I sat and watched the sky darken outside the window until I

heard the shush of the door across the carpet and Suzy came back in.

'Everything okay?'

'Yes. Mum was tired. It's been a long day.'

She nodded. 'And did you get anywhere, with the songs?' I'd told her I was trying something new today, but not why.

'Not really. I think she prefers her normal ones.'

'Never mind.'

I let go of Mum's hand and placed it carefully on top of her blanket, then brushed a stray hair from her face and kissed her lightly on the forehead.

'I should be off now.'

'Yes, Penny will probably be asleep for the night now.'

'Thanks Suzy. I know how much you do for Mum and I really appreciate it.'

'Well apart from the fact that it's my job, I do love it. She's special, your mum, but I know you know that.'

'I do. I just miss her.'

'I know. But she is in there somewhere. You just have to look a bit harder to find it these days.'

'Thank you.'

Suzy leaned over and pulled Mum's curtains tight against the night, and we left together, leaving the bedside light burning.

19

NOW

Blink-182: 'I Miss You'

Growing up, I'd always hoped I'd find someone who loved me the way my parents loved each other. My staid, serious father lit up whenever my mother was in the room, while my mum seemed to adore my father with something closer to fervour. I might not have understood how two such entirely different people had ever ended up together, but I'd certainly always believed their love was real.

Now I felt as though everything I had ever known had been a lie, that the foundations of my childhood, of my life, had fallen down around my ears. And I didn't know what to do about it.

To make matters worse, Mum's words seemed to be stuck on a loop in my brain, and I couldn't stop thinking about the implications for me and Greg, or for me and Adam.

Which was why I'd come for a walk across the Common to try and clear my mind and make sense of everything.

So far, it didn't appear to be working.

I continued stomping, following the path that wound up the hillside that Adam and I had climbed just a couple of weeks ago. It felt different during the day. Beside me, a little boy rolled down the grass, screaming with laughter, while his mum yelled at him to get up, that he'd get covered in mud. I passed several dog walkers and a couple of joggers, everyone bundled up against the cold wind. When I reached the bench overlooking the town I stopped and took a rest, and tried not to think about being here with Adam.

The town stretched out before me, the sky a translucent pale blue smeared with wisps of cloud that raced across it like they were in a fast-forwarding film. Trees bent to the left with every gust, and I shivered as the wind penetrated my jeans and chilled my legs. I pulled my scarf tighter and my hat lower and let out a long, slow breath to try and calm my nerves.

I watched a couple walking arm in arm a little way down the hill and I thought about Greg, who had always loved me so fiercely, who had been there for me from the moment we'd met. There were so many things I loved about him, that had become part of us over the years. I loved the way he ate his spaghetti, cutting it up into tiny pieces so it didn't slop all down his chin; I loved the way he always stood aside to let me through a door first, even though he dithered about it every time because he worried about seeming obsequious, condescending. I loved that he remembered people's birthdays and always signed his cards 'from the Donnellys' as if we were minor royalty. I loved his ridiculous trainer obsession, the way he lined them up in the wardrobe and refused to throw the boxes away, and I loved that he always took so much care when he cooked that his food exploded with flavour. I loved all these things and more, from the mundane to the marvellous.

On paper, he was the ideal man. But when the gambling had begun, the familiarity of him had started to change its appearance. Instead of being the comfort blanket it always had been, it began to feel stifling, like a noose around my neck – one that was growing tighter with every day that passed.

I understood it was partly Adam's arrival that had made these feelings more acute, but the discovery of Mum's mixtape and her memories of Johnny had also thrown me. I'd realised, from the look on her face as she'd talked, that the way Johnny had made my mum feel was exactly the way that I'd always felt about Adam.

Not Greg.

What a mess.

I shivered and pulled my phone from my pocket and typed out a message to Sam. This was exactly the sort of situation his bluntness was perfect for, and I knew I needed a stern talking to.

Come over, he replied, so I made my way back down the hill and snaked through town and out towards his flat. When I arrived he pulled me inside and closed the door.

'I'm just finishing this call, then I'm all yours,' he said, indicating the phone in his hand.

He disappeared into his bedroom and I made my way into the kitchen and flicked the kettle on. By the time it was boiled, Sam was back and pulling open the fridge door.

'Do we really want coffee?' he said.

'What are you suggesting?'

'Vodka?'

'It's eleven in the morning!'

'And your point is…?'

I shrugged. 'Why not? It's Christmas.'

'Atta girl.'

He poured two generous measures into glasses, added a splash of Diet Coke and handed me one. 'Sorry, no ice.'

I took a sip and grimaced.

'So, spill.'

I took another gulp of the too-strong vodka and then told Sam what had happened when I'd played the mixtape to Mum.

'She was utterly joyous,' I said.

'And that's bad because...?' A frown flitted across his forehead.

I rubbed my face, trying to find the words to explain. 'She'd never mentioned Johnny before, but this time it was as though her mind had finally been unplugged and all the secrets that had been trapped came pouring out. She told me a bit about who this Johnny was, said he was the love of her life.' I looked up at Sam now. 'She looked so different when she talked about him.'

Sam drummed his fingers on the worktop. 'She's a dark horse your mum, eh?'

'You're telling me.'

'And you say she's never mentioned this Johnny before?'

'Never. It's weird, because she doesn't know what day or year it is most of the time, so you'd think she would have at least talked about him before. But I've never even heard her mention his name.'

'Maybe she just buried it away a long time ago. You know, if you tell yourself something is true enough times, your mind starts to believe it, so I guess it works with trying to deny something too.'

'Perhaps. But it's – how can this have happened? How can she have been so happy with this Johnny and feel like she settled for Dad? They always seemed like the happiest couple in the world.'

'I know darling. But everyone's a mystery really. I mean, look at me. I bet you don't have a clue what I'm thinking most of the time.'

'I usually assume you're thinking about trying to find a hot young guy to sleep with.'

'Fair point.' He grinned and took a gulp of his drink. 'But that's not what's really bothering you, is it? Your mum's ex-boyfriend?'

There was a reason Sam was one of my best friends. I couldn't lie to him about anything. I shook my head.

'This is about Adam, right? He's the reason you're so rattled?'

I rubbed my hands over my face and groaned. 'Oh God.' I looked at him. 'After I turned the song off, Mum told me I should never let Adam go because he's the love of my life, the way Johnny was the love of hers, and to make sure I never settled for second best like... like she had.' I could feel tears threatening and I blinked them back. 'Why did Adam have to come back? Everything was just fine the way it was and now it's all such a bloody mess.'

Sam grabbed my drink and walked to the sofa with it. 'Erin, sit down.' He patted the seat next him. I did as I was told and took my drink from him and held it while he topped it up. He leaned forward until he was so close I could see the changing colour of his eyes and the stubble on his chin. 'I love you, Erin.'

'I can feel a "but" coming...'

'Shush. Let me speak.' He studied me intently. 'You know I love you, but you also must know that you're kidding yourself if you think you were happy with the way things were with Greg, even before Adam came back on the scene. What I mean is, Adam is not the reason you're so unhappy at the moment. He's just a symptom of it.'

I shrugged and stared at the floor.

'You and Greg. You're – different. I know he's always adored you, but you've never completely given yourself to him have you?'

'I have! I married him didn't I?'

'Sure. And I'm not saying you didn't – don't – love him. I'm saying your mum's right. He's not the love of your life. Never was, never will be. He's a lovely man, and you care about him deeply.

But it was Adam who set your world alight, and now he's back it's made you realise that's not quite what you have with Greg, however much you love him. And finding out your mum had exactly the same choice to make as you did has made you wonder whether you did the wrong thing, the way she says she did.'

He sat back and crossed his arms, pleased with himself. My heart was racing and I felt dizzy. As much as I'd wanted to object as Sam had been talking, to shout him down and tell him he was wrong, that I did love Greg, the truth was, he'd hit the nail on the head. Greg was not, and never had been, the love of my life.

Adam was.

'Fuck, Sam. What the hell am I supposed to do?'

'As far as I can see, you have two choices. One, you stay with Greg and stop thinking about Adam. Stop seeing him, stop talking about him, try and put him out of your mind completely and make your marriage work the way you've managed to for the last however many years.'

'And two?' I wasn't sure I wanted to hear it.

'Or two, you don't do that, and you end up breaking Greg's heart and tearing your marriage apart.'

I couldn't speak. I gulped down the rest of my vodka and the heat of it burned my throat. I swallowed and felt it pouring through my veins and round my head until it spun. My stomach churned and I suddenly felt as though I was about to vomit.

'Sorry E.' Sam placed his hand on my knee and I stared at it, not daring to think about what he'd just said. He was right, of course. If Greg found out that Adam was back and that I'd been spending time with him, it would break his heart, and if I ever told him how I felt about Adam, it would destroy him completely.

'It has to stop, doesn't it, me seeing Adam?' I sighed. 'I already made this choice, thirteen years ago. I just – I felt like it was a sign, what Mum said. About Johnny, and about how I shouldn't settle for second best. I felt – I felt like that was what Greg was. But he's better than that. He's a good man, and he deserves better.'

Sam didn't reply, and we sat for a minute in silence. I tipped my head back on the sofa and closed my eyes.

'Want to get shit-faced?'

I grinned. 'Samuel, you're a terrible influence.'

'That's my main aim.'

I rubbed his knee. 'Thanks darling but I really need to go home and see my husband.'

He nodded. 'Fair enough. Shame though; I could do with a session right now.'

We both stood and walked to the door. I wrapped my arms around him and squeezed him.

'Thank you Sam.'

'What for?'

'For being you. I needed to hear the truth, and I knew I could rely on you.' I pecked him on the cheek then turned and left.

* * *

Before I'd even fully got out of the car, the front door swung open and Greg was hovering, looking nervous. My breath stilled in my throat.

'Greg?' I said, walking towards him.

'Hey, I'm glad you're home,' he said, his voice soft.

'What's wrong? Has something happened?' Visions of him having a relapse, of losing everything we owned on gambling sites flashed through my mind, and I pushed them away, trying to ignore the thought that perhaps that would make things easier for me by taking the decision out of my hands.

'No.' He stayed in the doorway, his hands clasped in front of him.

'Well, what's going on then? Why are you being so mysterious?'

'I've got a surprise for you.'

'I'm not sure I like the sound of this.'

'It's nothing bad,' he said, shuffling from foot to foot. 'Why would it be?'

He looked so crestfallen at my reaction I felt a stab of guilt. 'Sorry, of course it isn't.' I looked up at him. 'So, are you going to tell me what it is?'

'In a minute.' He turned and headed into the house and I followed him, mystified. I glanced into the living room as we passed, and checked round the kitchen as we entered, but there was no sign of anything untoward.

'You need to go and get changed,' Greg said, turning to face me.

'What into?'

'Something warm.'

I frowned. 'Okay.'

'I'll wait here for you,' he said.

Taking that as my cue to leave, I headed upstairs to get dressed.

'Will this do?' I said as I re-entered the kitchen. There was a cool box on the worktop, but Greg was nowhere to be seen. I reached over to lift the lid.

'No peeking!' Greg's voice made me jump and I leaped back guiltily. He grabbed the cool box by its handle and hoisted it over his shoulder. 'Ready?' He held out his other hand and I grabbed it, enjoying the familiar warmth of his palm.

'I guess so.'

We made our way out of the house and I climbed into the passenger seat of the car as Greg put the picnic box in the boot. As we drove, I tried to work out where we were going. The houses thinned, dwindling to nothing, and the landscape opened up, the sky expanding above us like a giant umbrella. Rain spattered on the windscreen and the wipers squeaked it away every few seconds, the rhythm soothing. We were in deep countryside now, the lanes narrowing, although no-one else seemed mad enough to be out in this weather. I turned the heater up and the mist cleared from the bottom of my window. I pressed my forehead against it and watched the bare trees whip past like stickmen keeping guard.

Finally, Greg turned down a narrow track. It was full of potholes and it felt as though my brain was rattling around in my head as we inched along, branches brushing the side of the car. The raindrops had turned to fat, pillowy splodges now and the wipers sped up, sweeping them away frantically. The trees had closed in on us, ominous, threatening, as though trying to stop us from going any further. We trundled on regardless.

The rain had slowed to almost nothing by the time we rounded a bend and the canopy of trees opened up before us, revealing a stony sky and a darker lake, the sky reflected back angrily in its choppy waters. The clouds hung threateningly close to the treetops as Greg pulled up in front of a scruffy shack with grime-smeared windows, its wooden slats painted a faded pale blue.

'Ta-da!' he said, cutting the engine.

I looked round, confused.

'Where are we?' I said. I'd lived here most of my life but I'd never seen this lake before.

He shuffled round in his seat to face me and took my hands. His felt warm.

'Do you remember when we used to go rowing on the lake, back in Nottingham? Way back in the olden days, when we first met?'

I smiled. 'Of course. It was our thing. Although you rowed and I talked, mainly.'

He grinned. 'That's true. But I never minded.' He swallowed and looked down, then back up to meet my eye. 'The thing is, I loved you even then. Well, you know that.' He cleared his throat. 'The point is, for me, those were some of my favourite times. When it was just you and me, and no-one else could get to us. I wanted those hours, those days, to go on forever.'

He squeezed my hands gently.

'I wanted to recreate that feeling. I wanted...' He stopped, and when he spoke again there was a tremble in his voice that hadn't been there before. 'I wanted you to remember how much you loved me. Love me.' He dropped his gaze to the floor and I felt something inside me melt at his vulnerability.

'I do love you,' I whispered.

He seemed to flinch, as though he could detect something in my words that wasn't quite sincere, and pulled his hands away.

'Anyway, I know the weather isn't quite up to the long summer days when we used to do this, but I thought we could take a boat out, just the two of us.'

I looked out at the rough water, which churned and rolled against the bitter winter wind, and shivered. 'In this?'

'It'll be all right Erin. I'll protect you.'

I looked him in eye and it felt as though he was looking directly into my soul. I wondered whether he could see the turmoil I was in.

'Let's do it,' I agreed.

'Brilliant.' He climbed out of the car and stalked towards the shack, and tugged the door open. I followed him. 'A friend from work, Andy, owns a rowing boat which he moors here, and he said we can use it,' he called, his voice muffled from the depths of the shed. Seconds later he emerged looking triumphant, bran-dishing two dusty-looking oars.

'The boat's over there,' he said, pointing to a small jetty marching out into the water, utterly uninviting in this weather. Although the rain had stopped now, the wind still found a path through the shelter of the trees, and I shivered as another gust pelted me.

'Are you cold?' Greg said.

'A little.'

'Wait there.' He walked to the boot of the car, propped the oars against it, then pulled out a waterproof coat which he wrapped around my shoulders. He lingered there for a moment and I could feel his breath against my ear. I wondered whether he was going to say something, but then he pulled away. I couldn't work out whether I was relieved or disappointed.

'Okay, you ready?'

I glanced at the tiny rowing boat and the steely water, then nodded. 'I guess so.'

Greg climbed in first, taking the picnic basket with him, then the oars, then finally holding out his hand to help me in. As I stepped inside, the whole boat rocked wildly and I tipped towards him, the bodily contact sudden and unexpected. He helped me sit, then gripped the oars tightly, and pushed off from the bank of the lake. I watched as he rowed and for the first time in months I saw him as the man I'd fallen in love with all those years ago: the strong, capable man who would do anything for me, who looked after me. I pulled the coat he'd brought me tighter round my shoulders and felt a surge of love for him. He looked up then and saw me watching him and I stuck my tongue out.

'Charming,' he said, doing the same to me.

We sat quietly for a while, just the sound of Greg breathing, of the wind sliding across the water, of small waves splashing up against the side of the boat, and I let the rhythm soothe me. The water was so dark it was impossible to know what was hidden beneath the surface and I stared down into it and let my thoughts drift.

I'd felt untethered, these past few weeks. This moment here, on this lake, on a freezing winter day, was just what I'd needed to feel grounded again, and it struck me that was what Greg was so good at, the way no-one else was: knowing what I needed, and when. The days after Mum's diagnosis had been some of the hardest of my life as I'd struggled to deal with the news. Greg had been the one person who'd understood the depth of my feelings, that I was terrified of losing my mum forever. He'd held me and let me sob when the tears had come, had let me drink too much, and cry and wail, knowing it would be cathartic, healing. Adam, meanwhile, had hardly let the news cause a ripple on the surface of his otherwise smooth life. I shook that thought away. It was disingenuous to bring Adam into my thoughts now. This was about me and Greg.

The truth was, just like he always did, Greg had got today completely spot on. This was exactly the tonic I needed, to remind myself of who I was. Of who we were.

'Penny for them.' Greg's words broke my reverie and I smiled at him. We'd stopped now, and were floating in the middle of the lake. The shack looked a million miles away, the sky above us hung like a dirty blanket, the greyness breaking every now and then to reveal a promising chink of blue.

'Sorry, I was miles away,' I said, rubbing my hands together for warmth.

'I wish I'd been there with you.'

Oh Greg, you really don't. 'I couldn't even tell you what I was thinking about,' I said. 'So, what now?'

'Well, I'd planned a picnic.' He indicated the bag by my feet. 'But you look frozen. Do you want to go back and eat it in the car?'

The truth was I was chilled to the core and heading back to the car sounded like heaven. But this obviously meant a lot to Greg.

'No, let's stay.' I glanced upwards. 'You never know, it might still warm up.'

'Ever the optimist,' he said, grinning at me.

'So, what have you got in this cool box?' I said, leaning forward. I stopped. 'I assume I'm allowed to open it now?'

'Yes, go on.'

I lifted the lid. There, nestled among a few ice packs, was a bottle, some plastic tumblers and a couple of Tupperware tubs.

He pulled a flask out of his bag. 'I've got hot tea as well because – well, it's bloody freezing. But you recognise it, right?'

I pulled the bottle out and read the label. Asti Spumanti. 'I recognise it.' I smiled.

I took the rest of the items out of the bag and prised the lids off. Cheese slices, Jacob's cream crackers, a bunch of grapes, a tube of Pringles and a bar of Dairy Milk.

'The picnic we had on that first day—' He stopped. 'I just thought... Well, you know what I thought.'

I nodded. I did. 'Thank you Greg. This is lovely.'

'So, shall we start with the crackers or do you want me to pour a glass of this first?'

'Let's drink first. Might warm us up a bit.'

I dutifully popped open the cheap fizzy wine, poured us both a tumbler full and handed one to Greg. He held his in the air. 'A toast?'

'To what?'

He shrugged. 'To us? To the future? To – finding the old us again?'

I studied him, this face I knew so well. How I wished we could travel back and find that comfortable love we'd shared back then, that easy, blameless friendship without any of the complications of marriage. I held my tumbler up and clinked it against his. 'To us.'

We sat sipping our wine and it occurred to me I should tell Greg about the tapes I'd found at Dad's. It felt wrong to be keeping secrets from him. So I told him all about the mixtape with the secret note from J, and that Mum had admitted he was a man called Johnny, who she'd loved a long time ago. I omitted details about the old tape Adam had made me, or any of the things Mum had said about Adam being the love of my life, of course.

'She's a dark horse your mum, isn't she?' he said when I'd finished.

'That's exactly what Sam said. I can't believe she's never mentioned this Johnny in all these years.'

He rubbed his hands together and blew into them. 'Well I guess she just didn't think about him much once she met your dad.'

His eyes bored into me and I shuffled uncomfortably on the hard wooden bench as he searched my face. Was he making a point?

'I guess not.'

Greg leaned forward. 'Does it really bother you, that your mum has secrets?'

I shrugged. 'It did. But you're right; I suppose it's just that it didn't matter, once she met Dad.' There was a time I could have discussed it with him for hours, pulled the story to pieces, analysed it from every angle to try and work out why it was making me feel so shaken, as though everything I'd always known had been thrown into doubt. But because there was so much I *couldn't* tell him, it seemed safer to steer away from it completely.

I took another sip of my wine and leaned back, resting my elbows on the edges of the boat and tipping my head back, letting the iron sky fill my vision, eyes focused on the tiny patch of blue where the sun threatened to trickle through. Come on sunshine, I silently begged. Bring some hope.

Out of nowhere, a drumbeat started and I snapped my eyes open and looked at Greg. He was smiling at me, and as the familiar sliding guitar of 'I Miss You' by Blink-182 started I smiled back.

'Where did you get that from?' I said, indicating the tiny speaker propped up on the bench between us.

'I brought it with me.' He paused. 'Do you remember this?'

'Course I do.' I drummed my fingers on my knees. 'God I haven't heard this song for years. We listened to it so many times I'm surprised the CD didn't disintegrate.'

Greg laughed, and we sat for a few more minutes, lost in our thoughts. What better choice of song when things are going wrong in the present, than one that rewinds the years and takes you back to happier, more simple times? It was a clever tactic – and it was working.

I felt the connection between us, the one that had been shaken loose over the last few months until it was barely attached at all, gradually start to strengthen. These times, these moments, were perfect. They were essential and restorative. We needed more of them.

The song came to an end and I expected another one to start. But when nothing happened I looked at Greg to find him watching me, his eyes serious.

'You okay?'

He nodded. 'Yes.' He looked up at the sky too, and I waited for him to say something more. He coughed. 'Actually I wanted to ask you something.'

'Okay.' I felt my shoulders hunch with fear. Had he found out I'd been spending time with Adam before I'd had a chance to tell him myself? I could have kicked myself. How it must have hurt him. But when he spoke, I realised I'd got it completely wrong.

'I know—' He stopped, gathered himself. 'I know things have been tricky between us lately. And I know it's mostly my fault.' He looked down at where his hands were clasped in front of him, a plastic tumbler dangling from one as though he didn't have the strength it hold it any more. 'But I can't give up on us, Erin.' He looked at me, and there was a determination in his face I hadn't seen for a long time. 'I know I've let you down, but I want to make it up to you.'

'You are Greg. You're getting help for your gambling, aren't you? It's working, isn't it?'

He nodded. 'Yes, it is. But there's something else.'

I waited.

'I want us to have a baby.'

For a moment it was as though everything froze, suspended in that moment where nothing moved and nobody spoke. A bird hung in mid-air, trees paused their swaying, branches bowed, splinters of wood skittering on the current halted their journey, and my breathing slowed... And then a shaft of sunlight split open the bank of cloud that smothered us and shot its beam across the murk of the water and broke the spell.

'A baby? Are you serious?' I felt dizzy, breathless.

He met my gaze. 'Deadly.'

I couldn't speak. This was so out of the blue, and so at odds with where I was right now that I didn't even know how to process it, let alone give him an answer.

'But...' I stammered. 'I thought we'd agreed we didn't want children?'

'We did, once. But' – he sighed – 'that was then. We're in our late thirties now and this could be the only chance we get. Plus I think... I think it could be good for us. It could help us, mend us. It – it feels like the right time. Don't you think?'

The doubt in his voice was clear, but I was still reeling from the shock.

'How can this be the right time?' I said, my voice low.

He leaned forward and the boat rocked beneath me. A gust of wind blew us off course and I shivered. 'I know I've messed things up, Erin. I know I have. But you must remember how much we love each other. How important we are to each other. I can't lose that. Not because of one mistake.'

One mistake. If only you knew.

'But how is having a baby the answer?'

He dropped his head. 'I don't know.' He looked at me again. 'There was something else I wanted to say too.'

'Go on.'

'I think we should renew our wedding vows.'

I felt muddled, as though the world was spinning out of control, and I lowered my head between my knees.

'Erin? Are you okay?'

I nodded, but stayed where I was, trying to process Greg's suggestion. He wanted us to renew our wedding vows and have a baby. Meanwhile, I was worrying about whether I was in love with a man I hadn't seen for eighteen years, and angry at my husband for almost losing our house. We really couldn't be any further apart.

I raised my head. Greg was looking out across the water, and I studied him for a few seconds, his handsome face, the faint lines radiating out from his eyes. He'd hardly aged since the day we met, and the truth was, apart from the gambling problem, he'd barely changed either. He was still the kind, funny man he'd always been, with a heart of gold and a great memory for one-liners.

He turned to face me and the sorrow on his face was almost more than I could bear. How hard would it be for me to agree to renew our vows, and promise to think about having a baby? Surely it was the best thing for both of us, to put everything else behind us and look to the future.

And yet.

'I don't think I ever do want children, Greg,' I said gently.

'Oh.' His voice was heavy with pain. 'But...' He paused, his voice carrying a hint of hope. 'You will think about the vows? I just think – I think it will be good for us.'

And so, despite myself, despite every nerve ending screaming at me to say no, that it wasn't a good time, that I had too much to sort through in my own mind first, I found myself reaching for his hands and nodding. 'I promise to think about it.'

* * *

A hot bath and a glass of wine revived me when we got back from the lake. Both of us were frozen to the core, and sadly the warm feelings we'd rediscovered had evaporated following Greg's announcement, only cooling further on the drive home. Greg had gone to put a leg of lamb in the oven for dinner and the smell of rosemary and thyme drifted up the stairs as I came out of our en suite wrapped in a fluffy towel. I was determined to put the tension of this morning behind us and move on, to try to make things work between us, whatever it took. Because Greg was right, we couldn't lose everything we'd built over the last eighteen years.

I studied the carefully curated prints that hung from our

bedroom walls, depicting bands Greg and I loved, places we'd visited together – the Golden Gate Bridge, the towering majesty of the Taj Mahal; the jewels colours that sprang from the walls that we'd deliberately chosen to rebel against the ever-rising tide of grey. The cushion cover from a trip to Thailand discarded on the carpet, the ancient well-loved bedspread we'd been given as a wedding present, still rumpled with the imprint of Greg's body... All these memories clamoured for attention, as if trying to convince me that what we had – what we *have* – was worth saving.

I sat down and rubbed a towel over my hair, droplets scattering across my shoulders, across the dressing table...

I froze. There, nestled among the bottles of hair serum and perfume and the bowl of earrings, was the crotchet necklace that Adam had bought me. My fingers fluttered to my throat. I must have taken it off. But it wasn't the fact that it was there that was bothering me. There was something else. Rather than being thrown down carelessly on the dressing table, the necklace was folded neatly on top of a small piece of paper. The note that Adam had given me.

I thought I'd thrown the note away. But now here it was, like a siren of my betrayal.

My heart thumped and I gripped the edge of the stool.

I didn't need to pick it up, I could read the words from here: *Dear Erin. I might not remember you, but you're music to my ears. Merry Christmas. Love A x*

Greg had found it. And I didn't know how I was going to come back from this.

20

THEN

Snow Patrol: 'Chasing Cars'

The engine idled, thrumming through Erin's body. She felt queasy. Leaning forward, she tapped the chauffeur on the shoulder.

'Could you switch the engine off for a minute please?' she said. He tipped his hat, then the rumbling stopped and the car shuddered to a halt. But the nausea lingered. She swallowed and took deep breaths through her nose.

'You all right?' Beside her, Rose clasped Erin's hand. She continued to stare blankly out of the window.

'Come on Pearson. You'll be fine. You just need to get through the ceremony then you can relax.' Sam took her other hand from the other side. She looked at him, his hair smoothed back, his bow tie at a jaunty angle, and then at Rose, so pretty in her ice-blue dress, and gave a weak smile.

'Am I doing the right thing?'

A silence. Then Sam: 'Just a hunch, but it might be a bit late for that now.'

'Sam,' Rose said sternly.

'Sorry.'

Rose shuffled to face her. 'Listen Erin, this is serious. It's totally normal to be feeling nervous and scared—'

'How would you know?'

'Sam!'

'Sorry.'

She continued. 'But if you're genuinely feeling as though you're doing the wrong thing, then you have to say so now.'

Erin looked up at her. 'Really? It doesn't seem like the best time to be honest, sitting outside the venue ten minutes before the ceremony.'

'Agreed, it's not ideal. But it's still preferable to waiting until after-wards, or regretting it for the rest of your life.' She lifted Erin's chin and forced her to meet her eye. 'Tell me the truth Erin. Do you love Greg?'

'Of course I do.'

She did, of course she did. She loved his smile, and the way he held her hand, always insisting on walking on the outside of the pavement. She loved his long, slender thighs, strong from rowing and cycling, and the way his hair curled at the back when it got too long. She loved how he paid attention to people, remembered their names, asked them questions, and listened to their replies. There was so much about him that she loved, of course there was – she would never have let things get this far if there weren't. But now they were here and about to do this, it felt enormous.

Erin had had an anxiety dream last night, and several nights before that, where she'd been standing in front of everyone at the altar, holding Greg's hand and about to say her vows, when the doors had crashed open and Adam had burst in, yelling at them to halt the ceremony, that she was making a terrible mistake, that it was him she was meant to be with, like a scene from The Graduate. Then she'd looked up at Greg and realised she didn't know who he was, that he was an imposter, and that Adam was right. Each time she'd woken up at that exact point, feeling confused and shaken. And each time she'd looked over at Greg and studied his sleeping form and tried to remind herself why it was him she was marrying and not Adam.

Now she was about to walk down the aisle for real, and she was simultaneously dreading that Adam might turn up, and hoping that he would.

She breathed in deeply as Rose searched her face for clues that she might be lying, and then Rose nodded, clearly satisfied.

'Right. Let's get on with it then.'

'We'll be by your side the whole time,' Sam added.

'Thank you, you two.'

They climbed out of the car, then up the steps of the Town Hall, where Erin's mum and dad were waiting. Michael clutched Penny's hand tightly, while Penny locked eyes with her daughter.

'You look beautiful love,' she said, tears shining in her eyes.

Erin hugged her, grateful that she was well enough to be here. Although Penny was still fine most days just five years after her diagnosis, in situations that made her feel uncomfortable, she could sometimes become scared and confused. Erin was so relived she was here to see her big day.

Michael laid his hand on his daughter's arm. 'You ready Reeny?'

'I think so,' Erin said, her voice a whisper.

They made their way into the room where all their friends and family were waiting.

As they walked towards the front, Erin studied the back of Greg's head. She knew him so well it was almost impossible to know whether the feelings she had for him were love, or friendship and familiarity, but she could tell from his stance just how nervous he was. Did he think she might not turn up, that she might change her mind at the last minute? She hoped he didn't know how close she had come.

As she made her way down the aisle towards him she felt as though her heart was going to hammer out of her chest. As she reached the front and Greg turned to face her, she almost gasped to see the look of pure adoration in his eyes. He loved her so much. She'd always known that. And she loved him.

They were doing this.

As they said their vows, and promised to love each for the rest of their lives, Erin smiled, all the while keeping one eye out for Adam, for someone, to interrupt.

But no-one came.

They were husband and wife.

* * *

Later, after the meal and after the speeches, and after all the photos and the glass chinking and the toasting, it was time for their first dance. Greg took Erin's hand as 'Chasing Cars' by Snow Patrol began, and they swayed together gently on the dancefloor, Erin resting her head on her husband's shoulder, her eyes closed, trying not to think about another time, another place, another man... dancing like this, so close, to another song. Instead she focused on the here and now: on this time, this place. This man.

Their song.

And the man she loved. This was all that mattered.

21

NOW

The Cure: 'Friday I'm In Love'

I need to see you. E

I pressed send, then let out a long breath of pent-up tension. My phone beeped with an almost immediate response.

Can you come to the house? A x

I'll be there at 2.

It was done. I was going to see Adam, to tell him, in person, that this had to end. I couldn't see him any more.

I hadn't dared ask Greg about the necklace, and instead had thrown the note away, hidden the necklace and pretended nothing had happened. He obviously hadn't wanted to talk about it either because he hadn't said a word. But I knew that, after the promise I'd made to him to think about our wedding vow renewal, I couldn't betray him any more than I already had.

Which meant Adam had to go.

At 1.30 p.m. I popped my head round the living room door where Greg was watching trashy telly and finishing off the last of the Christmas cheese.

'I'm popping out for some fresh air,' I said.

'Okay.' He studied me for a moment, tilted his head, and I wondered what he was thinking. Did he believe me? 'Want me to come with you?'

'No, you stay. You look like you're well settled for the day.'

He held my gaze a moment longer, then nodded. 'Sure. Enjoy your walk.'

I pulled on my coat and boots and headed out into the icy air. The rain from the previous day had cleared and the sky was a translucent blue, shot with streaks of pale grey. A weak winter sun provided hardly any warmth, its heat dissipating before it reached ground level, and trees thrust their spindly arms into the sky. The pavement was slick, slippery in places, and as I tugged my hat over my ears and wound my scarf round my neck I tried to ignore the guilt that sat like a stone in my belly at the thought of how Greg would feel if he knew where I was going.

Fifteen minutes later I arrived at the gates of Adam's house and rang the buzzer.

'Erin, is that you?' came a crackly voice.

'Yes. Let me in?'

'Wait there.'

I waited for the blare of the gate unlocking, but nothing came. I peered through the bars. Had Adam left me here? I glanced round, hoping nobody I knew would see me. I yanked my hat even lower over my eyes and pulled up my hood.

It was several minutes before I heard the low thrum of an

engine. Slowly it got closer and closer until, just before it became an unbearable roar, Adam appeared over the brow of the hill, dressed in leather trousers, a helmet pulled over his head. He was on his motorbike.

He pulled up to the gate, climbed off and unlocked it, then rode through and cut the engine. The sudden silence made my ears ring. He took his helmet off and grinned at me.

'What do you think?' he said, and that was when I noticed he was holding out another helmet towards me.

'You're kidding?'

'Absolutely not. Go on Erin, you'll love it.'

I took the helmet tentatively. 'I thought you hadn't ridden since the accident?'

'I haven't.'

'So what—'

'I have to get back on some time. And I'd already planned to give it a go today. So when you texted I thought, who better to come with me on my very first time back in the saddle than Erin?'

I stared at the hulking machine sitting between us and then at his face. 'Are you sure this is a good idea? I thought—'

'I won't freak out, I promise. I've ridden it up and down the drive a few times and it's been fine. Nowhere near as bad as I thought it would be.' He glanced behind him. 'But if you're coming we'd better get going before my parents stage some sort of intervention. They think I'm being "completely irresponsible".' He made quote marks in the air with his fingers and rolled his eyes.

I hesitated a moment longer, torn between agreeing with his parents and wanting to get on the bike despite my promises to myself before I got here. Then I placed the helmet over my head, the sounds around me immediately becoming muffled. I waited for Adam to climb on and slung my leg over the seat, clambering on behind him and pressing my body as close to his back as I could.

'You'll have to hold on tight,' he yelled through the distortion of the helmet and I wrapped my arms round his waist and pressed my cheek against the soft leather of his jacket. I felt light-headed at the contact.

Then we were off, the roar of the engine filling my ears, the hulk of the machine vibrating beneath me, and Adam's body melded to mine as though it was always meant to be there.

It didn't take us long to get out of town, and soon we were zipping along country lanes, Adam only slowing to take corners cautiously on the slick tarmac. For the first time I saw his vulnerability, his fear of coming off the bike and hurting himself again winning over his desire to fly like the wind.

It felt as though we were riding for hours, but it couldn't have been more than fifteen minutes by the time Adam pulled over to the side of the road and stilled the engine. The silence was immediate, and my ears hummed. I pulled my helmet off at the same time he did, and when he twisted round to speak to me, his mouth was precariously close to mine. I felt his breath on my lips when he spoke.

'Ready?'

I glanced at the muddy fields that stretched bleakly to our right to meet the wispy sky, the high ground tipped with frost. A solitary bird pecked at the frozen earth, but otherwise there was no other sign of life. I nodded.

Adam took the helmet from me and hung it from the handlebar, then indicated for me to follow him as he pushed the bike away from the road and towards the trees. The darkness beneath the canopy of branches felt heavy, and every sound was muffled, even our footsteps, which crunched as we walked.

Adam stopped and leant the bike against a nearby tree and

before I knew it he had grabbed my hand and started dragging me further into the woods.

'Where are we going?' I said, my feet stumbling beneath me.

He didn't reply, but it was only a few more seconds before he stopped and I almost crashed into him.

'I found this place the other day when I was out in the car,' he said. 'I thought you might like it.'

The trees had opened up into a clearing overhung by branches, where logs were arranged in a circle, a patch of scorched earth and ashes in the centre. An old string of tattered bunting flapped in the wind, and a discarded foil barbecue was half-buried beneath one of the larger logs. And I was hit, suddenly, by a memory of being here, a long time ago, with Adam. There had been a party, a late one after a gig, and Adam had brought me here on his scooter. His band mates came, and when we'd arrived the fire had been roaring, crates of beers were being passed round, and music had blared out of speakers as people danced round the fire. I'd been mesmerised, and had felt shy suddenly, unsure of myself. These people were older than me, and so cool, they wouldn't want me here.

It had been a chilly, late-autumn evening and we'd spent most of the night near the fire, trying to stay warm. I blushed now as I remembered how he'd kissed me that night, how people had shouted at us to get a room as his hand had slipped under my skirt and up my thigh... I remembered the spliffs that had been passed round, the bottles of vodka, the world starting to spin. And then I remembered 'Friday I'm In Love' by The Cure playing, and Adam's lips pressed against mine, warm and dry and tasting of ash and Coke, and him telling me he loved me for the first time...

'We've been here before,' I said, looking up at him.

'Have we?'

I nodded. 'A long time ago. There was a party. We were – we were drunk. And stoned.'

He nodded, studying the clearing. He dropped my hand and stomped through the muddy ground towards the nearest log and sat down, his head in his hands. I followed him, sat beside him. Eventually, he looked up at me, his eyes empty.

'I'm so sick of not remembering anything,' he said.

I longed to reach out and comfort him, but I tried to remember why I was here, the decision I'd made. 'You will, I'm sure you will.'

He slammed his hand down on the stripped bark of the log and I jumped. 'You don't know that,' he said, his voice angry. 'Nobody knows that, and it fucking sucks.'

I didn't speak. Nothing I could say would make him feel any better so I sat and watched my feet, my boots buried in the damp, soft ground, old leaves and branches mixed with tatty cigarette ends and the odd crushed can, long discarded. A faint whistling sound penetrated the tree canopy where the wind was trying to battle through, and the air felt cold here, damp, frigid. I shivered, wrapped my arms around myself. Adam didn't seem to notice my discomfort. I knew Greg would have.

'Why did you bring me here today?' I said eventually.

He shrugged. 'You said you wanted to see me and I needed to get away from that house.'

'Right.'

I felt acutely aware of our proximity, of the fact that, even though we weren't actually touching, the air between us felt alive, electric. I shuffled further away.

'Happy New Year by the way.'

'Oh yes. Happy New Year to you too.' I felt tongue-tied and silly and wished I could just say what I needed to say.

'So.' He stopped, scuffed his foot in the mud and I was struck by how different he seemed from the old Adam. Less cocky, less self-assured.

'So,' I repeated back at him.

'I was glad to hear from you.'

'I wasn't sure if you would be.'

'I'm always glad to hear from you.' He looked at me. 'It's not as though I've got a lot of friends round here.'

'No, right.' I was flustered and annoyed with myself for being so.

'So, what did you want to talk to me about?'

I continued to stare down at my boots and let the seconds tick by. I'd been so sure that I knew what I wanted to say, that I couldn't see him any more. Even now, sitting here with him just inches away, I knew it was the right thing to do. The trouble was, I couldn't seem to make my mouth form the words.

'Erin?' He reached for my hand and when he touched me, even through the fabric of the gloves, I flinched as though I'd been electrocuted. He didn't let go, and eventually I tore my gaze away from the ground and looked him straight in the eyes.

'I can't see you any more.'

He nodded but said nothing, so I stumbled on.

'I – I don't think I should spend any more time with you. Like this, just me and you. It – it's wrong.'

'Because of Greg?'

'Of course because of Greg!' I could hardly concentrate on his words, all my thoughts trained on the feeling of my hand cupped inside his. I stared at his mouth.

'Sorry Erin. That was a stupid question.' He licked his lips. 'I just wish things were different.'

'I know.' My voice was a whisper. 'Me too.'

He dropped my hand and the air between us felt cold, the

wind whipping in to fill the spaces where his fingers should be. I shivered again.

'I'm sorry Adam. I just – I haven't even told Greg that you're back. If he knew we'd been spending time together it would break his heart.'

He sat for a moment, staring ahead of him at the long-abandoned firepit. I wondered whether he'd heard me. But then he half-turned towards me and his knee brushed my leg. He didn't move away, but instead studied my face, his eyes scrutinising every inch as though he was searching for something. Maybe he was. After all, he couldn't remember anything about me, or about us. Perhaps he was hoping that something about my face would bring those memories back. I held my breath.

'You're very beautiful,' he whispered.

'Thank you.' The words barely came out.

He lifted his hand to touch my face and I had to stop myself from groaning. The skin where we were connected felt like it might melt, hot with betrayal and desire. I should have moved away, put some distance between us, but somehow it felt impossible.

As quickly as it had begun, the moment ended and Adam moved away from me, our connection broken.

'I'm sorry Erin. That was totally inappropriate.' He ran his hand over his hair. 'I – I just feel this overwhelming urge to be near you. I can't stop thinking about you.' He looked down at the floor, then back up at me. 'I just wish I could remember anything about us. It must have been wild.'

'It was.' My voice was low, husky. 'It was incredible.'

He nodded, as though he hadn't expected anything else.

'I don't know what it is,' he said. 'I can just feel it. That there's something special here.'

I didn't reply.

'Why didn't we end up together?'

How could I explain it to him? That everyone warned me about him, said he couldn't be trusted and that, when I was away at university and he'd been touring round the country, he proved them all right by sleeping with groupies. And then, that night when he'd arrived at my university halls, drunk and angry, with a love bite on his neck.

Nothing I could tell him would ever fully capture the power of our feelings for each other, or properly explain why it ended.

'It just didn't work,' I said. The words were weak, diluted.

'Come on Erin. I'm lost here. I don't know who I am any more. No-one ever tells me anything. My parents don't want me to remember, and there's no-one else who will ever be honest with me. I...' He stopped. 'I need to know who I was, what I was like. Why you couldn't be with me, even though there's clearly passion here.' He looked up at me, his eyes wide. 'Please tell me. Everything, warts and all.'

'Okay.' I shivered, the damp from the log seeping through my trousers.

He turned to face me properly. Then I told him everything.

* * *

When I'd finished we sat in silence for a while. I'd told him about how we met, how passionate it had been between us, how we could never keep our hands off each other. But also how it was always about more than just desire. That there had been a connection we both thought could and would never be broken.

I'd told him about how he'd betrayed me and made me stop believing in soulmates, and fate, and how, when he'd left that night after I told him I didn't want to see him again, I'd sobbed and sobbed until I thought my heart would never mend. I told him how Greg, who had always been so kind and so loving, had been there for me.

I told him how we hadn't seen each other again after that.

'Wow. What an arsehole,' he said.

'You weren't an arsehole. You were just angry.'

'I get why I was angry at my parents. I mean, from the bits I've cobbled together, they didn't really want me around. My dad clearly disapproves of me and is hoping to mould me into some sort of perfect son now that I can't remember who I was before, and Mum is a cold fish who doesn't seem to have feelings for anyone. But you? It sounds as though you were the only good thing in my life, and I ruined it.'

'It's hard to explain. I think it was just the wrong time. For us, I mean.'

'And now it's all too late.'

'It is.'

He paused a moment and stared at his feet. 'Do you think if we'd met now, we would be together?' His question was so quiet I wasn't sure at first whether I'd heard him right. But a glance at his face confirmed I had.

'I don't know.'

He nodded sadly. 'I mean, it's still there, right?' He waved his hand between us. I didn't reply. How could I? To say yes would be to betray my husband. To say no would be a lie.

Instead I stood. 'I should probably get home.'

'I'm sorry Erin. I didn't mean to make you feel uncomfortable.' He patted the log beside him. 'Please stay a bit longer.'

Reluctantly, I lowered myself back down, making sure there was plenty of distance between us. I clasped my hands in my lap, closed to him. This wasn't going as planned. I opened my mouth to explain again why this was a bad idea.

'What if you told Greg you were helping me?' Adam said before I managed to say a word.

'What do you mean?'

'Well, you're a music therapist, right?'

'Sort of.'

'Well anyway. You work with people with memory problems and music, and I have amnesia. So what if you told him I was back, and that you had agreed to help me? That way you're not lying so there's no need to feel guilty.'

I stared at him. It would be the easiest thing in the world to say yes. But Adam must have been as aware as I was that it was more complicated than that.

'But—' I started, but Adam interrupted me.

'I know what you're going to say. That there's too much between us for that.' I gave a small nod. 'But we can keep it strictly professional.' He stopped, threaded his fingers together. 'I just – I don't want to stop spending time with you, Erin. Seeing you has been the only thing that's given me any pleasure at all since the accident, since I got back.' He looked up at me pleadingly. 'Please?'

I sighed heavily. 'Adam, I really want to say yes. With all my heart. But you don't know Greg, and because you can't remember anything at all, you don't know how much he hates you.'

'He *hates* me? Good God, what did I do to him?'

I sighed again. 'It wasn't what you did to him. It was what you did to me. Plus the fact that you even existed.' I hesitated, unwilling to reveal Greg's weakness. 'He spent the first few years of our relationship – of our marriage even – terrified that you were going to turn up and ruin everything, that I'd choose you over him every time and that he'd lose me.'

The wind blew between us, but there was no other sound for a few moments as Adam took in what I'd told him. Then he gave a slow nod.

'And would you?'

'Would I what?'

'Would you choose me?'

The trees closed in around me, the ground rose up and the air stilled and for a moment I was suspended, between before and after, my mind filled with the life Greg and I had built together and the pain on his face last night when I'd been unable to give him an answer to his question about renewing our vows.

'I don't know.'

It was partly the truth. Because my heart told me I absolutely would choose him, even now, even after all these years. But my head told me otherwise.

'Okay.'

I looked away, but could still feel his eyes boring into me, and I turned back to meet his gaze. The air between us felt charged; it crackled and sparked and for a moment it felt inevitable that we would end up together. Everything tipped, became blurred… and then Adam moved, shifting slightly along the log away from me and the world sprang back into sharp focus again. My head pounded.

'Promise me you'll at least think about it?' he whispered. 'About helping me?'

'I promise.'

The trouble was, I knew my decision was already made.

22

NOW

Shed Seven: 'Chasing Rainbows'

'I don't fucking believe it.' Greg's voice wobbled wildly, and he sat down heavily on the bed. I perched uneasily beside him and placed my hand on his thigh but he whipped it away.

'Please Greg, don't be like this.'

'Don't be like what? Don't be angry or sad that that – *fucker* – is back? Or don't feel utterly betrayed that my wife has been seeing him behind my back? That he's given her a *necklace* for fuck's sake?' He spat the words out with such venom I flinched as though avoiding bullets.

'Greg, stop it, please. You know full well it's not like that, otherwise why would I be telling you about it? God's sake, I'm even asking your *permission* to see him.'

I felt his body jerk violently beside me and it took me a moment to realise that he was crying. Greg rarely cried, and I moved my arm from his leg to his shoulder and pulled him towards me and let him sob onto my chest. Finally, when he was done, he looked up at me through red-rimmed, puffy eyes.

'Sorry. I didn't mean to get so emotional.'

'It's okay. But you do understand that I had to tell you that Adam was back, don't you? It would have been worse if you'd have bumped into him without warning.'

He nodded sadly. 'I know. I still want to punch the fucker though.'

'Don't.'

'But I do. What it's not just about him being back. It—' He stopped, choked. 'What was he doing giving you a necklace? And why – why did you keep it?'

As soon as I'd broken the news to Greg about Adam being back, he'd put two and two together, of course. 'I knew it was him the minute I found that note, but I'd prayed it wasn't,' he'd said, tears glistening in his eyes. Now he wanted some sort of explanation as to why another man had given me such an intimate, thoughtful gift – only I didn't have one. Not one that would ease his fears at least.

'I don't know. I didn't have the heart to throw it away I suppose.'

'But you wore it.' It was a statement rather than a question and I nodded, unable to say anything more.

'Will you let me explain? About Adam I mean.'

He wiped his cheek with a shaky hand. 'Go on.'

So I told him about Adam's accident, about his amnesia, and about how he wanted me to help him try to unlock some memories.

'He's desperate, Greg. He doesn't remember a thing about himself.'

'Probably better that way.'

'Please try not to let your opinion of him cloud your judgement. Just hear what I'm saying.'

He nodded and I took it as my cue to continue.

'He's desperately unhappy, and when I told him what I do for a living, he asked if I could help him. Simple as that.'

It wasn't the entire truth of course, but there was no point in telling Greg how many times Adam and I had seen each other, or how just being in his company had made me question the entire foundation of our marriage.

'But you work with dementia patients, not people with amnesia,' he said, his voice cracking. 'How can you help him?'

'I don't know for certain that I can. But I don't see how it can hurt to at least try.'

He shook his head. 'I've been dreading this day since our very first kiss.' He looked at me. 'You do know that, right? That every single day for the last eighteen years I've dreaded that man walking back into your life, and that I'd lose you to him.' He was shaking and I longed to hold him, comfort him, tell him he was wrong, that Adam meant nothing to me. But I couldn't.

'Yes, I do know that,' I said, as gently as I could. 'But this isn't about me and you or anyone else. This is about me doing my job.'

Greg shook his head again. 'You're either a fool or you're lying to me,' he said sadly. 'Because we both know that there's more to this than a purely professional relationship.' He let out a huge puff of air. 'But what can I do? If I say I don't want you to do it you'll probably do it anyway, and I'll seem like an utter arsehole.'

'If you say no, I won't do it.'

He looked me in the eye again. 'And yet if I do I'll come out badly so I guess I have no choice. You'll just have to do what you're going to do, and I'll just have to hope that you love me enough.'

'I do love you.'

'I know. But I also know how you felt about him, and I'm not totally convinced those feelings ever disappeared. I guess it explains why you're not sure about renewing our wedding vows.' He took a long, shuddery breath and stood up. 'But you help him if you feel you need to Erin. Just don't tell me anything about it, and please never, ever talk about him with me. Okay?'

'Okay.'

Then he walked out of the room.

* * *

I had no choice, no matter what Greg said. I was always going to help Adam. Two days later I was standing in Sam's living room with a bag of instruments, waiting anxiously for him to turn up.

'You're a complete fool, you do know that right?' Sam said as he placed two steaming hot mugs of coffee on the small side table.

'You might have mentioned it once or twice,' I replied, plonking the bag on the floor with a crash.

He lowered himself onto the sofa behind me and tucked his feet beneath him. I snuggled next to him but rather than putting his arm around me like he usually would, he stayed where he was, giving me nothing.

'Rose agrees with me you know. She's furious with you.'

'Yes, you've told me that too.'

There was a pause. 'So why are you doing it, E?'

I craned my neck to look up at him and was shocked by how sad he looked.

'You know why.'

He shook his head and I shuffled to face him. 'No, I know what you've told me. But I don't really understand it. I just don't see why you're risking everything you and Greg have for the sake of Adam Bowers.' He held his palms up.

'He needs me.'

'*Greg* needs you. He's practically begged you to stay with him.' He shook his head. 'At least I'm here to keep an eye on things.'

I nodded. He was right. It *was* good he was here. I had been unsure where to arrange to meet Adam again, keen to make sure it was somewhere safe, neutral. A location where no intense moments like we'd shared the other day could be repeated. So when I'd told Sam what I was planning, he'd suggested we came to his flat.

'Do you think that's a good idea?' I'd said. There had never been any love lost between Sam and Adam.

'I think it's better than any of your ideas,' he'd replied. And because I hadn't been able to argue with that, it had been agreed.

'Adam's probably terrified of seeing you anyway,' I said now.

'Good. He should be.'

I rolled my eyes but was prevented from saying anything further by the doorbell.

'I'll get it.' I leapt up before Sam could get there.

Adam was soaked through when I opened the door but his face broke into a smile when he saw me.

'Oh good, this is the right place.' He peered over my shoulder. 'Are we on our own?'

'No, Sam's here. I think he wanted to keep an eye on us.'

'Oh right.'

I stepped aside to let him in and waited while he removed his drenched jacket and boots. 'Don't worry, he won't bite.'

Adam looked up at me. 'Are you sure? After everything you told me about how I behaved I don't imagine he's thrilled I'm back.'

'I told you on the phone, he's fine. Really.' I walked back into the living room where Sam was standing, arms folded, looking stern. Adam stopped in the doorway behind me.

'Hello Sam.'

'Hello. I didn't think I'd see you around here again.'

I sighed. 'Come on Sam, this isn't *The Godfather*. Let's just be civil and get on with this shall we?'

Sam unfolded his arms and sighed too. 'Okay, I was just making sure you both knew I was here and I won't stand for any nonsense, all right?'

I grinned at Adam. 'See, told you he was a pussy cat.'

Sam flounced off to the kitchen, leaving me and Adam alone. I stepped closer to him, ready to explain what we were about to do. But before I could speak he took another step towards me so there was barely any space between us, and his eyes flickered with desire. I felt something stir in me, and was relieved when Sam yelled from the other room, 'Tea? Coffee?' and broke the spell.

I sprang back, turning away as Adam called back, 'Coffee please,' and busied myself with picking up the bag of instruments I'd dumped on the floor.

'I'm glad you agreed to help me again.' Adam's voice was low and came from just above my head. I stood and faced him.

'I'll try my best.'

He nodded. 'So you told Greg about me then?'

'Yes.'

'And?'

'He knows I'm here.'

He paused. 'I assume he's not happy about it?'

'Of course not. Why would he be?'

'And yet you came anyway.'

'I did.' I raised my chin and looked him in the eye. 'I said I'd help you, so I will.'

The air quivered between us as we stood facing each other.

'Right, shall we make a start?' I said, trying to disguise the tremor in my voice. I wished he didn't still have such an effect on me, it was making things a lot harder.

'Sure.' He sat on the sofa just as Sam re-entered the room and handed him a coffee, then took a seat next to Adam.

'Right, what happens now E?' Sam said, leaning forward with his elbows on his knees.

'Are you staying?'

'Yup. Got to keep an eye on you two.'

'You don't trust us?' Adam said.

'Nope. Especially not you.' He grimaced. 'You might not remember me, Adam Bowers, but I remember you very well and I'm not leaving this room for one minute. Got it?'

'Right.' To his credit, Adam didn't say another word, and simply turned back to me. 'I guess you're going to play some CDs like last time are you?'

I shook my head. 'I actually thought I'd try something else first.'

'Oh?'

I pulled a small keyboard from my bag. 'I'm going to play some more generic songs, some sounds I like to play to my patients.'

'Your dementia patients?' Adam sounded sceptical.

'I know it sounds weird, but it's how I like to start a session rather than going straight in for the kill, so to speak. To warm up a bit.'

'Like a jamming session,' Sam said, and I nodded.

'Exactly that.' I turned back to Adam. 'I'm going to play some notes and I want you to close your eyes and listen and tell me if you think of anything when you hear them.'

'Like what?'

'I have no idea, that's the whole point. Most of the time this doesn't trigger any memories, but it can help just to keep an open mind.'

'Okay,' Adam agreed.

The pair of them sat back on the sofa and closed their eyes. 'You're doing this bit *too* are you?' I said, squinting at Sam.

He peeled an eye open. 'You betcha.'

I rolled my eyes and placed the keyboard on the table. Sam had been right about one thing at least. His presence would definitely guarantee nothing inappropriate would happen between Adam and me. It couldn't be less conducive to passion if he sat in the middle of the floor and started clipping his toenails.

I took a moment to study Adam's face while he wasn't watching. His strong jawline, the curve of his cheek, the dark sheen of his hair, shorter now, but still all so familiar. I tore my eyes away and propped my keyboard on my knees and played a few simple tunes, watching Adam for any reaction at the same time.

After a while he snapped his eyes open.

'Anything?' I said.

'Not a thing.'

I shrugged. 'That's okay. I wasn't expecting much, I just thought it might be useful to warm up a bit rather than diving straight in this time.' I put the keyboard down and dug around in my bag for my tape recorder. 'Okay, I've got something else I want to try.'

Adam peered suspiciously at the machine in my hands. 'Are we attempting a bit of time travel?' he said.

'Something like that.' I ignored the confusion on his face and pulled the mixtape he'd made me from my bag. 'Do you recognise this?' I held the cassette up for him to see and he shook his head.

'Uh oh,' Sam said. I threw him a look and he stood. 'Sorry. I'm probably just getting in the way. I'll leave you to it, but' – he waggled his finger back and forth between us – 'I'll only be in the next room and I don't want any funny business, all right?'

'Go,' I said, shooing him away, and he slunk off through the door.

'Sorry about him,' I said, as the door closed behind him. 'He's just protective of me. And Greg.'

'It's fine. I get it.'

I nodded. 'So, this tape.' I took a deep breath. I hadn't been sure whether or not to tell him about the tape, just in case it worked too well, and triggered memories I wasn't sure I wanted him to remember just yet. But in the end I'd decided it was worth the risk if the songs it contained helped him. 'This is a tape you made me back – well, back when we were together.'

His eyes widened and a smile spread across his face. 'And you've still got it?'

I felt my face redden. 'No. Well, yes, but I hadn't seen it for years. I found it in a box at my dad's house on Christmas Day.'

'Oh, right.' He reached for the box and read the note on the front, opened it and looked back at me. 'Wonder why I didn't write a song list on it?'

I shrugged. 'No idea. But don't worry, I've listened to it. I think we should give it a go.'

'Okay.'

My hand shook as I loaded the tape into the cassette player, and then we both waited as I pressed play. Seconds later Ash, 'Girl From Mars' started and I watched as Adam listened carefully. It conjured immediate images of him standing on stage singing to me, but would it do the same for him? It seemed unfathomable that it could all be meaningless to him, lost in the past – but I also knew that was highly likely.

When it came to an end, I pressed pause.

'Well?' I said.

Adam looked at me sadly and shook his head. 'Nothing.'

'Don't worry, there are plenty more,' I said, trying to hide my disappointment. If these songs didn't trigger a memory in him, then I wasn't convinced any of the other ones would either. But I wasn't about to give up yet.

I played the next song – 'Chasing Rainbows' by Shed Seven, one of his favourites – and another, and each time I was transported back instantly to another time, another place, when Adam and I were together. Most were happy memories, when I'd felt safe knowing that Adam had loved me. And when those songs were playing I watched Adam expectantly, hopeful that this time, something might spark. But each time he looked back at me with the same blank look of sadness and disappointment and my heart lurched again. I'd been so sure this was going to be the break-through we needed, that at least one of these songs would trigger a memory in him, even just a spark to remind him of who he once was, and who we once were. But so far, nothing.

'Do you want to stop?' he said, his voice low.

'Do you?'

'I think we probably should. I mean, this clearly isn't working.'

I nodded. 'I know. I'm sorry.'

'It's not your fault.'

'How about one more?'

He shrugged. 'Okay. But then we have to officially admit defeat.'

'For today.'

'What do you mean?'

'I'm only agreeing to admit defeat for today.' I leaned forward to make my point. 'I know this is disappointing, and it is for me too. But Adam, this can sometimes take weeks before it works.'

'And does it always succeed in the end?'

I shook my head. 'Not always. But there are times it seems as though it's not working, and then suddenly *poof*, a memory comes, just like that. It can be fleeting, a tiny spark, but it doesn't matter. Once a memory has been ignited, you know the possibility is there.'

He nodded slowly. 'Okay.'

'So, ready?'

'Yup.'

I took a deep breath, pressed play, and waited. Nirvana's 'Heart-Shaped Box' began, the song Adam had been playing the day I'd found him busking; the song that had launched me instantly back to the day we'd met at the party. I watched Adam intently as it played, trying to work out whether anything was happening beneath his eyelids, any sign of recognition, but his face gave nothing away. Finally, the song came to an end and he slowly opened his eyes and searched me out.

'Did it work?' I felt my heart hammer with anticipation. 'Did you remember something?'

He gave a slow nod. 'I think I did.'

My belly flipped. 'What was it? What did you see?'

He closed his eyes once more as though trying to conjure it up again. 'I was playing the guitar, and there was a crowd of people round me, and I was lost in the music, and then I looked up and there you were. Except I didn't know it was you, I just felt you watching me, as though there was a connection between us, drawing us together.'

I waited for him to carry on but he didn't say anything else. He opened his eyes and looked at me hopefully. 'Sorry, that's it.'

'Oh.'

'You're disappointed.'

'I—' I stopped. 'I was hoping for something from your past. But this – this is from the day we met – just before Christmas I mean.'

He nodded slowly as realisation dawned. 'Which means this hasn't worked. It hasn't unlocked any past memories.' His voice was flat with disappointment.

'Not yet, no.'

He looked so dejected I wanted to reassure him that it would be all right, that the memories would come, sooner or later. But I also didn't want to lie to him or give him false hope, so instead I simply said: 'Just give it time.'

He made me jump when he smacked himself in the forehead. 'Stupid, stupid brain.'

'Adam, stop it, you'll hurt yourself,' I cried, leaping to my feet. But his hands were bunched into furious fists and his face had transformed in a heartbeat from a calm, patient Adam into an angry, defensive, frustrated Adam I hadn't seen before – or at least not for many years.

Watching him as he paced up and down the room, his body tight, full of pent-up aggression, I was transported back to another night, another time when I'd seen him behave in just the same way, when his frustration had bubbled over to boiling point and he'd been so close to exploding I'd felt nervous of being around him for the first time ever. Not scared. He was never that bad. But sometimes – something someone had said, or a slightly over-hard shove as he was walking past someone in the pub, or a comment about his band that wasn't entirely complimentary, and he'd lose it for a few seconds. His body would coil with tension, just like it had now, and I was reminded of how volatile he could be. I wasn't sure I liked it. It was such a far cry from what I was used to, being with Greg for so many years, I wasn't sure how to handle it.

I sat back down and waited for him to calm. Moments later, as though a switch had been flicked, he almost deflated in front of my eyes.

'God I'm so sorry Erin. I don't know what came over me. I

just...' He rubbed his eyes with his still-clenched fists. 'I just hate what I've become. I hate that my mind has done this to me.' He slammed his fist into his palm, sat down next to me again, so close we were almost touching, then looked up. 'Was I always like this?'

'Like what?'

'Like this, so furious, so aggressive?'

I shook my head. 'Not aggressive, no. But you could be fiery at times.'

He looked down at the desk and didn't reply for a moment. 'I don't think I was a very nice person, was I Erin?' His voice was so quiet I had to strain to hear him.

'You were nice Adam.'

He looked up at me. 'But?'

I wasn't sure what to tell him. 'But you were angry.'

'At what?'

I took a deep breath. 'Life. Your father. The world. But it was a long time ago when I knew you. You were young, a teenager. We – we've all changed, since then.'

He shook his head. 'I don't think I've changed as much as you think.'

'What makes you say that? I haven't seen you lose your temper at all until today.'

'Not with you. Why would I? But since I got home I've been permanently angry with my parents. Blamed them for the fact my life is so miserable. But tell me this Erin. If I was such a wonderful person, before, why has no-one been to see me? Why haven't friends flocked round to wish me well, to see how I am since the accident? Why haven't I got someone who loves me?' He stopped, rubbed his face. 'Does that strike you as the life of someone who was a nice person?'

I didn't know what to say. After all, what Adam and I had had between us all those years ago hadn't been friendship. It had been passionate, love, lust. It had been obsession. Now, as I listened to Adam, it struck me that, actually, perhaps he was right. Perhaps he hadn't changed as much as I'd thought he had. Perhaps, after all, the memories I'd had of me and him back then weren't exactly how things had been between us. Perhaps I'd been seeing the past through rose-tinted glasses and, in fact, things may not have been greener on the other side if I had ended up with Adam.

I felt overwhelmed with the thoughts racing through my mind, so I stood abruptly, keen to leave and get some space to order my thoughts.

I pushed my chair back and Adam's head jerked up at my sudden movement.

'I need to get going,' I said, trying not to meet his eye.

'Okay. I'm sorry.' He stood slowly and stretched himself up to his full height. I tried not to notice how handsome he still was, how my body still responded to him, and focus on the fact that I needed to get away from him. I moved towards the door to go and find Sam but before I got there he was suddenly in front of me, blocking my way. He was so close now I could see the amber flecks in his dark eyes, and a wave of desire coursed through me. 'You won't give up on me, will you Erin? Please?'

I couldn't speak so I just shook my head.

'Thank you.' He looked down at his feet. 'I just – can I ask you something else?'

My heart fluttered. 'Of course.'

'I need to move out of my parents' house. I need my own space. Will you – will you help me find somewhere?'

'Yes of course but – didn't the doctors think you should stay with someone?'

He shrugged. 'Yeah. For a while. But I'm fine. You can see I'm fine. I don't need them.' He puffed out his cheeks. 'To be honest if I don't get out of there soon I'm going to go mad.' He looked at me.

'I know it's a lot to ask but I don't really know anyone and I – I don't really know where to start to look for a house.'

Realisation dawned. Of course he didn't know how to do these things, because he'd always had them done for him – or had his parents' house and money to fall back on. But now he needed to do this by himself.

'I'll help if I can,' I promised.

'Thank you. I need space to remember who I am, even if it's not who I want to be.' He swallowed, then whispered, 'And I need to remember who we were, even if we can't ever be together again.'

The thought hovered for a moment. It would have been so easy to close the tiny gap between us and let our lips brush, let ourselves get lost in the connection that was still there, as strong as ever. Everything in my body was urging me to do it, to reach out to him, to touch him. It took everything I had to step away.

And just in time too, as at that moment the door swung open and Sam came into the room. I sprung away as though I'd had an electric shock and Sam looked from me to Adam and back again. 'It looks as though I came back just in time.'

'Adam was about to leave,' I said, my face flaming.

Sam fixed him with a stare. 'Great. I hope it worked. Nice to see you.' Then he bundled Adam out of the living room and into the hall and left me standing alone. I closed my eyes and took a couple of deep breaths, trying to clear my mind.

The door slammed shut and then Sam was back in the room.

'I knew I should never have agreed to this,' he said, and when I opened my eyes he was standing right in front of me, his face serious.

'Nothing happened Sam. I promise.'

'Only because I came back when I did.' He turned and threw himself on the sofa. 'God Erin, what are you *doing?*'

Anger flared through me then. 'I'm not *doing* anything. I'm helping an old friend who's struggling, and you can choose whether to believe me or not, but nothing happened. Yes, I feel drawn to him, but I didn't let anything happen because – well, because of Greg. Because it would have been wrong.' I sat down next to him, suddenly exhausted, and he swivelled to face me and took my hands.

'I'm sorry E. I didn't mean to shout at you. I just worry about you. You know that.' He shook his head. 'It's not you I don't trust, it's him. Adam. He broke your heart once, and I just don't want him to waltz back in here, destroy your life and then fuck off again. I can't let it happen. I won't let it happen.'

I studied our hands which were lying between us, Sam's nails more manicured than mine, and felt a tear drip down my cheek.

'Thank you Sam,' I whispered.

He wiped the tear away with the back of his finger and planted a kiss on my cheek. 'Don't be daft. I've always got your back. You know that. Rose too.' He grinned. 'Speaking of Rose, she's going to be furious when I tell her what she's missed today.'

And despite myself, I couldn't help but laugh at my stupid, loyal, wonderful friend.

23

THEN

No Doubt: 'Don't Speak'

'What time is he arriving?' Greg said, trying his hardest to keep the disdain out of his voice.

'About three,' Erin replied, trying just as hard not to notice it.

Greg gave a small nod and looked back at the textbooks spread out across the library table. He wasn't really taking any of it in and he was pretty sure Erin wasn't either, despite her insistence that coming to study was the best thing to take her mind off the news she'd just heard.

Greg gathered his things together and shoved them into his rucksack. 'Come on, let's get out of here.'

Erin looked up at him. 'Where to?'

Greg shrugged. 'No idea. Just somewhere else.'

Erin picked up the book she'd been staring at for the past half an hour and followed her friend out of the library and onto the street, ducking through the door he held open for her. They stood outside on the pavement for a moment, deciding where to go.

'Pub?'

'Pub,' Erin agreed, and hooked her arm through Greg's. The local was only a couple of minutes away and they walked there in silence, but as they reached the entrance Greg stopped dead. 'What's wrong?'

Greg looked serious.

'I just—' He shuffled his feet. 'Come here you,' he said, and before she knew what was coming he wrapped his arms around her and held her tightly. Her cheek pressed against his chest and she felt herself relax as he held her there, safe in the cocoon of his body. She didn't know how long they stayed like that, but when he released her she instantly missed the comfort of him, and didn't move away. She looked up and realised there were tears in her eyes.

'It's shit, what's happening to your mum, Erin,' he said. 'Utterly shit. I know you don't want to talk about it any more and that's fine and I'll respect that, but I'll always be here to listen if you change your mind, you know that, right?'

Erin nodded, feeling a single tear slip down her face. She let it drip onto her chest, a dark spot blooming out across the dark green fabric.

'Thank you. I don't know what I'd do without you.'

Greg smiled sadly. If only she knew how many times he'd imagined being the most important person in her life. Yet no matter how hard he tried, he'd always take second place to Adam, the arsehole boyfriend who really only cared about himself. He shook the thought away. He had Erin to himself for another three hours before Adam got here, and he wasn't about to waste a single second of it thinking about him.

'You'd become a wreck, that's what you'd do,' Greg said, taking her hand. 'Now, let's go and get shit-faced and forget about everything else for a couple of hours shall we?'

'That, Gregory Donnelly, sounds like an excellent plan,' she said, grabbing his hand and following him into the warmth of the pub.

* * *

They were three pints down by the time Erin noticed her phone. There were eight missed calls and a text.

'Shit,' she said, fumbling with the buttons. The text was from Adam, telling her he'd wait for her in the student union bar, seeing as she wasn't answering her phone.

'Adam?' Greg said, the name tasting like poison in his mouth. He couldn't help the way he felt. Even putting aside the way he felt about Erin, he would still dislike the guy intensely. Adam was selfish and annoying and far, far too full of himself, and however hard he tried, he just couldn't understand what a girl like Erin saw in a man like Adam, rock star or not.

Erin nodded.

'Got to go?'

'Yeah.' She stood and downed the dregs of her pint. 'Coming?'

'Adam won't be too impressed if I tag along.'

'He won't care. Anyway, I want you to come.'

Greg didn't need telling twice. Even though it felt like a burning hot iron was being pressed on his heart every time he saw them together, spending more time with Erin still made it worth it. He hadn't got very far with his mission to win her from Adam – in fact, he wasn't sure he'd made any progress at all – but he wasn't about to throw in the towel just yet. He finished the last half of his pint and stood too.

'I feel a bit wobbly.' Erin laughed, as they scurried towards the union.

'You're such a lightweight.' Greg could feel Erin's hand swinging beside his and although he longed to take hold of it, now didn't feel like the time.

'You're twice the size of me,' she said, shoving into him.

'Yeah fair point.'

The street was busy, full of shoppers and tourists, and it took them another five minutes to get back to the union. As they approached, Erin grabbed Greg's hand and pulled him round to face her.

'Thank you,' she said, simply.

'For what?' His voice came out as a croak.

'For – being you. I—' Her voice caught, and she coughed. 'The call from Dad really shook me,' she said. 'Mum, she – she's just so young. She's...' She stopped again, searching for the right word. 'She's amazing. She funny and kind and vibrant and – I just can't believe this is happening to her.'

Greg nodded, not sure what to say.

'I didn't know what I needed, afterwards,' she continued. 'But it turns out you did.' She stepped forward and kissed his cheek and he felt it burn where her lips had touched it. He wished he could bottle this moment, keep it to relive over and over again whenever he felt down, or sad, or lonely.

'I'd do anything for you Erin,' he said, his voice low.

'I know. I would for you too.' She smiled.

The moment sat between them briefly, and Greg pictured stepping forward and kissing her properly, telling her not to walk up those stairs to where Adam was waiting, and to come to bed with him instead. He could see it all, and he wanted desperately with every fibre of his soul to say it. And maybe he would have done, but at that moment there was a shout and they both turned in unison to see Adam standing there, swaying slightly at the top of the stairs. Erin snatched her hand away from Greg's and he watched, his heart heavy, his hand hanging limp in the cold air, as her face transformed. If only she'd look at him like that.

'You coming?' she said, tugging his sleeve.

'You don't want me hanging around you two love birds,' he said, concentrating on keeping his voice even.

'Please come G,' she pleaded. 'I'm feeling a bit fragile; I need you there.'

He hesitated a moment, although he didn't know why. He knew he'd go with her, no matter how much he didn't want to see them together. He'd go anywhere with her.

He nodded and trudged up the stairs, letting Erin go ahead to get their greeting out of the way, and he didn't look up until he was at the top, where the pair of them seemed to be attached to each other, Adam's tattooed arm slung proprietorially around Erin's shoulders as though he was staking his claim. Greg's stomach clenched.

'All right Greg?' Adam said, the plummy vowels sounding forced with the chummy expression.

'Hello Adam,' he said, coolly.

'Greg's coming for a drink with us,' Erin said.

'Oh, I was hoping we could go straight back to your room,' Adam said, nuzzling into her neck. Erin pushed him away, giggling.

'No, not yet,' she said. 'I – I'm not really in the mood right now.'

'It's all right, I can wait,' Adam said. Then he turned and headed towards the bar. 'Drink?'

'Please,' Erin said, and Greg followed her to a free table to wait for Adam to get back with their drinks. No Doubt, 'Don't Speak' played in the background and Erin smiled. 'I love this song,' she said. 'It always reminds me of Rose and Sam.'

'I love it too.'

'Now I'll always think of you when I hear it too, and how kind you were to me today.'

'It's what friends are for,' he said, meaning it. He really would be happy with always being her friend, if it was all that was on offer. 'Anyway' – he glanced at the bar – 'are you sure you want me here? I should probably leave you to spend some time together.'

'No, please stay,' Erin said again, watching Adam chatting easily to the barmaid. He'd been served immediately, of course, and Greg wondered how on earth he always got people to do his bidding for him wherever he went. 'I just feel like I need to get drunk – drunker – and blot everything out tonight, and I'd like you to do it with me.'

'I don't think Adam agrees with you.'

'Maybe not, but it's not up to him.' Her shoulders slumped. 'I love him but he – well, he used to be really thoughtful, but now – I don't know. He's changed since he started touring and I sometimes feel like he doesn't give a shit about anything outside of his little bubble. I don't think he means it but I just don't know how he'll react when I tell him about Mum. Whether he'll even really care.'

Greg wasn't sure what to say. It was the first time he'd ever heard Erin express any doubts about her usually blameless boyfriend. And even though he couldn't imagine anyone not caring about the news, maybe it would be a good idea for him to stick around after all, and be here to pick up the pieces just in case Adam did fuck it up.

Greg jumped when a pint was placed sloppily in front of him, beer swilling over the sides. He wiped the table with his sleeve as Adam slid into the booth beside Erin and kissed her greedily.

'So, what have you two been up to?' Adam said, pulling away and taking a sip from his pint. 'You're always together whenever I get here; are you stuck together?'

'Greg's my friend,' Erin said, her voice sharper than usual. 'He's good to me.'

'I'm good to you,' Adam said and it took everything Greg had not to laugh. Erin might have complete faith Adam, but Greg didn't trust him as far as he could throw him. He didn't believe for one second that when Adam was out on tour with his band, with girls throwing themselves at him after every gig, he wasn't making the most of every second. Adam craved the attention, he lapped it up. It was just the sort of man he was, despite what Erin chose to believe.

'Greg was just helping me drown my sorrows,' Erin said.

'Sorrows? What sorrows?'

Erin didn't answer for a minute so Greg said, 'Erin had some bad news today.'

Adam frowned and looked at Erin. 'What's the bad news? Are you ill?'

'No Adam, I'm not ill.' She glanced at Greg. 'Dad rang. My mum –

she's not been herself. She keeps forgetting things and she got lost the other day.'

Adam didn't say anything, so she carried on. 'Doctors think she's got dementia.'

Adam frowned. 'Isn't that what old people get?'

Erin flinched but Adam didn't seem to notice. 'Yes, usually. But this is early onset.'

Adam took a sip of his beer and swallowed. 'So what does that mean?'

'I'm not sure. She'll get worse. They don't really know.'

'Oh right. Well that doesn't sound too bad then. You know, if she's just forgetting a few things.' He laughed. 'I mean, I forget things all the time.'

'That's because you're usually off your face,' Greg snapped, and Adam whipped his head round angrily.

'What the fuck?'

'Greg,' Erin said, and gave a small shake of her head.

Greg held his hands up. 'Sorry. That was out of order. I just meant to say, it's more than just a bit of forgetfulness. Erin's really worried about her mum.'

'And I suppose you were comforting her, were you?'

'Greg was there for me when Dad rang,' Erin said.

'Course he was. He's always there when you need him, isn't he? Good old Greg.' Adam held his pint up in the air. 'Here's to Greg, always on call in a crisis.'

Greg stood, knocking the table as he did, spilling beer. 'I'd better go; sorry Erin. I'll see you tomorrow?'

'If we get out of bed,' Adam said, smirking.

'Adam stop it,' Erin said, standing. 'Sorry Greg. I don't know what's got into him. You go. I'll see you tomorrow.' Then she turned back to Adam, and Greg left, his heart heavy. He'd never in a million years

understand what she saw in that moron. She deserved so much better. He could only pray that one day she'd see it for herself.

24

NOW

Buzzcocks: 'Ever Fallen in Love (With Someone You Shouldn't've?)'

'I still can't believe you let Adam come to your flat,' Rose said from behind the driver's seat. I peered in the rear-view mirror and saw her face pulled into a pout.

'You're just pissed off because you missed all the drama,' Sam replied, reaching behind from the passenger seat and poking her in the ribs. She squealed and moved away.

'Oi Samuel, can you stop that?'

'Stop what?' He smiled at me innocently.

'Stop poking Rose and stop saying there was drama.' I glanced at him quickly before looking back at the road. 'You know perfectly well that nothing happened.'

'Only because I came back in time.'

'Oh for God's sake you two, stop bickering.' Rose poked her face through the gap between the seats. 'Anyway, forget the fact you both went behind my back' – Sam rolled his eyes – 'and tell me. Are you sure your mum won't mind us coming with you today?'

I shook my head. 'Honestly, she'll be thrilled to see you. I've checked it with Suzy and she says it's fine too.' I glanced round again. 'But don't be insulted if Mum doesn't recognise you. She doesn't know who I am half the time.'

'Don't worry, there's no way she can forget me,' Sam said, popping a handful of Minstrels into his mouth with a grin.

'Fool,' Rose said, swiping at his head. He ducked out of the way just in time.

'Honestly you two, it's worse than having a couple of kids in the car.'

'Sorry Mum.'

The truth was, I was glad these two were with me today. I felt nervous about seeing Mum, and I wasn't sure why. Maybe it was a sense of foreboding. Her words from my last visit – *never settle for second best; always follow your heart* – seemed to be stuck in my brain on a loop, and I suppose I hoped that speaking to her again, finding out a bit more about her and Johnny, might give me some more clarity about my situation. It certainly couldn't do any harm.

The light was fading now and the roads were narrowing to lanes so I kept my eyes trained ahead of me, my hands gripping the steering wheel tightly. We stayed silent for the rest of the drive until we finally pulled up in the car park. The darkness was drawing itself across the sky like a veil, and when I climbed out of the car, the cold hit me in the face like a wet flannel. It was a still evening, and beyond the home, the gardens stretched out into the blackness. I tightened my scarf, and beside me, Rose linked her arm through mine. 'Ready?'

'I guess so.'

We headed into the home, where Suzy was waiting to greet us the second the door opened, as promised. It was warm in here, the ancient radiators pumping out a dry heat so that I had to peel off layers the moment we stepped inside.

'Suzy, you remember Sam and Rose don't you?' I said.

'Yes, but it's been a while,' she replied, shaking their hands. 'Hello again.'

'How is she?' I said, shoving my hat and scarf into my bag.

Suzy's lips tightened. 'She's... okay.' My stomach dropped. Suzy was an eternal optimist, and always thought Mum was on great form even when she seemed utterly lost to me. In Suzy's world, *okay* was not good. She must have seen the worry on my face, because she hurried to reassure me before I could say anything else. 'Don't worry, there's nothing wrong. She just seems a little – I don't know. Melancholy.' She glanced at Rose and Sam and back to me. 'She's been a little tetchy since you were last here actually. I don't know what you said to her.' She smiled to show she wasn't telling me off, but guilt pierced me. I'd never meant to upset Mum by playing her the mixtape. I was beginning to doubt the wisdom of what I was doing here.

'Are you sure she'll be okay to see us all today?' I asked.

Suzy hesitated, then nodded. 'Yes, I think it will cheer her up.'

'Thanks Suzy.'

'Do you want me to go and check on her first?'

'No, I think we'll be fine, thank you.'

'Great, see you later then.'

The three of us made our way to Mum's room and when we got there I paused with my hand resting against the door. 'Just let me see how she is,' I whispered, and Rose and Sam both nodded. I pushed the door open and peered round the door. 'Hello?'

No reply. I stepped inside, but couldn't see Mum anywhere. 'Penny?' I said, panic rising in my voice. Had she gone wandering again? 'Where are you?'

'Hello?' Her voice was muffled and I couldn't work out where it was coming from. Then I spotted her, on her hands and knees in front of the chest of drawers, her arm stuck into the bottom drawer. I hurried over.

'What are you doing down there?'

She looked up at me, confusion clouding her face. 'I...' She stopped, a tear streaking its way down her face. 'I don't know.'

I helped her up, closed the drawer and walked her over to her chair. She was unsteady on her feet and it struck me again how frail she'd become. She was only fifty-seven, but this disease had ravaged her physically as well as mentally. My heart broke a little bit more.

Once she was sitting down, I crouched in front of her and took her hands in mine. 'Penny, I've brought some friends to see you today. Can they come in?'

She looked at me searchingly and I could tell she was trying to work out who I was talking about. Her gaze wandered over to the door and I looked round to see Sam's face poking into the room. 'Oh, it's you,' she said, and a sudden smile lit up her face, transforming her. I beckoned them both in and they leaned down and pecked Mum on the cheek in turn then sat on the bed beside her. I sat in the other armchair.

'Hello Penny,' Sam said.

'Hello Sam, hello Rose, haven't you grown,' she replied, and my heart swelled with happiness that she remembered who they are, even if it was only momentarily. These were people she'd known since they were young teens, and if that was how she remembered them, that was fine. At least they were there, somewhere, in the mist of her mind.

'So, how are you today Mum?' I said, hoping it was now safe to call her that without upsetting her. 'Suzy says you've been a bit grumpy.'

'Does she?' Her face crumpled. 'I don't think I have.' She

looked round the room as though searching for something. 'Is Adam coming?'

'No,' I said gently, throwing Rose and Sam a look. 'Not today.' I swallowed to clear my throat.

'Oh that's a shame. I do like him.' She turned to my friends, who were watching our exchange with interest. 'He's a lovely boy isn't he, that Adam? Loves the bones off my Erin he does.'

Rose looked horrified, but Sam just leant forward and said, gently, 'Yes, he does Penny. You're absolutely right.'

Silence descended again. I watched Mum's gaze roam round the room, and wondered what was going on in that muddled mind of hers. I was also trying to work out how to broach the subject of Johnny. If the music I'd played her from the mixtape had upset her so much the other day, I wasn't sure whether I should risk playing it again. Far from helping her, as playing music was intended to do, it seemed to have left her feeling more confused than ever.

'Have you brought some more music for me today?' Mum said suddenly, as if reading my thoughts.

'Oh...' I started.

'We have,' Sam said, smoothly.

'Oh good,' Mum said, her eyes lighting up again. She turned to Sam. 'Johnny made me a tape you know.'

'I know.'

'Do you?' She smiled at him. 'So are we going to listen to it again?'

Sam didn't look at me, but kept his eyes trained on Mum. 'Would you like to?'

'Yes, I think I would,' she said.

Sam turned to me. 'Do you think we could, Erin?' he said, and I was suddenly so grateful for his presence. I always found my anxiety levels soaring whenever I came to see Mum – on the approach because I was worried how she was going to be when I got here, and while I was actually here because I was panicking about doing something to upset her. I'd spent so much time with dementia patients you'd think I'd be used to it, but somehow, when it was my own mum, it felt as if there was so much more at stake.

'Go on then, let's try one song,' I agreed, bending down to find the tape and cassette player in my bag. I set it up and looked at the three expectant faces watching me. 'Ready?' All three heads nodded, so I took a deep breath and pressed play.

As the opening guitar riff of 'Ever Fallen in Love' by Buzzcocks began, I saw Mum's face relax, just like it had last time, and she smiled. It was clear she was gone again, miles away, lost years in the past. I flicked a glance at Sam and Rose as I waited to see whether she'd say anything about Johnny again, although I had no idea what to expect this time.

It didn't take long.

'Oh, this takes me back,' she said, fixing her gaze on a spot on the floor in front of her. 'It was playing on our first date.' She stopped again, and I held my breath, hoping she was going to tell us more. 'We went to Brighton, you know, me and Johnny, to the pier. It was blowing a gale, and he was late. I almost went home, I was so cold. But then there he was, bold as brass, marching up to me.' She clasped her hands together. 'He was so handsome. I'd never been on a date with anyone before, never thought Johnny would want me. But he did, and now here he was and he grabbed my hand and pulled me along the pier behind him, towards the arcade. That's where this was playing, this song. And that's why he put it on the tape for me, you know. It was one of our songs.' She smiled again. I thought she'd finished, but then she started speaking again, quieter this time. 'It was so loud in there, I could barely hear my own voice, but it was the best afternoon of my life.

Johnny stood behind me as we slotted pennies into the machine, and I thought I was going to die from happiness. Then he kissed me, for the very first time, in front of all those people, by the slot machines, and the whole world disappeared.' She stopped suddenly, then turned her gaze to me, her eyes blazing. 'I was in love. I'd never loved anyone like that before. And I never have since.'

Shaking, I reached over and switched the music off and the sudden silence made the air hum. For a few seconds none of us said a word. Rose and Sam were watching me; I was watching Mum.

'Oh!' Mum sounded dismayed. 'Can't we have any more?'

'In a bit,' I said. I felt rattled by what Mum had said, by the lingering feeling it had left in me. I just didn't know whether I was more bothered about Mum and Dad not being everything I'd always thought they were, or whether it was touching a nerve about my own situation.

'So, tell me about this mixtape,' I said now, resting my chin on my fist. The direct approach didn't always work with Mum, but I was hoping that, having listened to one of the songs from the tape already, her mind might be more open to talking about the past.

A slow smile spread across her face, and she stared into space, before starting to talk.

'Johnny made it for me. He was so lovely.' She stopped, and I let her mind wander for a moment without interruption. 'He loved me, you know. We were going to get married.' She dropped her gaze to the carpet and fell into silence again.

'So, when did he make this tape for you?' Rose prompted, and I smiled at her, grateful for her help.

Mum looked up at her, her eyes blank, unseeing. 'Just before I had to leave him.' Her face dropped and for a moment I thought she was going to cry, but then she took a deep breath and carried on.

'I loved him, but my father, he didn't think he was good enough for me.' She stopped, cleared her throat, anger making her voice louder. 'He said he wanted me to find someone better, someone who would give me a good life. Someone like Michael. And Michael was lovely, he really was but Johnny was – he was the best man I'd ever known. We were going to run away.' Her voice dropped to a whisper and we all leaned in to hear. 'It was all planned out. He'd made me this tape, and we were going to run away in his car, and go to Gretna Green. But then that night my father caught us as I was sneaking out, and he told me I had a choice. If I went I could never go home again. If I stayed and forgot about Johnny, he wouldn't disown me.' A tear rolled down her face, but I left it, unwilling to interrupt her train of thought now for fear I'd never get it to return to this moment in time again. I needed to know the truth.

'So what did you do?' My voice was a whisper too.

'What could I do? I was young. I had nothing. And even though Johnny had promised me the earth and I believed he'd do everything he could to give it to me, right then he had nothing either. So I stayed and married Michael, a lovely man with prospects just like my father wanted.' The tears were rolling down her face now. 'But Johnny was still the person I dreamed about at night. And oh—' She stopped now with a cry. 'Michael was a good man. He was my friend, and he loved me. I loved him too. But there was one thing Michael wasn't.' She looked me dead in the eyes. 'He wasn't Johnny.'

The room was utterly silent as Mum's words settled.

My mind whirred with so many thoughts. Greg wanting to renew our wedding vows and trying so hard to make amends.

Adam's outbursts, his unpredictability and the way he made me feel. Mum's regrets for the love she'd lost.

And Dad, my lovely, kind dad. How much had he known about this Johnny? Had he ever known he'd been Mum's second choice and if he had, how much did it bother him?

I let out a long breath and sat back in my chair, suddenly exhausted by it all. I watched as Sam reached out to Mum and took her hand, and Mum turned to him with a smile. 'Hello, who are you?' she said, amiably.

'I'm Sam,' he replied patiently. 'Erin's friend.'

'Are you her boyfriend?' Mum had always known Sam was gay but, not wanting to contradict her, he just shook his head.

'No, just her friend.'

'Oh good. I'm glad she has some lovely new friends.'

I caught Rose watching me from the corner of my eye. Her face was filled with sadness and I forced a smile.

'Okay?' she whispered and all I could do was nod.

* * *

It wasn't until we were almost home that I felt ready to address what had just happened.

'What the hell am I going to do?' I said as we drove long frosty roads, the moon almost full and bright above us, lighting the way. I was glad we were in the car so I didn't have to look my two best friends in the face and see the worry and confusion I knew was in their eyes.

'What does your heart say?' Rose said.

'Oh heart schmeart,' Sam said. 'We all know if Erin followed her heart she'd never have married Greg in the first place, and would have run off to find Adam wherever he was in the world instead.'

'We don't know that!' Rose cried.

'To be fair, he's probably right,' I admitted, and it was the first time I'd said it out loud. Even saying the words felt like stabbing Greg in the back, but if I couldn't admit the truth to these two, who could I admit it to?

'See,' Sam said triumphantly, smacking the dashboard with his palm. 'Samuel Evans is always right about matters of the heart.'

Rose and I burst out laughing at the same time and Sam looked at us indignantly. 'Oi, it's not that funny,' he said, sticking out his bottom lip.

'Oh Sam,' I said, reaching across the gearstick and patting his leg affectionately. 'We all know perfectly well that not only is that statement not true, but that actually it's pretty ridiculous. But we love you anyway.'

'Charming.' He folded his arms across his chest but I could tell he was only pretending to sulk.

'Anyway, that doesn't help me.' We were only a few minutes from home and I had no idea how to process everything I was feeling, or how I was going to face Greg. Or my father, come to think of it.

'I think you need to write a list,' Rose said.

'You're such a teacher,' Sam said, rolling his eyes.

'I *am* a teacher,' Rose countered.

'Carry on,' I said, trying to placate Rose. 'What should this list say?'

She shot Sam another glance and looked back at me. 'You need to write down all the reasons for staying with Greg – you know, that you love him, he loves you. He's kind, you have a mortgage together, he's trying so hard to make everything right again. Anything you can think of. Then you need to do the same for all the reasons for not staying with him. The fact you don't love him as much as you feel you should, that you can't stop thinking about Adam, that Greg's lost loads of your money. Then you need to weigh everything up.' She stopped and held her finger up. 'But, you should make it about you and Greg first, and forget Adam in all of this. Because you need to take it one step at a time. Make sense?'

I heard Sam snort beside me and I smacked his thigh. 'It does Rose, yes. And you're right. Whether I can trust Greg and want to stay with him has to be separate from anything I might feel for Adam.'

'Except it isn't.'

'Sam, that's not helpful,' Rose said.

'It's true though, isn't it? I mean, before Adam came along again you were more than ready to forgive and forget Greg's gambling. But now you don't know whether you can, or even want to, and that's no coincidence.' He stopped and looked at me, eyebrows raised in challenge. 'I'm not saying it's wrong. I'm just saying that the two things *are* connected. So I think you need to consider that as well. And remember what your mum said, about not having any regrets. She obviously does, but it's too late for her. It's not too late for you.'

'You're right.' My hands were gripping the steering wheel so tightly my knuckles had turned white. I tried to take a deep breath and relax, but it didn't work. I was too tightly wound. 'This is all connected.' I sighed. 'You know what I need to do before I make any decisions though, don't you?'

'What?'

'Talk to my dad.'

'That wasn't what I expected you to say.'

'I know. But I have to, don't you see? I need to find out whether he always knew that Mum settled for what she saw as her second choice when she married him, and if he did, whether he minded.

Whether now, looking back, he thinks she should have made a different choice.'

'He's never going to say he thinks that, surely? He adores your mum.'

'I know he does. But it was all a long time ago, and he might see things differently now to how he saw them back then.' I shrugged. 'It might just help me work things out.'

25

NOW

Bob Dylan: 'Like a Rolling Stone'

I'd come to see Dad alone this time. Thanks to work it had been a couple of days since I'd been to see Mum, and my mind had been spinning with what she'd told me ever since. Inevitably, things with Greg had been difficult at home, but I had at least spent some time making a list, as Rose had suggested.

The trouble was, every time I thought about hurting Greg, or tried to picture telling him I was leaving, guilt flooded through me. Images of the two of us together throughout the years kept playing over and over in my mind, as if my mind was trying to torture me, or guilt-trip me into staying.

Sitting here outside my father's house, I thought back to the first time I'd brought Greg home to meet my parents, when Mum had asked me whether he made me as happy as Adam did. Although at the time I'd wondered why she couldn't just be happy for me, now I think Mum had always known that I was settling for 'good enough', and that Greg didn't set my heart alight the way Adam had – because she had done exactly the same thing when she'd married my father.

My poor dad.

My poor mum.

I consoled myself with one thought. They *had* been happy. It might not have been the passionate love story that my father had craved, but there had always been affection, respect, joy, and maybe that would have been enough for them both, even if Mum hadn't fallen ill.

I checked my reflection in the rear-view mirror and sucked in a lungful of air, trying to steady my nerves. I knew that, if Dad didn't know about Johnny, what I was about to ask him could rip his whole life to smithereens. But if he *did* know about him, then I needed to ask him what he thought Mum should have done – and what he thought I should do. I wasn't sure now how I was going to even begin to navigate this.

I climbed out of the car, opened the gate and headed up the pathway, ignoring the weeds that were standing tall despite the frost and cold, and rapped on the door. Seconds later, Dad's silhouette appeared behind the glass and the door swung open.

'Hello Reeny, this is a lovely surprise.'

'Hi Dad,' I said, planting a kiss on his cheek.

'Come in,' he said, stepping backwards and almost toppling over a pile of newspapers.

'Have you got rid of anything else yet Dad?' I said as we picked our way along the hallway to the living room.

'I'm working on it,' he said, and I rolled my eyes. 'Is that what you've come to do? Throw some more of my things in the bin?' He sounded tetchy.

'No not today.' We reached the small, cleared area in the living room and he turned to face me.

'I assumed that's why you'd come over.'

'Aren't I allowed to come and see my dad without an ulterior motive?'

He pursed his lips. 'Of course you are. Sorry.'

'It's all right.' I knew he was sensitive about his hoarding, felt ashamed of it, so I didn't say anything more.

'Anyway, let me put the kettle on. Tea or coffee?'

'Coffee please.'

I sat as he shuffled out of the room, the tapping of his stick on the tiles following him like a faithful puppy. To my surprise, Dad had some music playing in the background – his favourite, Bob Dylan's 'Like a Rolling Stone' – and I was glad I'd made the effort to get his CD player working for him on Christmas Day.

'Here you are Reeny,' Dad said, handing me a plain white mug of black coffee.

'Thanks Dad.'

Slowly, he lowered himself into the armchair opposite me. I watched as a pile of boxes just a couple of feet away from his chair swayed precariously, then settled again.

Dad took a sip of his coffee. 'So, to what do I owe this pleasure?'

'I...' I started, but was suddenly terrified. I didn't know where to begin. I didn't even know whether I should begin. What exactly was I trying to achieve? 'I just wanted to come and see you.'

He nodded but didn't look convinced.

'Are you sure you don't want me to get some help clearing this stuff? It's going to take me forever on my own.'

'I didn't ask you to do it.'

'I know. That's not what I'm saying.'

'I'm fine. Don't fuss. I'm working through it, but I can't just throw things out willy-nilly. It has to be done properly.'

It has to be done before you get crushed to death by it all, I wanted to say, but bit my tongue. Instead I nodded. 'Well let me know if you want me to get someone in to help us sort through it all.'

He nodded. 'Your mother would have disapproved of course.'

'What?' I was blind-sided for a moment. Dad had found it difficult to talk about Mum since she'd moved into the care home – he missed her so deeply he usually found it easier to simply avoid talking about her altogether rather than thinking about how much she'd changed. But now he'd brought her up twice in as many visits.

'Your mother wasn't the tidiest person in the world, as you know, but she was a stickler for cleanliness. She'd be furious at me if she could see this mess.'

'Dad, it's more than just a mess. You know that, right?'

'Yes, yes, of course. But it's nothing I can't sort out.' He sighed, as though exhausted by it all. 'Your mother would have simply thrown everything in the bin.'

'She would.' I smiled, then took a deep breath. It was now or never. 'I went to see Mum a couple of days ago.'

'And how was she?' His voice was even but I could see it hurt him to talk about her.

'She was okay. She was—' I stopped. 'She was a bit confused.'

'Oh dear.' He steepled his fingers beneath his chin and studied me. 'Did something happen love? Come on, it's obvious you've got something to say, so spit it out.'

He was right. It was time to stop pussyfooting about.

'Dad, do you know who Johnny is?'

I didn't know what reaction I expected, but as I watched what little colour there was left in Dad's face drain away, I realised it wasn't this. I'd expected a straight-forward no, or a denial of some sort. Not this look of horror.

'Dad?'

He looked up at me, his eyes heavy. 'Has your mother been talking about him?' His voice was a hoarse whisper.

'Yes.'

He hung his head. 'I'm surprised it's taken this long.' He snapped his head up again. 'You haven't been playing her music again have you?'

'I have,' I admitted.

He shook his head. 'I knew, when you said you were going to try this music therapy business that something like this might happen.' He sighed. 'Although she gets confused, your mother has always known she loves me, even when she doesn't recognise me. All these years of her mind deteriorating and I'd been expecting her to remember Johnny, and to ask me why it was me visiting her and not him. But it hasn't happened. Until now.'

'Oh Dad, I'm sorry.'

He shook his head. 'It's not your fault. It was bound to happen.' He looked up again. 'Anyway, I don't suppose it really matters. Not to your mother, at least. She probably won't remember him again by tomorrow.'

'But it matters to you?'

He nodded. 'I suppose it does. What did she say about him exactly?'

How much should I tell him? It was clear that he knew about Mum and Johnny, and that he knew Mum had loved him. But how much had she actually told him?

'She said she loved him, before you and her met.'

He nodded slowly. 'She did.' I waited for him to continue, not wanting to push him too much. 'I always knew she loved him more than she loved me.' His breathing was heavy. 'But her father didn't want her to marry someone like him.'

'Like him?'

'He didn't have a good job; a labourer I think. Her father

wanted her to marry someone with prospects. Someone who could give her a good life. I met her at work shortly before she ended it with Johnny, and we became friends. We'd go for walks together at lunchtime and she'd talk about him, how happy he made her, how he wanted her to marry him. And then – well, her father gave her an ultimatum. Leave Johnny, or move out. She left him but I could see how heartbroken she was when she made her choice.' He sighed heavily. 'I always wondered whether I was just in the right place at the right time.'

'But Mum loves you, Dad.'

He nodded. 'Oh I have no doubt of that. I loved her instantly. I mean, who could fail to fall in love with her? She was so bright, so vivacious, so full of fun. She shone everywhere she went.' His eyes were wet now, lost in the past. 'And even though I knew she didn't love me in the way she'd loved Johnny, I tried to forget that, and tried to give her the best life I could. Over time, she did love me. I have no doubt of that. But it wasn't the kind of love to set the world on fire.' His voice trailed off now and I swallowed. Bob Dylan still played gently in the background and we both sat and listened for a few moments, remembering, perhaps, the times this had played over the years when we'd all been here together, a happy family. But had my childhood been one big lie? How many people had been hurt by this decision? How different would Mum's life have been if she had been allowed to follow her heart?

'I'm sorry Dad.'

'It's okay Reeny. It's surprisingly good to tell you about it after all this time.' He smiled weakly and I reached over and held his hand. He looked down. 'When your mother told me she was pregnant, I was the happiest man alive you know.' He sniffed. 'When she told me, I knew right then that everything would be okay. That Penny would never leave me, and that we'd make a perfect little family for ourselves.' He looked up at me. 'I always wanted to give you a brother or sister but in the end it was just the three of us. I think—' He stopped. 'I think your mother wanted to give herself options. I think she felt so much love for you, she didn't dare to have another child, in case she ever wanted to leave.'

'Mum would never have hurt you.'

'Not deliberately. But your mother would have left me in a heartbeat if Johnny had ever come back on the scene, and I always knew that. Baby or no baby. I never stopped believing that.'

'Oh Dad.' I squeezed his hands and took a deep breath, thinking about Greg and how he'd said the same to me over the years. 'Do you – do you ever think she made the wrong decision?'

He looked up at me, his eyes filled with pain. 'Honestly? Sometimes I do. I mean, I would have been heartbroken if she had chosen him over me. But if she hadn't have fallen ill, I'm not sure we would have made it to old age together. I think she was always waiting for a time to leave.'

'To look for Johnny?'

'Maybe. But not necessarily. Maybe just to look for that sort of love again.'

I stared at my father for a moment. This old man in front of me had surprised me today. He'd never talked to me this way before, and quite honestly, I hadn't expected anything from him when I came here. But now he'd told me this I felt I knew him better. I also felt as though I wanted to wrap my arms around him and protect him.

'Do you want to go and see her?'

Dad looked up at me in bewilderment. 'See who, love?'

'Mum.'

He waited so long before replying that I began to wonder whether he'd even heard me. There was a look in his eyes that I couldn't read. And then he nodded his head.

'Do you know what, I'd love to.' He rubbed his neck. 'When?'

I shrugged. 'We could go now, if you like?'

'Could we?'

'Let me just ring Suzy, make sure it's okay, but if it is then why not? I haven't got any other plans today.'

Besides, I wasn't keen on going home straight away anyway. I wasn't sure what that said about the state of things at home. I left the room and rang Suzy's number.

* * *

'Do you think she'll be pleased to see me?' Dad's voice trembled as we pulled into the driveway and I swivelled my head to look at him. He'd been silent all the way here and I was beginning to think I'd made a huge mistake by suggesting this trip.

'I'm sure she will Dad,' I said.

He nodded and said no more until we'd parked and were standing outside the front door of the care home. 'Ready?' I hooked my arm through his and felt him trembling.

'Ready.'

I pushed the door open and made my way along the familiar corridor towards Mum's room. Suzy wasn't around this morning but she'd told me it was all right to bring Dad, so we didn't wait around. As we reached Mum's door, I felt Dad's grip on my arm tighten.

I knocked gently. No answer. I pushed the door gently and peered round. Mum was sitting in her armchair, eyes closed, gently snoring.

'Come on,' I said, tugging Dad's hand and leading him inside. I perched on the edge of Mum's bed and left the other chair for Dad, but when I turned back he was standing stock still in the middle of the room, staring at Mum. His eyes glistened with tears.

'You okay Dad?' I said, my voice low.

He looked at me and smiled sadly. 'She looks so peaceful when she's asleep, doesn't she? Just like the old Penny.'

I followed Dad's gaze back towards Mum. Her mouth was slack, but her whole face looked more relaxed, her skin less tight, the lines and wrinkles smoothed with the sedative of sleep. 'She really does,' I said.

He sat down and we stayed quiet for a few minutes, waiting to see whether Mum would wake up. Slowly, her eyelids began to flutter and she opened them and peered round the room. Her gaze landed on Dad first.

'Hello Michael love,' she said, her words slurred but the recognition instant. She sat up straight and smoothed her skirt down over and over.

'Hello Penny,' he said, leaning over and reaching for her hand. She let him, and their hands hung, slack, between the two chairs. The love in their eyes was plain to see, and, satisfied Mum was content in Dad's presence, I stood.

'I'll just go for a walk,' I said. 'Give you some space.'

'Thank you love,' Dad said.

I stepped into the hall and headed to the front door again. Outside, the wind had picked up and it pummelled me as I walked towards the gardens. It felt cleansing after the stuffiness of Mum's room and I breathed in the freezing January air. As I walked along, hands stuffed into the pockets of my huge winter coat, I let my mind chew over all the things I'd learned over the last few days, weeks. I thought about Dad, and everything he'd told me. He had known about Johnny. Not only that but he'd always known that Mum had once loved Johnny more than she'd loved him. And yet he'd given her the chance to love him anyway, along with a good life. The best life.

While mine and Greg's situation wasn't quite the same, there were striking similarities. Two men – one a good man who I loved, who I had history with, who loved me unconditionally. The other a disruptive spectre from my past who seemed to have a hold on me in a way I couldn't explain.

Would Mum have been happier if she'd have followed her heart and married Johnny, or did Dad save her from that life? Was Dad right? Would Mum have left him one day anyway?

And where did that leave me and Greg?

Because there was one important difference between our two stories: Johnny had never come back.

But Adam had.

* * *

It was almost dark by the time we set off for home, and Dad seemed tired as he sat in the passenger seat.

'You can have a snooze if you like,' I said.

'No, it's all right love.' He turned his head to face me and I saw a glimmer of a smile on his lips. 'Thank you for taking me to see your mum today. It's been too long.'

'It's fine Dad. I was happy to.' I stopped. 'She seemed happy to see you too.'

'She did, didn't she?'

'And no more talk of Johnny.'

'No. It seems she's forgotten all about him again.'

I nodded and concentrated on looking out for approaching headlights on the narrow lane. A headache was forming behind my eyes and I rubbed them, my vision blurred when I looked back at the road.

'Was there another reason you wanted to know about Johnny?' Dad's voice in the darkening car made me jump.

'What do you mean?'

'Reeny, I know you and Greg are having problems.' Did he?

How? I never talked to my father about anything like that. As if he'd read my mind he said: 'It's perfectly obvious when you're together. And despite what you think, I do take notice of you.' He smiled. 'I wonder whether something has happened to make you so curious.'

How much should I tell him? On the one hand, it would be good to have someone close to talk to. But on the other hand, I didn't know whether voicing my worries would only make them more real.

'Adam's back in town,' I said, deciding to take the plunge.

He hesitated a moment as if trying to place the name.

'Ah, I see,' he said, realisation dawning. 'And you think this could be your second chance, do you? The one you threw away, like Mum did with Johnny?'

I was surprised at his astuteness. 'I honestly don't know Dad. I just – Mum said something the other day about Adam, told me I shouldn't settle for second best.'

'The way she had you mean?'

I shook my head. 'She didn't say that. It's just – she thought Adam was still my boyfriend and she told me not to listen to anyone else and to follow my heart.'

I wondered whether I'd gone too far. But then Dad shook his head and turned to face me.

'You know I was never keen on Adam, don't you?'

I nodded, keeping my eyes on the road.

'He was everything I didn't want for my little girl, at the time. And when you met Greg I was so pleased. He's the sort of man most men would want their daughter to marry.' He sighed. 'But now, looking back, I'm not so sure I was right. I've often wondered whether your mother would have been better off if she'd have married Johnny after all.' He raised his hand to stop me when I started to object. 'Hear me out. Of course I'm glad she chose me.

But you're my daughter, and I only want what's best for you. I want you to be happy.'

'But that's just it. I don't know what will make me happy.'

He studied me for a moment, then said, 'You can only follow your heart.'

* * *

When I got home Greg was in front of the TV but he wasn't watching it, instead scrolling through his phone. He glanced up as I came in, then looked straight back down at the phone without saying anything.

'Everything okay?' I said.

'Uh huh.'

'Greg.'

He looked up sharply and glared at me. Was he challenging me? I sat down next to him, forcing him to shuffle along the sofa to give me space.

'What's going on?'

He shrugged. 'Nothing. I'm just playing.' He indicated his phone and I was relieved to see it was only a game of snake occupying his attention and not a gambling site.

'Right.' I stared down at the carpet. There were so many things I could say right now, but I couldn't seem to get anything to come out.

'Where have you been?' His voice was steely, and he sounded nothing like my warm, loving husband.

'I went to see Dad, remember?'

He nodded. 'Ah yes of course. How is he?'

'He's fine.' I shrugged. 'I took him to see Mum.'

He looked back down at his phone but I noticed he wasn't

playing snake any more. I sifted through my mind for the best thing to say, but before I could, Greg spoke first.

'I thought you were with *him.*' The last word was said with such venom I flinched. I'd rarely seen Greg as furious as he was now. Normally, when he was angry about something, he was like an open book, the fury obvious, and the cause just as plain. But this tightly coiled, volatile Greg was something new, and I didn't know how to handle it. What had I done to him?

'No Greg. I told you when I was with Adam.'

He gave a tight nod.

'And did it go well?'

'I thought you didn't want to talk about him ever again?'

His jaw clenched as he replied. 'I don't really. But I can't stop thinking about you—' His voice caught. 'You and him together.'

I reached my hand out for his but he pushed it away. 'I was just trying to help him. You know that.'

'Yep.' He looked at me, his face leaden with pain. 'But you were together weren't you? Just the two of you.'

'Sam was there too.'

He stood so suddenly I almost tipped off the sofa. He didn't look me in the eye but stared somewhere over by the door. 'I can't do this Erin.'

I jumped up so I was standing next to him but he still wouldn't meet my eye.

'Greg, look at me.' His eyes flickered over me and then away again. I placed my palm against his chest and this time he didn't push me away. 'Greg, there's nothing going on between me and Adam.'

He was silent for a moment and I wondered whether he'd even heard me. But then he looked down and met my eyes. 'I'm sorry Erin, but I don't believe you.'

'But I—'

'No.' He stepped away from me and clutched his hands in front of him. 'You might not have technically cheated on me, but it doesn't matter. It's – it's the thought of you with him, telling him things about us, about me, about our lives... It's tearing me apart. I know your feelings for him are still there. I *know* they are. I've always known it, but when he wasn't here, in our lives, in my face, I could handle it. I felt safe, knowing you'd chosen me.' He sobbed now and swiped roughly at his cheek. 'But I can't do it Erin. I can't pretend I'm okay with this.'

'Greg—' What could I say? I could lie to him and tell him that Adam meant nothing to me, that I was over him. But what would be the point? Greg knew as well as I did that the gambling was one thing – it had caused a rift in our marriage, a huge one that would have been a lot of work to overcome even at the best of times. But with Adam back, that rift now seemed almost unfixable. As though anything we did to mend it would only be like sticking a plaster over a broken bone.

'Would you stop seeing him, if I begged you?' Greg's voice was small, all the anger drained away.

'I don't know.'

He stared at me for a moment, as though trying to read my mind. Then he gave a nod and stalked out of the room, leaving me standing there, alone.

Velvet Underground: 'Venus in Furs'

'Pleeeeease Mum,' Erin begged.

'Your nagging will be the death of me young lady,' Penny said, sighing. But Erin knew that meant she was going to give in and she clapped her hands with glee.

Erin had been desperate to watch her parents' wedding video ever since she'd heard them talking about it a few days before. She'd always coveted the wedding photo on the mantelpiece and had tried to picture them on the day – where they were, how they sounded, who was there. But now she could see it for real and she couldn't wait.

Erin snuggled into her favourite armchair and waited while her mum loaded the video, then watched as the images formed on the screen. She smiled as her mum swam into focus, impossibly young and beautiful, her blonde curls pinned up, tendrils tumbling round her face. Confetti rained down around her.

'You look like an angel,' Erin whispered.

'She really did.' It was her dad's voice and she looked round to find him wrapping her mum in a hug and kissing her cheek. Penny smiled at him, then they both looked back at the screen, where their former selves were emerging from the church, the wind whipping Penny's veil, Michael looking handsome and serious in his dark suit. They both seemed so carefree, and Erin could hardly believe this was only ten years ago.

'Where did you find this?' Michael said, a smile tugging at his lips.

'It was in the cupboard under the TV,' Penny said. 'Erin begged to watch it so I gave in.'

'I'm glad you did,' Michael said, and the three of them watched as the youthful Penny and Michael waved at their guests, then disappeared down the road in a car. The screen went dark, then the video switched to a different venue – this time the wedding reception. The newlyweds took to the dancefloor, the clunk of the guitar, the low, intoned vocals and the pitter patter rhythm of 'Venus in Furs' by The Velvet Underground accompanying them as they swayed together, their first dance.

'This was your dad's choice.' Penny laughed, as young Michael spun his bride around on the screen. 'I wanted "When Doves Cry".'

Michael held his arms out. 'Dance with me now?' he said. Penny looked uncertain, but finally relented, taking his hand and stepping in front of the TV. Erin watched as the real- life Penny and Michael swayed and twirled along with their decade-younger selves, and she saw the unmistakeable look of infatuation in her dad's eyes, both then and now. And she saw how her mum responded, giving him everything he needed.

As the song ended and her parents moved apart, she knew without a doubt that that was what she wanted. For someone to look at her with as much love in their eyes as her dad did when he looked at her mum.

What girl wouldn't want that?

27

NOW

The Offspring: 'Bad Habit'

I knew something was wrong the second I got back from work. Greg's car wasn't on the drive, so I assumed he was out but when I stepped into the semi-darkness of the hallway, lit only by the small lamp filtering through from the living room, he was standing there, waiting for me. Music played too loudly in the background and I recognised the heavy, rapid-fire drumbeat as 'Bad Habit' by The Offspring, one of Greg's favourite songs.

'Greg?' He stared at me with hollow eyes as I placed my bag down and slipped off my coat, but he didn't say a word.

'Greg?' I repeated loudly over the music, taking a step towards him. He didn't move away but I saw his body stiffen and I stopped before I reached him, feeling my own body react.

'Greg, has something happened?' I glanced over my shoulder towards the front door. 'Where's your car?' I was shouting now and I stepped briefly into the living room and turned the volume right down until you could hear nothing but a tinny guitar playing, then returned to the hallway. Greg dropped his head, and I saw his shoulders begin to shake. I didn't move to comfort him, just waited until he looked back up at me, and saw that his eyes were filled with – what? Pain? Regret? Fear? Maybe all three.

'I—' he started, but his throat was blocked, his voice thick with tears. He coughed and started again. 'I'm sorry.'

'What for? What have you done?' I felt the panic rise in me. What had happened? What could he possibly have done that he was finding so difficult to tell me?

'I've lost it.'

'It?'

'My car.' He threw his hands up and let them smack back down to his sides hopelessly. 'I've lost it.'

My stomach constricted. 'What do you mean, you've lost your car?'

He sniffed, and wiped his face with the back of his hand. 'Can we sit down?' He indicated the living room.

'Just tell me what you've got to tell me here.'

He nodded sadly. 'The car got – re-possessed. Because—' He choked. 'Because I borrowed more money to gamble and I...'

'You lost it.'

'Yes.' His eyes searched mine out beseechingly but I refused to let him off that easily. I could feel the anger rising in me like a roar and I didn't know how to make it stop.

'How could you?' The words felt like shards of glass as they left my throat.

'I—' He stopped, as if he realised there was no point trying to make excuses any longer.

'You promised me. You said you'd never do anything like this again.'

'I know and I meant it. I *do* mean it. I – it was just one slip.

That's all. I'll make it up to you, I'll pay it all back and more, and buy a new car. This isn't the end of the world.'

I looked up at him sharply, the blood running icily in my veins. 'I beg your pardon?' My voice was cold, sharp.

'I said it's not the end of the world. I mean I know you're angry, but I'll make it right. This is just a setback. That's all.'

I shook my head, trying to loosen my thoughts, to separate my feelings from the excuses he was making. 'No.'

'No?'

'I mean no, Greg, you're wrong. This *is* the end of the world. For me at least.' I looked him in the eye. 'For us.'

'But Erin...' He stepped towards me, his arms outstretched and I took a step back, away from him. I didn't want him anywhere near me.

'No Greg. You promised, and you let me down. Again.' I picked up Dog, nuzzled my face into his soft fur as he squirmed. 'You asked me to renew our wedding vows only days ago. And now this. I – I just don't think I can forgive you again,' I whispered.

'You can't mean that. I mean, we can sort this out, can't we? We can get over it, make it work? Make *us* work.'

I shook my head and looked down at the polished floor-boards, at the tiny hole in Greg's sock. 'I honestly don't think there's any coming back from this. Not again.'

Greg took a step back as though he'd been slapped, and wrapped his arms round himself. 'You don't mean that. You just need a bit of time.' His voice was low, as though he didn't have the energy to speak. I didn't reply, so after a couple of beats he walked past me, took his coat from the hook, picked up the running trainers he'd left there since his last run, and let himself quietly out of the house.

I waited until I was sure he'd gone, and then I crumpled onto the bottom stair and sobbed. I sobbed for me, for Greg, for everything we'd been and everything we could have been. I sobbed for what I felt sure was the end of the marriage that had meant so much to me for the last thirteen years.

Because Greg was wrong. I didn't need more time.

It was too late for that.

28

NOW

Viola Beach: 'Boys That Sing'

I knew I wasn't helping myself, but after the showdown with Greg, I really needed to see Adam again. My mind was a mess; it felt like a canvas onto which a child had thrown an entire palette of paint and swirled the colours round with their hands until they formed a brown smudge, interspersed with occasional splashes of brightness. Adam, Greg; Greg, Adam.

It was impossible to think straight. Because despite my anger with Greg, was I really ready to call it a day?

I'd asked Adam to come to my office. It felt more business-like, more proper. As I waited for him, my shoulders were hunched, my hands were bunched into fists, and my feet bounced up and down on the tiled floor. I felt as though I might explode.

And then he was there, and the world lit up.

'Hi,' he said. He was smiling at me uncertainly as he

approached my desk. I stayed on the other side, the solid wood a safety barrier between us. And it struck me then how different he seemed to the old Adam. The old Adam would have strutted in here like a peacock, ruffling his feathers, showing off, the preening and the parading all defences to shield how lonely he'd felt, how unloved by his family. Now, those defences had been stripped away and he was open, vulnerable.

Unfortunately, it only made him more attractive.

I smiled back. 'Thanks for coming.' I tried to sound formal, hoping it would help me avoid making any irrational decisions or doing anything stupid. 'Take a seat.'

He sat down opposite me and I folded my arms. The air between us fizzled and I knew he could feel it too.

'This is nice,' he said, looking round the small office I shared with a colleague. It was deliberately simple with nothing too distracting.

'Thank you.'

'Do you see patients here?'

'No, that's usually in the treatment rooms down the corridor.' I gestured vaguely in the direction of the door. Adam nodded.

'So?' He spread his hands out questioningly. 'I've brought my guitar like you asked.' He indicated the case he'd leaned up against the desk. 'What next?'

I took a wobbly breath. 'I'm happy to keep helping you,' I said, the words coming out in a rush. Adam's face lit up.

'Really?' He swiped at his eye. 'Honestly, you don't know what this means. I was so worried—' His face flushed, something else I'd never seen the previously confident Adam do. He ran his thumbnail along the grain of the desk. 'I was terrified I'd messed it up. That I'd scared you off.'

'You didn't.'

He looked up to meet my gaze. 'I'm glad. I mean, I know you're married and I know nothing can happen between us. So I'm sorry. Truly.' He held his hand up in a mock-salute. 'I promise to keep this strictly professional.'

Despite having planned to say that myself, I still felt the disappointment crush me as though someone was sitting on my chest. I nodded.

'Thank you.'

The moment sat between us for a while, with neither of us speaking. But Adam didn't look away and I felt my body heating up under his gaze as though it would burn right through into my soul. The tick of the ancient clock above the door was the only sound in the room, apart from the roaring in my ears.

I reached down and pulled a notebook out of the drawer beside me, breaking the spell.

'I'm going to take notes while we work,' I said, forcing the words through my parched throat.

'Okay.' He leaned forward and rested his elbows on the desk. 'What do you need to know?'

'First I need to write down what we've tried up to now.' I scribbled on the pad. 'And then I'm going to ask you for a few more details about your medical diagnosis, and what the doctors say regarding your chances of recovery.' I looked up at him and tried to ignore the smile on his face.

'Yup, that all sounds very professional and proper.' There was no disguising the laugh in his voice now.

'Adam,' I warned. 'This is serious.'

'Sorry.' He crossed his arms and waited. When I'd finished writing I looked up at him again. 'So come on. Tell me as much as you can.'

So he told me again about his accident, about how doctors didn't know whether he would ever regain his memory. He told me some more about his recovery, and how he'd been on his own in the hospital for three days before his parents had come to see him, and about how he kept waiting and waiting for someone else to visit. He told me about trying to discover his old self through social media, and the scraps of information he'd found out from the few friends who had visited, and how quickly he'd realised he didn't want to go back there, to his old life, no matter what happened next. And he told me how lonely he'd been since he'd been back.

'It's almost as though I had no friends before. Not real ones anyway,' he said. 'I mean, I have all these numbers in my phone, but I don't know who any of them are. A couple of people have messaged me to see how I am but even that petered out after the first couple of months.' He rubbed his face. 'I'm really scared I could just be a horrible person, Erin.'

'You are not a horrible person,' I said.

'But how can you be sure of that?'

'I know you, remember?'

He shook his head in frustration. 'Yeah, but you said yourself we haven't seen each other for years. And it doesn't sound as though I was very nice to you even when we were together.' My face burned. 'But if I mattered to anyone at all, how come nobody has come to see me more than a handful of times, or rung me?' He hung his head and looked down at his lap. 'How come nobody seems to care?'

'I care.'

His head snapped up again. 'I don't get why.'

'Because we're friends.'

'Are we?'

I stared at him, uncertain how to respond. Because of course we were never just friends. We were always far, far more than that, and I'd loved him with every ounce of my being, even if he hadn't treated me as well as he should have done. He was young, back then. We both were. I felt sure he'd changed, grown up.

'Anyway, sorry. I promised not to do that.' He wrung his hands together in his lap. 'I just feel like I need to know who I am. Even if I don't like what I discover, I need to know. And if you can help me that would be amazing.'

I leaned forward so we were facing each other square-on across the tabletop. My pulse thumped in my temples at his proximity and I forced the words out in a whisper. 'I promise I'll do my best. But you need to understand that there are never any guarantees.' I looked away for a moment, distracted by the intensity of his gaze. 'I want you to find your memories again too. I just don't want you to get your hopes up.'

'I won't. I haven't.' He took my hands and I almost jumped from the seat at the shock that bolted through me. But I didn't pull away.

'Right, let's give this another go shall we,' I said, finally removing my fingers from his. I didn't know where to look.

'Are you going to play me some more songs?' he said.

'Yes, I am. But first I wondered whether we should try something else.' I pointed at his guitar. 'Could you – would you be able to play something?'

'Like what?'

On safer ground now, I explained my idea. 'I have no idea whether this will work, but I just thought if we started the session a different way this time, with you playing some music of your own, it might help.'

He nodded slowly. 'Okay. Although I have to warn you that it hasn't worked so far, when I'm busking.'

'No, I know. But listen. I have a patient who's never really responded to music in the months I've been seeing him. But yesterday during our session he grabbed a tambourine and started shaking it about, singing a long-forgotten song. For the first time since I'd started working with him he got completely lost in whatever memory the song had brought back to him.'

'And you think it could work for me?'

'I have no idea but it's worth a go.'

'So what shall I play?'

'I want you to think of a song that you've played recently, but one that you know well – a song you already knew when you picked up the guitar after your accident and didn't have to relearn. Maybe a song that means something to you.'

He frowned. 'And then what?'

'And then, instead of performing it to me, try to really concentrate on the lyrics as you sing – on the melody, the timbre, the rhythm. Try and really lose yourself in the song.'

Adam took his guitar from the case and held it, thinking for a moment.

'Forget I'm even here. Just do it without any forethought or expectations,' I said.

'Can I face the other way?'

'Whatever works.'

He turned away from me so I could only see the back of his head, and then he started to strum. As he haltingly sang the lyrics to 'Boys That Sing' by Viola Beach, I saw his body begin to sway and his foot tap, and I imagined that he'd closed his eyes. I tried not to think too much about the meaning as he sang about how he'd never find another girl like her. I just waited, and when the song came to an end, we both sat in the silence for a moment. Then Adam turned round.

'Well?' he said.

'How was that?'

He nodded. 'It was good. I – I didn't remember anything.'

'Okay. Is there a *but*?'

'Yes, I think so.'

'And...?'

He paused. 'But I felt *something*. It wasn't a memory, nothing concrete like that. But I did what you said and I really focused on the song, the lyrics, and everything as I played. And I felt – melancholy.' He nodded. 'Yes that's probably the best way to describe it. I felt as though I had a hole in the centre of me that I desperately wanted to fill with happiness and joy, but...' He broke off. 'You're going to think this sounds stupid.'

'Try me.'

He swallowed. 'I felt sad, empty, but a little bit hopeful. As though this was the way I'd felt before. Not how I feel now. Does that make any sense at all?'

I nodded encouragingly. 'That's great Adam.'

'Do you think so?'

'I do.' The truth was I wasn't sure, but it did feel like a breakthrough, however small.

'So what do you think it means?'

'Perhaps something in there' – I jabbed my temple – 'is starting to dislodge. Perhaps those memories that have been locked away since your accident are in the very early stages of revealing themselves.' I shrugged. 'At least that's the hope. And if not, at the very least you might be forming new memories, starting from now.'

'Right. So what do we do now?'

'Now, we just keep trying.'

He studied me for a moment, his gaze drawing me in until I couldn't look at anything else in the room. Thoughts of Greg, of music, of Mum, Johnny, Dad, of trying to be professional – all of it drifted away through the slightly-open window, leaving behind nothing but this moment, right here, right now.

I heard the slow scrape of a chair across the floor, and I held my breath as Adam stood and walked round the desk towards me. I couldn't move, my whole body coiled like a spring, and I sat, hands in fists, waiting for him to approach. The air was so thick with tension I could barely breathe as he crouched down beside me and slowly, achingly, reached out a hand until it touched my fingers. I sprang back, a jolt of desire bursting through me as he gently lifted my chin with his other hand, until I was forced to look right at him. He was scrutinising me, as if trying to work something out, and I was on fire, my whole body shot through with desire from my head to my toes.

He moved forward, inch by agonising inch, his fingers now stroking my cheek. His mouth was so close I could feel his warm breath on my face and I felt like I might melt from the inside. His lips brushed my mouth and I let out a groan, pressing myself into him, responding hungrily as he deepened the kiss, his tongue searching out mine. The taste of him was so unfamiliar, and yet the feel of his lips was so right, and for a few, suspenseful seconds I could feel the intensity of all the years we'd been apart pressing down on me as if nothing else mattered but this moment: us, together, his hand running down my neck, to my shoulder and down towards my chest...

I sprang back, my breath coming in gasps.

'I can't do this.'

He didn't respond, but moved away slightly so the gap between us expanded, the space dense with longing. I gulped in air and tried not to look at him.

'I'm sorry Erin.' His voice was rough, scratchy. 'I know that was wrong, but I just – I couldn't help it.' His hands were trembling and he shoved them into his pockets. 'I just – you deserve better.'

'Better?' My throat was like needles and I swallowed.

'Better than Greg. Better than being let down.' He stopped. 'I don't know what I was trying to do. It just felt right at the time. I'm sorry.'

I shook my head, my heart rate starting to slow. 'Me too.'

'Can we…' He looked at his feet. 'Can we still do this again? The music thing, I mean.' His face turned pink. 'I really need this to work.'

'I honestly don't know. You'll have to give me some time to think.'

He nodded. 'Sure.' Then he stood up and walked back to the other side of the desk, picked up his guitar and left without looking back.

* * *

Never let Adam go.

Never settle for second best, Erin. You'll always regret it.

Always follow your heart.

Your mother would have left me in a heartbeat if Johnny had ever come back on the scene.

There was one thing Michael wasn't. He wasn't Johnny.

I was a wreck. As well as trying to shake the memory of Adam's kiss, Mum and Dad's words tumbled round my mind like odd socks in a washing machine, and I couldn't seem to grab hold of one thought before it disappeared from reach again. I thought back to the moment I'd found the mixtape in Dad's house and wished I could go back and leave it where it was.

But then, would it really have made any difference? Maybe it was only ever a matter of time before my feelings would have become confused anyway, and all the mixtape and Mum's memories of Johnny had done was speed it all up.

My daydreaming was broken by the buzz of my phone.

Rose. I considered ignoring her but she was tenacious if

nothing else, and I knew if I didn't answer she'd simply turn up on my doorstep.

'Hi Rose.'

'What's happening? I've been trying to get hold of you for ages. I've sent you about three hundred messages.'

'Have you?'

She sighed dramatically. 'Come on E, don't hold out on us. What did your dad say? Did you speak to Greg? What have you decided?'

I listened to the empty hum of the line between us and breathed deeply. 'Is Sam there as well?'

'Yes. You're on speakerphone.'

Of course I was. They were my best friends, why wouldn't they want to know what had happened since the dramatic moment with my mother at the care home? And they didn't even know about Greg losing the car yet. It had all been too much to think about in the last two days.

I explained everything. What my father had said, and how he'd always believed Mum would leave if Johnny came back.

What Greg had done.

Then I told them about Adam.

'You *kissed* him?' Sam's voice was so high pitched it was a wonder I could even hear it.

'Strictly speaking he kissed me.'

'Semantics, Erin. Fuck, what are you going to do?'

The million-dollar question.

Did I do what my dementia-riddled mother suggested and follow my heart? Did I leave my husband, who I loved but wasn't in love with and who had betrayed me over and over again, to be with the man who had always set my heart alight, but who had plenty of faults that I wasn't sure I could live with, and who didn't remember who I was? Or did I stay with my husband, have a baby, and spend the rest of my life wondering what if?

It was the ultimate coin toss, and I had no idea which way I wanted it to go.

'I don't have a clue.'

29

NOW

Joy Division: 'Love Will Tear Us Apart'

The phone call came as I was walking back from work. I answered it with trepidation, but when I hung up I felt an unexpected sense of relief. Then I made another phone call of my own.

'Erin?'

'Adam.'

'Everything okay? I wasn't sure I'd hear from you after what happened.'

'It's fine.' I cleared my throat, keen not to talk about it. 'I've found a flat for you to look round.'

'You have? Where?'

'In town, above the shoe shop.'

'That's great. When can I see it?'

'Now, if you like. About half an hour?'

'I'll see you there.'

'Adam?'

'Yes?'

'There's something else.'

'Go on.' I could hear the hesitation in his voice and a part of me felt pleased that the uncertainty was on his side these days. Rose and Sam had been right when they'd reminded me that Adam hadn't always been good to me. I'd spent a lot of the time we'd been together feeling insecure and worried that he'd leave me at any moment. It felt good to finally have the upper hand, however awful that sounded.

'I might have found you a job as well.'

Adam had made it clear he didn't want his parents' assistance any more if he could help it but, having never held down what he called a grown-up job, he wasn't sure what he'd be qualified to do.

'What is it?'

'Teaching kids guitar. At the local music group.' I swallowed. 'It would only be a few hours a week to start with but they said they're always desperate for people and there could be the chance to do more hours during the holidays. I said you'd pop in and see them. I thought it would give you the chance to get some separation from your parents and start again.'

'That's amazing, thank you Erin.' He paused. 'I don't know what to say. I thought you'd want nothing more to do with me after the stunt I pulled last time. I am sorry.'

'It's okay Adam. Honestly. Just meet me in half an hour.'

I ended the call and took a deep breath. Adam had asked me to help him and I'd agreed. I didn't know where this was going to lead, but increasingly I was beginning to feel that maybe this would be the end of it. That maybe, once he had his new job and his new flat and a slice of independence for himself, that he'd realise he didn't need me after all.

I couldn't work out how I felt about that. A few weeks ago I would have felt bereft. Now, I wasn't so sure. The truth was, since the kiss, something had shifted in me. It no longer felt as though Adam and I had found each other, as though we were meant to be. Rather it felt, somehow, as though I'd lost everything. I was at sea, stranded. Adrift.

I didn't feel like going home and explaining to Greg why I was going out again. In fact, I felt less and less like going home every day, the atmosphere between us so thick it was like wading through treacle. Things had never been this bad between us, and I was scared we'd never get back to how we were.

Or if I even wanted to.

I began walking towards town to meet Adam. I bought a coffee on the way and by the time I got there the letting agent was already waiting outside. My head hurt and my stomach felt tight as we waited for Adam to arrive. But when he finally turned the corner and walked towards me I realised the tension that had been there since I'd first seen him four weeks before, that had reached breaking point two days ago in my office, had dissipated. I felt my shoulders relax and took a deep breath.

The flat was nicer than I'd expected, newly renovated and available immediately.

'I'll take it,' Adam said, as we left a few minutes later.

'Don't you need to think about it?' I said.

He shook his head. 'Dad's so desperate to see the back of me he'd pay for this flat forever if I asked him.' It was meant as a joke but I could hear the sadness in his voice. But alongside the sympathy I felt for him lay a little nugget of something else. Irritation? Annoyance? Adam had never needed to consider how he was going to pay for something – everything had always just come to him. Private school, somewhere to live, cash to spend. He had never had a worry about money or that sense of pride in something he'd been able to buy for himself through sheer hard work. He'd never understand how devastated I felt about Greg losing our car, and almost losing the house we'd both worked so bloody hard for. Adam's upbringing had made him, to be honest, selfish, in more ways than one, whether he meant to be or not.

'Fine, if it works for you, go for it,' I said, keeping my voice cool, detached.

'That's great. I'll get the contracts drawn up for you, and once you've paid a month's deposit and the first month of rent you can move in,' the letting agent jumped in, determined to close this easy deal.

As we left, Adam grabbed my arm and pulled me towards him. He stood inches from me and I felt my breathing quicken at his proximity, despite everything. 'I – I wanted to thank you. For everything you've done for me,' he said.

'I would have done it for anyone.'

His shoulders slumped. 'Well, anyway, I appreciate it. Really. I don't know how I would have got through these last few weeks, without you. I just hope I haven't fucked things up. For you and Greg.'

I shook my head. 'You haven't fucked things up, Adam. I've made a perfectly good job of doing that by myself.'

He slid his hand down to take mine then, and I found myself wanting to pull it away, to put some distance between us. It was impossible to think clearly when he was there, right in front of me.

'I'm sorry to hear that.'

I shook my head and took a step away. 'It's not your fault. It's nothing to do with you.'

'Oh. Well, that's good then.'

I hitched my bag up onto my shoulder. 'I need to go home now. Let me know if you need any help moving in.'

'I...' he started, then stopped, his face dropping. 'Thank you Erin. For everything.'

'You're welcome.'

And then I walked away from him, my heart hammering but my head held high.

30

NOW

Elbow: 'Grounds for Divorce'

If you love someone enough, most things are forgivable.

I couldn't forgive Greg.

I'd thought I could, but in the end, I'd found the tiny seed of resentment had blossomed into a huge, thorny hedge that I was simply incapable of getting over, however hard I tried.

'I'm leaving.'

Greg stared at me as though I was speaking a foreign language.

'You can't.'

'I'm sorry Greg.'

He slumped onto the sofa like a deflating balloon. I longed to go over to him and put my arms around him and tell him everything would be all right. But I stayed where I was and waited for him to say something. Finally, he looked up.

'This is because of him isn't it?'

I shook my head. 'No. This is because of us.'

'I don't believe you.' His voice cracked at the edges. 'I know I screwed up, but I think you'd already made up your mind.'

Maybe he was right. Of course Adam *was* part of the reason I was leaving Greg. But not for the reasons he thought.

'I'm not leaving you for Adam.'

'Sure.' I studied his face, the face I'd loved for so long. I thought about the first time I'd seen him, when we'd become instant friends. I'd loved him with a gentle brotherly love, and the warmth of my feelings had only spread and grown as the years had passed. But lately, the warmth had begun to seep away, stripping away the flesh of our love with it, until all that remained were the bare bones without anything left to hold it together. The gambling had been one thing – a coconut thrown at an already unstable coconut shy. But the parting shot, the one that had destroyed it once and for all, had been Adam's return. Because it had made me realise that mine and Greg's love wasn't what I needed any more. It wasn't enough.

That was why hurting him was breaking me. He was still that funny, caring man he'd always been. But he deserved better than to be with someone who didn't love him as much as they should.

I sat down beside Greg and he moved away an inch as though touching me would scald him.

'Greg. Look at me, please.'

He continued to stare ahead at the rug.

'Greg, this is not about anyone else. This is about us.'

'Is it the gambling? I promised you I'd stop and I will.' His voice sounded like broken glass. 'I'll get the car back, I swear.'

'It's partly the gambling. But it's about more than that.'

He looked at me. 'You've never loved me the way I love you, have you?' He shook his head. 'I've always known it, deep down. I just – I always hoped it would be enough. What we have. Had.'

I didn't know what to say. He was right. It had been enough, for a long time.

'Do you want me to leave you alone?'

He nodded. 'Yes please.'

So I stood and I walked stiffly out of the house we'd shared for so many years. As I went down the path, out of the gate and onto the street away from the house – from our home – I felt a deep sadness tugging at my heart, and my chest felt hollowed out. But beneath that sadness was another feeling, rising up to meet it, to challenge it.

Happiness. Freedom. A lightness I hadn't felt in a long time.

And, most importantly, a sense of a new beginning.

Because since Adam had kissed me and Greg had lost the car, one thing had become absolutely crystal clear to me.

I didn't need either of them to make me happy.

I didn't need anyone except myself.

As I walked, the sky dipped to meet me and the trees bowed as I passed. The pavement might have been a dull grey but it felt as though it should be lighting up with every step, red, yellow, green blue, like walking on an arcade dance game. It was a flip of a coin in the end, only this time, the coin didn't fall and show me the answer, but continued to spin, revealing all of its faces and all its endless possibilities as it hung there, suspended. And I knew this was the right thing to do.

Because this time, it was only about me.

* * *

I didn't know where I was planning to go but I had a vague idea that I'd go and see whether Sam or Rose were in, spend some time having my broken heart tended to by my best friends. But as

I approached town I heard a familiar sound, and I slowed, tuning in my ears to see whether I was right.

My steps became heavier as I got nearer, and I wondered whether I ought to just turn around and walk in the opposite direction. But I kept going, kept moving, determined to see this through.

There he was. Adam. His back was turned slightly to me which meant he hadn't seen me yet, affording me the opportunity to watch him for a moment, unseen.

I studied the familiar profile of his face, the flex of his bicep as he strummed, the way his leg moved up and down as he perched on his stool, marking out the beats like a human metronome, and I felt the familiar swell of desire. But there was something else beneath it, something that had been sitting like a stone in my belly for weeks now, ever since Adam had come back, that I hadn't recognised until this moment, hadn't wanted to recognise.

I tuned in to hear the song Adam was playing. It was 'Boulevard of Broken Dreams' by Green Day – and a vague memory floated into my mind as it played. A memory, and a feeling, of sadness, and of hurt. This song had been playing one night just before I'd left for university. I'd been feeling heartbroken and melancholy about leaving Adam behind for weeks, and now the time was nearly here, I was getting cold feet to the point where I was considering not going to university at all, even though I knew my parents would be furious. But how could I leave him? How could I be without him? It would be like trying to live without air.

Adam and I had been in his bed, this song playing in the background. I was snuggled into the crook of his neck as he smoked a roll-up and the smoke kept blowing into my eyes. I waved my hand in front of my face for the hundredth time and tipped my chin up to look at him.

'I'm going to stay,' I said.

He looked down at me. 'Don't be daft. You've got to go.'

I shuffled so I could see him better. 'But I can't leave you. I...' I had been embarrassed suddenly in case he didn't feel the same. 'What if you stop loving me?'

'Now you *are* being ridiculous,' he said. 'Why would I do that?'

Because you'll have women throwing themselves at you every night, I thought. *Because you have women all over you now, when I'm here, and you find it hard enough to resist.*

Because I'm not sure I can trust you.

Because I worry you'll hurt me.

Of course I hadn't said any of those things but I'd felt them, and I felt them again now, standing here in the cold watching Adam play this song. The truth was, however much I'd loved Adam, I'd never been sure he'd loved me as much. The depth of my feelings had felt like drowning to me, but Adam merely seemed to be treading water, his eyes always on the distance, waiting for something or someone better to come along.

These thoughts swirled round my head as I watched Adam now, and the smoke slowly started to clear so that I could see what had been eluding me all this time.

This wasn't about whether I should be with Greg or Adam. This was about me, and what I wanted.

This was about my future.

As I walked away, Adam started playing a new song, and I couldn't help but smile. 'Grounds for Divorce' by Elbow.

It was a sign that I was making the right choice. And this time, it was for no-one else but me.

A LOVE TO LAST A LIFETIME PLAYLIST

"Something" – **The Beatles**
"Bitter Sweet Symphony" – **The Verve**
"Club Foot" – **Kasabian**
"Heart-Shaped Box" – **Nirvana**
"Wild Horses" – **The Rolling Stones**
"The Chemicals Between Us" – **Bush**
"Hey Jealousy" – **Gin Blossoms**
"Numb" – **Linkin Park**
"Old Man" – **Neil Young**
"Last Nite" – **The Strokes**
"Like A Prayer" – **Madonna**
"Don't You Want Me" – **The Human League**
"Maps" – **Yeah Yeah Yeahs**
"Monkey Gone to Heaven" – **Pixies**
"Black" – **Pearl Jam**
"Everywhere" – **Fleetwood Mac**
"Time After Time" – **Cindy Lauper**
"Girl From Mars" – **Ash**
"Pretty in Pink" – **The Psychedelic Furs**

"Friday I'm In Love" – **The Cure**
"Chasing Cars" – **Snow Patrol**
"I Miss You" – **blink-182**
"Chasing Rainbows" – **Shed Seven**
"Don't Speak" – **No Doubt**
"Ever Fallen in Love (With Someone You Shouldn't've?) –
Buzzcocks
"Like a Rolling Stone" – **Bob Dylan**
"Venus In Furs" – **The Velvet Underground, Nico**
"Bad Habit" – **The Offspring**
"Boys That Sing" – **Viola Beach**
"Love Will Tear Us Apart" – **Joy Division**
"Grounds for Divorce" – **Elbow**

Listen to the playlist by using the link or scanning the code below
on Spotify...

https://spoti.fi/3WYd62f

ACKNOWLEDGMENTS

If someone had told me back in early 2015 that today I'd be writing the acknowledgements for my SIXTH book, I would never have believed them. Because writing books for a living honestly is a dream come true, and my brilliant readers are the ones that mean I can keep doing this. So thank you, from the bottom of my heart.

Although the idea and the words are mine, when it comes to writing a book, it really does take a team – and this is the perfect time to thank those people who have helped me shape this novel into what it finally became.

This book, for some reason, was the most difficult one I've written yet. I don't know why. It involved three complete rewrites (from scratch!) and many, many edits. It was almost as though Erin, Greg and Adam didn't want me to tell their story. But I persevered. Through its successive versions, the book changed almost beyond recognition – but the one constant that remained was the importance of music and memory. And that bit was great fun to research and write.

Early in my research I spoke to psychologist Dr Victoria Williamson who helped me to work out the details of Erin's job, as well as the importance and power of music in helping people retrieve missing memories. We discussed many things, including the fact that most music psychologists wouldn't actually be music therapists as well, but I decided I wanted Erin to do that for the purposes of the story, so that is down to me! But Dr Williamson's help was invaluable in shaping that element of the story, so I'm enormously grateful to her for letting me pick her brain. I also must mention a book, *This Is Your Brain on Music* by Daniel Levitin, which was brilliant as well and helped me in my research.

Friends are always great sounding boards, and this time my enormous thanks must go to my lovely and very talented friend Rachel Bath who let me talk through the story with her when I hit a stumbling block, and helped me realise what I was really trying to do with it. At a later stage, fellow author Christie Barlow helped me work out what wasn't working about the story and then helped me to unpick the problem. It was like a eureka moment when she pointed out the obvious issue and from that moment I never looked back!

Thanks to the very funny Flic Everett who came up with the name of Adam's band, and also to my brilliant friend Serena who always reads everything I write very early on, and helps me to see the book through someone else's eyes. Your comments and ideas are always helpful, and your support is invaluable.

Of course, I have to thank the wonderful team at Boldwood Books. My amazing editor Sarah knows how to push me to make sure we get the very best from the story, and even though she always apologises for sending through what she sees as lots of comments and suggested changes, I'm never upset or worried – in fact I welcome it, as she always helps get the best out of me. So thank you Sarah, for your brilliant brain. And thank you to Nia and Claire for helping my books find their readers. Without you all I wouldn't be able to do this wonderful job.

And finally, as always, thank you to my lovely family. Tom, Jack and Harry, you're my world. And thank you to Mark, whose shared love of music has meant so much to me over the years and has, no doubt, been a factor in this book being written in the first place. Here's to many more years of amazing gigs together, little brother.

MORE FROM CLARE SWATMAN

We hope you enjoyed reading *A Love to Last a Lifetime*. If you did, please leave a review.

If you'd like to gift a copy, this book is also available as an ebook, digital audio download and audiobook CD.

Sign up to Clare Swatman's mailing list for news, competitions and updates on future books.

https://bit.ly/ClareSwatmannews

Explore more from Clare Swatman.

ALSO BY CLARE SWATMAN

Before We Grow Old

Dear Grace

The Mother's Secret

Before You Go

A Love to Last a Lifetime

How to Save a Life

ABOUT THE AUTHOR

Clare Swatman is the author of five previous novels, which have been translated into more than twenty languages. *A Love To Last a Lifetime* is her sixth novel. A former journalist, she spent the previous twenty years writing true life stories and health features for *Bella* and *Woman & Home*, amongst many other magazines, but now writes fiction full-time. Clare lives in Hertfordshire with her husband and two teenage sons.

Visit Clare's website: https://clareswatmanauthor.com

Follow Clare on social media:

 facebook.com/clareswatmanauthor

twitter.com/clareswatman

 instagram.com/clareswatmanauthor

Boldwood

Boldwood Books is an award-winning fiction publishing company seeking out the best stories from around the world.

Find out more at www.boldwoodbooks.com

Join our reader community for brilliant books, competitions and offers!

Follow us
@BoldwoodBooks
@BookandTonic

Sign up to our weekly deals newsletter

https://bit.ly/BoldwoodBNewsletter

Printed in Great Britain
by Amazon

17114928R00180